A GOOD STORY

and Other Stories

A GOOD STORY

and Other Stories

Donald E. Westlake

Five Star
Unity, Maine

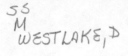
Five Star Mystery.
Published in conjunction with Tekno Books and Ed Gorman.

June 1999
Standard Print Hardcover Edition.

Five Star Standard Print Mystery Series.

The text of this edition is unabridged.

Set in 11 pt. Plantin by Al Chase.

Printed in the United States on permanent paper.

Library of Congress Cataloging in Publication Data
Westlake, Donald E.
    A good story and other stories / by Donald E. Westlake.
— 1st ed.
        p.   cm. — (Five star mystery series)
    ISBN 0-7862-1943-2 (hc : alk. paper)
    1. Detective and mystery stories, American.   I. Title.
II. Series.
PS3573.E9G65 1999
813′.54—DC21   99-25259

Table of Contents

SINNER OR SAINT

Everyone agreed that the Reverend Mister Wimple, the new minister, had done wonders for the town, none of them more wondrous than the taming of Miss Grace Pettigrew, who had been known to argue with the grocer over the price of Dixie cups. At the age of seventy-four, she still mowed the entire length and breadth of lawn surrounding her rundown manor, employing for the task a handmower badly in need of repair, to save herself the expense of hiring a boy to do the job, and she could have easily shattered the Lanesville Merchants and Farmers Bank, as she often threatened to do, simply by closing her account. It was even rumored that Miss Grace Pettigrew had been so softened by the good Reverend that she was about to make a handsome donation to the new hospital building fund, Reverend Mister Wimple's pet project ever since he had first arrived in Lanesville some eight months before. The wildest rumor of all had it that Miss Pettigrew's donation was to be the famous and almost priceless Pettigrew diamond, valued at something over one and a quarter million dollars.

The rumor was quite true. At this very moment, old lady Pettigrew (as the coming generation referred to her) sat quietly and patiently in the Reverend Mister Wimple's office, her hands folded demurely in her lap, a pious, gentle look on her crotchety old face. In the purse on the floor beside her chair lay a cigarette box of the flip-top variety, containing a lot of stuffed cotton and, in the very center of all the cotton, a large and flawless diamond, the family diamond, named for the Pettigrew who had first smuggled it out of Africa and into Baltimore some two hundred years before. Miss Grace

Pettigrew, three score and fourteen, had reformed.

The Reverend Mister Wimple came to his office and paused on the threshold, smiling beatifically at the diamond-toting sinner before him. The Reverend Mister Wimple was a tall man, stocky, well-upholstered though not fat, rosy-cheeked and bulb-nosed, bristly-eyebrowed with gentle eyes and a great shock of white hair rising above and to both sides of a high, shining forehead. His well-scrubbed hands were folded across his full stomach; he had pleasant laugh lines around his eyes and mouth, and upstairs in the medicine cabinet in the bathroom there was a bottle of white hair dye.

Reverend Wimple stood unnoticed in the doorway behind Miss Pettigrew, and his eyes rested absently on the purse Miss Pettigrew had set on the floor beside her chair. Reverend Wimple knew what was in that purse, knew what Miss Pettigrew was about to say to him and what he was about to reply, and it was the culmination of almost a year of difficult and heart-breaking labor. Reverend Wimple paused in the doorway, smiling and elated, allowing the warm feeling that comes from success to spread through his body like alcohol, and in his mind he traveled backward in time and space to two men speaking in hushed tones in a cool and quiet library in a cool and quiet state penitentiary, and he smiled the more broadly.

The two men were prisoners and partners. The taller, heavier and older of the pair was named Joe Docker and his profession was that of the confidence man. He had sold gold-mine stock, oil-well stock, pension plans, municipal statues and methods for beating the horses in every state of this broad and fertile land except Alabama. It wasn't that he had anything against Alabama. He just hadn't happened to go there yet.

Joe Docker's partner in crime was named Archibald

(Lefty) Denker, and he was a jack of all trades. Through the years, many of them lean ones, Lefty Denker had unfortunately developed a quirk of the eye and lip which could only be called shifty, a circumstance which handicapped him in the confidence man trade, where the operative word is "confidence." No one trusts a man who looks like Lefty Denker. Nature, however, moves in devious ways, and always makes up for a handicap by replacing the loss by a special skill of some sort. Lefty, his friends swore, could get into Fort Knox with a used toothpick. His hands were living creatures, and locks, pockets and all kinds of machinery were known and conquerable.

And so the team of Docker and Denker prospered. Where Docker's voice and looks could not obtain entry, Denker's hands could. It was only due to the negligence of a menial in an auto rental agency, who had neglected to fill the gas tank before renting a sedan to Joe Docker, that the car had stopped in the middle of a four-lane highway with five state police cars in hot pursuit. The pair had found themselves wards of the state, with a mailing address at the big house and a future that suddenly looked rather drab.

Joe Docker was a man devoted to his job, and he refused to allow himself to become disheartened. He had long known that a good confidence man is a good conversationalist, and that a good conversationalist is a man who is well read. On this conviction, Joe began to haunt the prison library, where he read everything he could find, books, magazines, old newspapers, everything. He spent so much time in the library, in fact, that he was soon made a trustee and an assistant librarian. This post was due, in part at least, to Joe's long and pleasant conversations with the chief librarian, a hatchet murderer named Simpson, a tiny, bespectacled gentleman who blinked constantly and had the Dewey Decimal System memorized, including his own improvements thereon.

Lefty, meanwhile, in order to keep his own hand in, got himself assigned to the prison machine shop, where he wiled away the idle hours in building and dismantling locks. Occasionally, he and Joe would get together in the library, the only place inside the prison where one could safely whisper, and Lefty would plead, sotto voce, "Joe, let's get outa here. I been studyin' the locks."

Joe would smile and shake his head. "Lefty, you're too eager. Take it easy. You're eating well. You've got a bed. Why complain?"

"It's the principle of the thing, Joe. I been studyin' the locks and I could get us outa this joint with my fingernail. Not only that, I been busy down at the machine shop. I made myself a coupla tools. Little things, you know."

"That's not good, Lefty. What if the bulls find them?"

"Joe, what am I, a beginner? I could hide a tank so these bulls wouldn't find it."

Again, Joe would smile. "Pride," he would say, shaking his finger in mock sternness, "pride, Lefty, has been the downfall of —"

"Joe, let's scram outa this place. I don't like state pens."

"Patience, Lefty. Wait till we have somewhere to scram to. Wait, in a word, until we have a plan, a motive, a reason, a goal."

"I got a goal. I wanta get outa this joint."

And so the idle months passed, Joe improving his mind, Lefty improving his hands, until one day Joe read a notice in a pictorial published by one of the smaller religious denominations. Joe pocketed the notice and continued to putter around the library beside Simpson, whose conversation was almost totally limited to a mumbled string of numbers. Each time Simpson looked at a book, he automatically and unconsciously placed it in the Dewey Decimal System and just as automatically and unconsciously spoke the appropriate number aloud. Libraries being by nature full of books, and Simpson being, by job, normally in the library, his unconscious was kept pretty busy saying numbers, and poor Simpson had a sore throat he couldn't explain.

Eventually, Lefty came down to the library for the normal afternoon chat, and he and Joe sat down at one of the tables.

Joe smiled and handed Lefty the magazine, opened to page fifty-two. "Look at that," he said, pointing at a small, black-encircled notice near the bottom of the page.

Lefty read the notice, an announcement of the death of the pastor of the Lanesville Rural Church, concluding with the remark that a replacement had not as yet been made, and then he looked at Joe, a puzzled expression on his face, and he said, "So what?"

Joe leaned forward dramatically, thrust out his lips, and very carefully pronounced, "The Pettigrew Diamond."

Lefty clicked his fingers. "The old lady! The one that called the FBI."

"Fortunately," Joe said, reminiscently, "gold-mine stock is not a Federal affair. By the time she had contacted the proper agency, we were well away from Lanesville."

Lefty grew serious. "You thinkin' of tappin' her again?"

"This time," Joe told him, "I want the diamond. Nothing less. The diamond."

"She'll remember us."

"She never saw you."

Joe said, "I've been racking my brains all morning. Think, Lefty. Who was I then in Lanesville? Wasn't it then I had the black moustache and the black hair?"

"The monocle?" asked Lefty.

"No, I don't think so. I think the moustache."

11

Lefty thought. "You're right. The moustache."

"Now," said Joe, "think about this. Clean-shaven, white hair, round spectacles — like Simpson's, there."

Lefty looked at Simpson, over by the main desk, blinking rapidly and mumbling digits. He nodded.

"It sounds good," he said. "Who are you? Broker? College president?"

"Don't be silly." Joe tapped the magazine. "I'm the new minister."

When they broke out they found a closed gas station about a mile from the prison. Lefty bent over the door for a moment, then pushed it noiselessly open, and he and Joe slipped inside just as the sirens began to wail behind them. Lefty whispered, "They know we're out."

"No," said Joe. "They know we're out of our cells, that's all." He closed the door behind them. "That's the advantage of relocking doors. It takes an extra second, but it gains an extra hour. First they'll look inside, then they'll look out-side."

Lefty had found a flashlight. He turned it on, but Joe said, "No, Lefty! The place will be full of cops."

Lefty doused the light. "We gotta see, Joe," he said.

"We'll see," Joe told him, and he turned on the lights.

Lefty let out a screech. "What are you doin'?"

"We're opening for business."

The fluorescent lights flickered on, and Joe headed for the main switches. He turned on the lights out at the pumps, the lights in the rest rooms, the lights in the tube shop. Within seconds, the area was flooded in light, and Lefty stood blinking in the center of it, panic-stricken.

"Lefty, go unlock the pumps, will you?"

Dazed, Lefty went out and unlocked the pumps, then came back shaking his head. "Joe, you got gall," he said.

"You got lots and lots of gall."

"Here's a new Chevy in the wash rack," Joe told him. "Go on into town and get us some clothes, will you? And get me my white hair dye."

"Where's town?"

"I don't know. Let's take a look at a road map."

Together, they bent over a map and found out where they were. Then Lefty backed the car out, and Joe called, "Be sure you fill it up this time."

Lefty blushed and filled it up. Joe took a look in the cash register, which was empty, and called Lefty back in. "Open the safe here, will you? I may have to make change."

"Sure thing," said Lefty. Once the safe was open, he got back into the Chevy and drove off. Joe sat down behind the desk and counted the take from the safe.

Within half an hour a car stopped at the pumps and Joe, by now dressed in a pair of coveralls, filled it up at the driver's direction. He checked the oil and water, put air in the tires and changed a twenty-dollar bill. Then another car stopped.

Business was relatively brisk. One of the customers, obviously a local resident, looked curiously at Joe. "When did Dick decide to stay open late?" he wanted to know.

"When he hired me, I guess," Joe told him. "Good amount of trade at night."

Fifteen minutes later a state police car pulled in and two troopers sauntered over to the office. Joe stayed seated behind his desk. He waved as the troopers entered, and said, "Hi, boys. What can I do for you?"

"Seen two suspicious-looking characters wandering around tonight at all?"

Joe thought. "No. Afraid not. What's up?"

"Couple prisoners escaped from the state pen."

"Thought I heard the siren a while back."

"Better keep a wary eye out. They're desperate, will be needing money and transportation."

Joe looked worried. He got to his feet. "Maybe I better close up."

"Wouldn't be a bad idea."

"Thanks for the warning, boys."

As the troopers drove away, Lefty drove in. He got out of the car looking frightened and wary. "Wasn't that a cop?"

"Uh huh. Dropped by to let me know two convicts broke out of jail tonight."

"Yeah?"

"Desperate men. Maybe we ought to close up."

"Yeah," agreed Lefty. "Maybe we oughta."

They changed clothes, and Joe spent some time in the men's room with the bottle of hair dye. Finally, they turned off all the lights, locked the door and the pumps, climbed into the Chevy and, with the aid of a commandeered road map, headed toward Lanesville, Joe driving, Lefty squirming in the seat beside him.

Lefty was worried. "What about road blocks?" he wanted to know.

"What about them?"

"You can't talk your way through a road block, Joe. You ain't got a driver's license."

"I don't intend to talk my way through road blocks. I don't have to." Joe tapped the road map on the seat between them. "Look at all those blue lines. One of them will get us to Lanesville."

"You're the boss," Lefty said doubtfully.

"I've been thinking about a name," Joe said thoughtfully. "What about Amadeus —"

"Who?"

"Amadeus."

"What's the first name?"

"That's the first name. Amadeus. And for the last name, how about Wimple? Amadeus Wimple. How does that sound?"

"Cheez, Joe —"

"The Reverend Mister Amadeus Wimple."

Lefty thought about it. "It does sound kinda-impressive," he admitted.

"I thought so."

"What about me?" Lefty wanted to know. "Who am I?"

"I don't know. My son? No, not my son. Something — something in keeping with the role of minister."

"Maybe I could be assistant minister?"

Joe glanced at Lefty, noticing again that unfortunate quirk of eye and mouth that branded the poor man as one of civilization's undesirables, and he regretfully shook his head. "No, Lefty, I'm sorry. No one would ever believe you had the call."

"Okay, so what am I?"

Joe clicked his fingers. "I've got it! You're a juvenile delinquent."

"A what?"

"The court paroled you to me at my request. I have undertaken to rehabilitate you."

Lefty shrugged. "Okay by me," he said. "Just so I don't have to get a newspaper route."

Ahead of them were lights across the road. A road block. Joe stopped the car. "Let's see the road map, Lefty. We're about to switch to another blue line."

The Reverend Mister Amadeus Wimple brought himself back to the present. Here he stood, in the doorway of his office, in his home next to the church, and waiting for him was Miss Grace Pettigrew and the fabled Pettigrew diamond.

Reverend Wimple folded his hands across his belly, resisting the impulse to rub them together, and paced slowly and deliberately into the room.

Miss Pettigrew turned as the minister's shoes squeaked his arrival. Her face softened to a blur of joy and she purred, "Good morning, Reverend Wimple."

The minister smiled. "Good morning, Miss Pettigrew." Pausing behind his desk, he gazed benignly out the window at the garden between his cottage and the church, a garden maintained by the Ladies' Aid to supply flowers for the church. "A beautiful sunny morning," he said. "A lovely morning on which to be alive."

"Amen," said Miss Pettigrew reverently. She bowed her head.

Reverend Wimple seated himself behind his desk. He spread his arms wide and rested his hands at the edges of the desk blotter. Beyond Miss Pettigrew he saw Lefty peeking through the doorway, and for a fraction of a second a cloud of annoyance came across his sunny face. Almost immediately, the cloud withdrew and Reverend Wimple beamed on Miss Pettigrew. "What can I do for you this beautiful morning?" he asked.

"You remember, Reverend Wimple, that we discussed the new Municipal Hospital a few days ago."

The minister nodded. "Yes, I remember."

"And you showed me the architect's plans and the estimates."

Reverend Wimple sighed. "Yes. Almost three million dollars. I don't know how we'll ever do it. The Ladies' Aid has been a great help. White elephant sales. Cake sales. Card parties. Bingo. Lawn parties. But it isn't enough. It just isn't enough." The minister shook his head sadly. "I don't know if we ever will have enough."

"Reverend Wimple," said Miss Pettigrew, "since you first came to this town, you've done wonders. Everyone agrees about that. You're a good, fine, honest man, interested in the people around you. You're the first minister this town ever had who made me *want* to come to church."

Reverend Wimple raised a disclaiming hand. "Oh, Miss Pettigrew . . ."

"No, it's true. I hate to say anything bad about a man of the cloth, but as far as the other ministers we've had here were concerned, I wasn't a person at all. I was just one big donation. You're different. You're completely unselfish. And you see people in terms of themselves, not in terms of the collection plate."

"Oh, Miss Pettigrew, you're far, far too harsh."

She subsided somewhat. "Perhaps. But I'm right about you. This hospital you're trying to build. That's the kind of thing I mean. So completely humane, unselfish. The ministers before you tried to raise building funds, too. But not for hospitals. They all wanted to redecorate the church or some da — some such thing."

"I wouldn't call redecorating a church a selfish act, Miss Pettigrew," the minister said gently.

"Still, there's a difference. Well, maybe you won't like this — I know how modest you are — but I've written the Archbishop about you."

Reverend Wimple's eyes widened for just a fraction of a second. Then he gripped his chair arms and fought with his facial muscles. They wanted to move his face from pleased serenity to hysterical shock, but he wouldn't let them. He continued to look bland and pleasant, though he was fighting too hard to be able to speak.

Miss Pettigrew continued, "I wrote him and told him all the wonderful things you've done since you arrived in

17

Lanesville. And I told him about the hospital, and that I was going to make a donation."

"You — wrote the Archbishop? I don't know what to say." Reverend Wimple looked embarrassed, modest and boyishly pleased. "I hope you didn't overpraise me."

"I really don't believe that's possible." Miss Pettigrew reached for her purse. Opening it, she took out the cigarette package. "I wrote to the Archbishop that I was making a donation for your hospital, what I was donating and why. And I told him that what this world needs is a few more ministers like you Reverend Wimple."

The minister ducked his head, blushing. "Please, Miss Pettigrew. No more flattery."

She was opening the cigarette box, pulling cotton out of it. Finally, a small, glittering stone appeared. Miss Pettigrew picked it up gingerly and set it down on Reverend Wimple's desk. "Here," she said, "is my donation. The Pettigrew diamond."

The Reverend held tightly to his chair arms and gazed at the gleaming stone in the center of his green desk blotter. He could not speak.

"It is worth," said Miss Pettigrew, "one million, three hundred thousand dollars. It is one of the twelve largest diamonds in the world. I hope it will help you get your hospital."

"Miss Pettigrew," gasped the minister, "I'm speechless. I'm overwhelmed." He surged out of his chair, his face a portrait of pure joy. "Oh, Miss Pettigrew! The hospital — We *will* have it! We *will* have our hospital!" Rounding his desk, he held her hands tightly. "Thank you," he said softly, and it seemed he might cry from happiness. "Thank you, you dear lady."

Miss Pettigrew felt her own throat tightening. She looked away and pulled her hands out of his grip. "Nonsense. A donation. It's a worthy cause." Hastily, she rose and gathered up her purse. She put the cigarette package and the cotton on his desk. "You can keep it in that. I — I have to shop."

Reverend Wimple stopped her at the door. "Miss Pettigrew," he said, "I want you to know how much I appreciate — how much this means to me."

"I know. Yes, thank you." Then it occurred to her that it was silly of *her* to thank *him*. She was getting flustered, and Grace Pettigrew hated to be flustered. "I — good morning. I'll find the door. You'd better put the diamond in a safe place. Good bye." She hurried out into the sunlight, and Lefty slipped by the Reverend and leaned in awe over the diamond lying on the desk. "You got it," he whispered. "She walked right in and handed it to you!"

"Beautiful," said Joe Docker. "A masterpiece." He looked at Lefty. "Lefty, I should have gone on the stage. I *am* Reverend Wimple."

Lefty shoved the diamond into the cigarette box, packed cotton in after it, and said, "Let's get packed and get outa here."

Joe looked surprised. "We can't leave yet."

"What? Why not? We got the rock."

"Lefty, be sensible. We leave now, sell the diamond to a fence, we get maybe forty per cent of its value. It's hot, and the fence has to cut it up into smaller rocks. That's a beautiful diamond. I'd hate to see it cut up. More than that, I'd hate to get a lousy forty per cent."

"What else can we do?"

"I'm about to sit down and write a letter to a reputable diamond dealer in New York. I'm the Reverend Mister Amadeus Wimple, and I was given the Pettigrew diamond as a donation. It's for sale. At full value. After he buys the diamond, then we can leave."

Lefty shook his head. "Nix, Joe. We can't do it. I was out there listening. The old broad wrote the Archbishop. He knows he didn't send any Reverend Wimple down here. There'll be cops all over the place."

"Maybe. We'll just have to take the chance."

"The *chance?*"

"Lefty, a guy in the Archbishop's position, he's got a secretary. Maybe two secretaries. They're the ones who read all the mail. There's a good chance the Archbishop will never even see that letter. And if he does, will he remember he never sent a minister named Wimple out to this two-bit town church? He didn't remember the church needing a minister, did he?"

"Joe, I hate jail."

The Reverend Mister Amadeus Wimple folded his hands across his belly. "Archibald," he said, "I'd like some coffee. I'm going to write a diamond merchant now. Would you make the coffee for me?"

Lefty considered further argument, but finally gave up with a shrug. He slumped out of the room, headed for the kitchen. Joe Docker opened the cigarette box and withdrew the diamond. He held it in the palm of his hand, gazing lovingly at it. Finally, he put it away again, sat down behind his desk, and wrote a letter.

Reverend Wimple had been pacing back and forth in the front hall, going over his sermon for the coming Sunday, when the doorbell chimed the first line of "Rock Of Ages." Opening the door, the Reverend found himself looking at a burly, crewcut, scrubbed-clean young man in clerical garb, and his first thought was, The legitimate replacement.

"Reverend Wimple?" asked the young minister.

Wimple nodded.

20

"How do you do? I'm Paul Martin, your assistant." Noticing the strange expression on the pastor's face, Reverend Martin added, "Didn't you get the Archbishop's letter?"

"Letter? No — no, I didn't." Recovering himself, Reverend Wimple stepped aside and said, "Come in, come in. Excuse my rudeness. You surprised me."

The young minister smiled as he stepped over the threshold. "I imagine so. I wonder what happened to the letter? Well, things are in their state of chaos in the Archbishop's office. You know how it is."

"Yes, of course. Come on into the parlor. You say you're my assistant?"

"That's right." The two ministers walked into the parlor and sat down in easy chairs. "Someone at the Archbishop's office suddenly realized," Reverend Martin explained, "that the size of the congregation here warranted a pastor *and* an assistant pastor. I wonder if things will ever get straightened out at the Archbishop's." He smiled. "I was assigned there once. Spent four months. You've never seen such a madhouse. They have an archaic filing system dating back to the Catacombs. It's a wonder they ever get things straight." He leaned forward confidentially. "As a matter of fact, did you know they've lost your records?"

"They have?"

Reverend Martin nodded. "Every last one. You'll probably be getting a letter from them on it one of these days. Unless they find the records again, of course."

"Of course."

"By the way, my luggage is still at the station. I walked up. Would you have a car, by any chance?"

"No, I'm afraid I don't. But I'm sure I can get your luggage for you." Joe Docker was recovering and Reverend Wimple was beginning to run smoothly again. "I think you'll find this one of the most pleasant congregations you will ever run across," he told his new assistant. "None of those theological battles that keep pastors shifting from one congregation to another, none of the radical youth element that can be so plaguing and embarrassing. A very pleasant congregation. I'm sure I can call some of my flock to pick up your luggage."

"Thank you very much."

Lefty walked into the room then, appearing as shifty, guilty and generally undesirable as ever, and Reverend Martin looked at him with obvious surprise.

"Ah, Archibald," said Reverend Wimple. "Come meet the new assistant pastor."

"The what?"

"Archibald Denker, Reverend Paul Martin, my new assistant pastor. Archibald," said Reverend Wimple to Reverend Martin, "is a poor unfortunate youth, originally from New York, who was in almost constant difficulty with the police. I came into contact with him in a bus station, where he tried to pick my pocket." Lefty scuffed his foot and looked guilty. "I convinced the court," Reverend Wimple continued, "to place him in my custody, and I have done my best to rehabilitate him. I actually believe I have had some limited success."

Reverend Martin offered a comradely smile to the unfortunate youth. "How do you do, Archibald?" he asked.

"How are ya?"

"Archibald," said Reverend Wimple, "would you show Reverend Martin to his room? I think he'd like the room to the left at the head of the stairs."

"Sure thing."

"You go on up now, Paul, and freshen up. I may call you Paul, mayn't I?"

"Why certainly, Reverend Wimple."

"And I am Amadeus. Now, you go on upstairs and freshen

up. I know how tiresome traveling by train can be. When you're ready, come on down and we'll get to know each other over a cup of tea."

"That would be very pleasant. Thank you very much."

Reverend Wimple watched his new assistant follow Lefty upstairs, and then he collapsed on the sofa and began to chuckle weakly. He was still there, sprawled on the sofa, a foolish grin on his face, when Lefty came back downstairs.

Lefty scurried into the room, sat down beside Joe, and said, "We gotta lam outa here."

Joe said, "Huh, huh, huh, huh."

"Who is that guy?" Lefty wanted to know. "Who is he?"

Joe pulled himself together, and Reverend Wimple answered, "He's my new assistant, Lefty." He looked at Lefty and tried to suppress a grin, but he couldn't help it. "He's my new assistant. And he used to work in the Archbishop's office, and he was telling me that things are in a mess down there. Confusion and chaos everywhere. Lefty, do you know what a mess they're in down at the Archbishop's office?"

Lefty shook his head.

"They've lost my records! He told me so. They've lost every one of my records. Isn't that a panic?"

"You mean they think you're legit?"

"Legit? Why, Lefty, they've sent me an assistant!"

Upstairs, Reverend Martin stood in the bathroom, reflectively drying his face and hands. "God, he's good," he thought. "He looks more like a minister than most *real* ministers do." Reverend Martin left the bathroom and trotted downstairs. He looked at the bogus minister sitting in the living room, and he smiled. "I'm ready for that tea now, Amadeus," he said.

There was no trouble with the representative from the diamond merchant. He came with a certified check, and he left with the diamond. He was a gray little man with a black briefcase handcuffed to his right wrist. He was a dour, sour little gray man who squinted at the Pettigrew diamond through a jeweler's glass, said, "Huh," and handed over the check. He was a grim, unsmiling little man dressed in gray who refused an offer to break bread with the pastor and his new assistant and who drove off in a brand new but quite naturally gray car without having said twenty words all the time he was there.

Lefty found Joe in his bedroom, sitting on the bed and holding the check with both hands. Joe was staring at the check with positively the strangest expression Lefty had ever seen on any face anywhere. It was a look of triumph and a look of pleasure, but it was at the same time a wistful look of something lost, something gone, something dead and destroyed. Lefty stood in the doorway, awed at the expression on Joe's face.

Joe looked up, and said, "Close the door." He spoke very softly, as though he were in a cathedral.

Lefty closed the door.

"Look at it." Joe held out the check. "Look at it," he said, in a whisper; and in the same exultant whisper, he added, "We did it, Lefty."

Even Lefty could tell it was a charged moment. "Yeah," he said huskily.

"Lefty," said Joe, in an awed and hushed voice, "Lefty, we're immortals. The size of this job — We'll be the biggest names in the annals of crime. Bigger than the Brinks job. Bigger than any of them. The whole world will remember the Docker-Denker Caper."

"Maybe they'll call it the Pettigrew Caper," said Lefty.

"Who cares what they call it? It's the top. The Yellow Kid

Weil, Richardson, none of them, none of them never pulled a con as big as this. Lefty, the biggest con haul in history, and it's ours!"

There was a soft knock at the door. The two immortals looked at each other, then Reverend Wimple got to his feet and opened the door. Reverend Martin was standing there. He said, "I've got to go downtown for razor blades. Would you like me to put the check in the hospital account at the bank for you?"

Reverend Wimple smiled. "Thank you, but to tell you the truth I want to reserve that pleasure for myself. You understand."

"Of course. This must be a great moment for you."

"Oh, it is. It is."

"The hospital a reality after all. You know, Amadeus, I've been assigned one place and another, here, there and everywhere, for the last four years, and I want to tell you sincerely and honestly that you are the very best minister I have ever seen. No, that's not flattery, I mean it." Reverend Martin's face bore a puzzled expression as he spoke. "I want you to know," he said, "that I intend to pattern my ministry after yours. You have been a wonderful education for me." Embarrassed, Reverend Martin turned away.

Joe Docker stood in the doorway, listening to the sound of Reverend Martin trotting down the stairs, and he felt a great loss, a great ache, and a great emptiness, and he had to remind himself that he was about to become the most famous con man in history, that he was now immortal.

Lefty said, "We gotta pack." He pushed by Joe. "Come on, Joe, start packin'. We gotta be gone by the time Paul gets back."

Joe made a sudden decision. "Lefty," he said, "you pack and get away. I've got one more thing to take care of. Remember that diner we stopped at on the way in?"

"Yeah?"

"I'll meet you there. If I'm not there by sundown, I'll meet you at George's in Detroit just as soon as I can."

"What are you talkin' about?"

"Lefty, this is only half of it, only half the take. The rest is downtown, in the bank, in the hospital account."

"You goin' after that, too?"

Joe Docker laughed. "Sure, I'm going after that. We don't want to leave anything behind, do we?"

"Why can't I go with you?"

"Lefty, I usually know what I'm doing, don't I?"

"Yeah, sure, only —"

"Well, I know what I'm doing this time, too. Now you get moving. I'm going down to the bank."

"Okay."

Lefty trudged away toward his room, and the Reverend Wimple, looking very solemn, very intent and perhaps a bit frightened as well, left his home and turned toward downtown. He walked all the way, graciously refusing rides from various members of his congregation, and arrived at the bank long before closing time. He filled out a slip, took it to a window, and deposited the check in the special hospital account. Then he walked across to where a short, pudgy gentleman in a wrinkled suit was filling out a withdrawal slip, and said, "You've been following me for the last three weeks. Would you like to walk with me this time?"

The pudgy man looked surprised. He considered denial, but then shrugged. "Okay," he said.

"Fine."

As they walked out of the bank together, the pudgy man said, "Make a withdrawal?"

"No. A deposit. I deposited the money for the Pettigrew

diamond. By the way, my name is Joe Docker."

"Bert Smith."

"You Federal?"

"No," said Bert Smith. "State. You got a record, Joe?"

"Long as your arm. I'm a bigger plum than you know. I'm an escaped con."

Bert raised an eyebrow. "Is that so?"

"Are you the only one on this case? I mean, at the moment."

"Yeah. Why?"

"My partner's lamming."

Bert stopped. He looked surprised. "Was that a dummy check?"

"No, it was the real check. Lefty isn't taking anything out of this town except Lefty."

Bert looked hurriedly around, as though he expected to find a pay phone on a nearby tree.

"Forget it," Joe told him. "Lefty's an expert at cutting out. You'll never even get a whiff of him."

Bert stared hard at Joe Docker, and then shrugged. "You're an oddball," he said.

They started to walk again. "I suppose I am," admitted Joe. "Tell me, my assistant, Reverend Martin — is he a cop, too?"

"No, he's a regular minister. But he's there to keep an eye on you."

"How did you get onto me?"

"Combination of events. Your Archbishop got a letter telling all about what a great job you were doing. He'd never heard of you. Then, we got an anonymous phone tip that something was buggy in the Lanesville Rural Church. We put one and one together and got you. But now I've got nothing on you. Not on this job, anyway. You deposited the haul."

"That's right."

"You could of told me to go fly a kite. You could of taken a plane, and by the time I found out you were wanted for prison break, you'd be nothing but a memory."

"I could even have cashed the check in some other town."

Bert nodded. "You could have. Why didn't you?"

"I don't know."

"What's with your partner?"

"Look. I don't understand myself why I did it. How could I get him to understand? I told him I'd meet him. I won't make it. He'll read the papers."

They had reached Reverend Wimple's house. Joe said, "Come on in."

Bert said, "I intended to."

Inside was pandemonium. Three uniformed cops, locals, were running around with fingerprint powder. Reverend Martin was pacing the floor, rubbing his hands agitatedly together. Miss Grace Pettigrew was sitting in a corner, talking away at the policemen, Reverend Martin, and the world in general, complaining about police inefficiency and stupidity and that this was the second time they had allowed a criminal who had swindled her to make good his escape. And, in state in the living room, sitting silently and majestically, was the Archbishop.

At Joe's and Bert's entrance, everybody shut up and stopped running around. The Archbishop rose and said, "You got him."

Bert shook his head. "No. He went down to the bank, deposited the check, and came back here. *He* brought *me*."

Everyone looked amazed. The Archbishop was the first to recover. "Mister Wimple?" he said.

"Docker."

"Is that your real name? I prefer Wimple. You impersonated a minister. At least, I have no record of your ordination.

You weren't sent here by me. Frankly, it was assumed that you were a swindler."

"I realize that."

"I'm told you have done very fine work during your stay here."

Reverend Martin piped up, "Excellent work, Archbishop. Magnificent work."

Grace Pettigrew scuttled close to Joe and stared in his face "If you weren't here to steal my diamond, why did you come?"

"I did come to steal your diamond. I changed my mind."

The Archbishop said, "You changed your mind?"

"Yes."

Reverend Martin said, "Archbishop, don't you suppose Mister uh, Docker, could be sent to the seminary and then continue as minister here?"

"I'm sorry," said Joe Docker. "I'm wanted for prison break."

There was general consternation, but the Archbishop waded through the startled chatter, took Joe Docker by the arms and gazed into his eyes. "You have good in you," he said. "Some day, you will be a free man again."

Joe nodded. "Two years. I'm due for parole. Unless they give me another sentence for the breakout."

"In your absence," said the Archbishop, "Reverend Martin will carry on for you. Your congregation will eagerly await your return."

Grace Pettigrew was back. "We'll hire the best lawyers. Expense means nothing."

Joe looked at them. "Are you sure —"

A voice beside him said, with mild reproof, "Joe, you know how much I hate jail."

Joe turned. "Lefty! What did you come back for?"

Lefty shrugged his shoulders and looked shifty and guilty. "Same reason you didn't take the dough. No reason. I felt like it, and no locks to pick — everything is open."

Bert Smith, state cop, tapped Joe Docker, wanted criminal, gently on the arm. "Reverend," he said, "would you mind if I used your phone?"

ONE ON A DESERT ISLAND

There is a perennial cartoon idea which begins, "Two men on a desert island. One of them says . . ." And there follows a more or less funny gag line delivered by one of the men. This situation can be potentially funny because, after all, there are two people present. But how would it be if there were only *one* man on that desert island?

Jim Kilbride was one man on a desert island, the largest of a group of four islands off by themselves in the middle of the Pacific, south of the major sea lanes. A mile wide by a mile and a half long, the island was mainly unshaded sand, washed by the ocean during high tide, but with two small hillocks near its center on which grew stunted trees and dark green shrubbery. On the eastern side of the island there was a small curving indentation in the beach, forming a natural cove in miniature, a pool surrounded by a half-circle of sand and a half-circle of ocean. A few birds soared among the islands, calling to one another in raucous voices. The caws of the birds and the whisper of the surf against the beach were the only sounds in the world.

Jim Kilbride happened to be on a desert island, alone, as a result of a series of half-understood desires and unexpected events. He had once been a bookkeeper, snug and safe and land-locked, working for a small textile firm in San Francisco. He had been a bookkeeper, and he had looked like a bookkeeper: short, under five foot seven; the blossomings of a paunch, although he was only twenty-eight; hair straight and black and limp; a round and receding forehead that shone beneath the office lights; round eyes behind rounder spectacles, steel-framed and sliding down his nose; a tie that hung from his neck like the frayed end of a halter; and suits that had looked much better in the department-store window, on the tall and lean and confident mannequins.

He was James Kilbride then, and he wasn't happy. He wasn't happy because he was a cliché and he knew it. He lived with his mother, he never went out with women, and he rarely drank intoxicants. When he read sad tales of contemporary realism, about mild and unobtrusive bookkeepers who lived with their mothers and who never went out with women, he felt ashamed and unhappy because he knew they were writing about him.

One day his mother died. This is where all the sad tales either begin or end, but for James Kilbride nothing changed. The office remained the same, and the bus took no new routes. The house was larger now, and darker and more silent, but that was all.

His mother had been well insured, and after all the expenses there was still quite a bit left over. Something from his reading, or from some conversation over lunch, something from somewhere gave him the idea and the impetus, and he surprised himself considerably one day by buying a boat. He also bought a sailing cap, and on Sunday, alone, he went sailing in the near waters of the Pacific.

But still nothing changed. The office was still bright with incandescent lights, and the bus took no new routes He was still James Kilbride, and he still lay awake in bed at night and dreamed of women and of another, livelier happier sort of life.

The boat was a twelve-footer, with a tiny cabin. It was painted white, and he named it *Doreen*, the woman he had never met. And on one bright Sunday, when the ocean was bright and clean and the sky was scrubbed blue, he stood in his little boat and stared out to sea, and the thought came to him that he might go to China.

The idea grew, until it possessed him. Then it took months, months of thought, of reading, of preparation, before at last he knew one day that he was actually going to do it, that he would really go to China. He would keep a diary of the voyage, and publish it, and become famous, and meet Doreen.

He loaded the boat with canned food and water. He arranged for a leave of absence from his employer (for some reason, he couldn't bring himself to quit completely, even though he intended never to return), and one fine Sunday he took off, smiling at the wheel, and steered the little boat out to sea.

The Coast Guard intercepted him, and brought him back. They explained a variety of rules and regulations to him, none of which he understood. On his second try they were more aggressive, and told him that a third attempt would result in a jail sentence.

The third time, he left at night and managed to slip through the net they had set for him. He thought of himself as a spy, a dark and terrible figure, fleeing ruthlessly through the muffled night from some enemy land.

By the third day out, he was lost. He paced back and forth, his sailing cap protecting him from the sun, and stared out at the trembling surface of the sea.

Ships, black silhouettes, passed far off on the horizon. Islands were mounds of mist far, far away. The near world was blue and gold, the silence broken only by the muted play of wavelets around his boat.

On the eighth day there was a storm, and this first storm he did manage to survive intact. He bailed until the boat was dry, and then he slept for almost twenty-four hours.

Three days later there was another storm, a fierce and out-raged boiling of water and air that came at dusk and poured foaming masses of black water across the struggling boat. The boat was torn from him like a hat in a high wind, and he was left lashing his arms about in the water, fighting and clawing and choking in the grip of the storm.

He reached the island in the night, borne by the waves into the slight protection of the crescent cove. He crawled up the sanded beach, above the reach of the waves, and gave in to unconsciousness.

When he awoke the sun was high and the back of his neck painfully burned. He had lost his sailing cap and both his shoes. He crawled to his feet and moved inland, toward the scrubby trees, away from the burning sunlight.

He lived. He found berries, roots, plants that he could eat, and he learned how to come near the birds as they sat preening themselves on the tree branches and then stun them with hurled stones.

He was lucky, in one way, because in his pocket were wa-terproofed matches that he had put there before the storm hit. He built himself a small shelter from bits of branch and bark, scooped out earth to make a shallow bowl in the ground, and started a fire in it. He kept the fire going day and night; he only had eight matches.

He lived. For the first few days, the first few weeks, he kept himself occupied. He stared for hours out to sea, waiting expectantly for the rescuers he was sure would come. He prowled the small island until he knew its every foot of beach, its every weed and branch.

But the rescues didn't come, and soon he knew the island as well as he had once known the route of the bus. He started drawing pictures in the sand, profiles of men and women, drawings of the birds that flew and screeched above his head, pictures of ships with smoke curling back from their stacks. He played tic-tac-toe with himself, but could never win a game.

He had neither pencil nor paper, but at last he started his book, the story of his adventures, the book that would make him more than the minor clerk he had always been. He composed it, building it slowly and exactly, polishing each word, fashioning each paragraph. He had freedom and individuality and personality at last, and he roamed his island, reciting aloud the completed passages of his book.

But it wasn't enough, it could never be enough. Months had passed and he had never seen a ship, a plane, or any human face. He prowled the island, reciting the finished chapters of his book, but it just wasn't enough. There was only one thing he could do to make the new life bearable, and at last he did it.

He went mad.

He did it slowly, gradually. For the first step, he postulated a Listener. No description, not even age or sex, merely a Listener. As he walked, speaking his sentences aloud, he made believe that someone walked beside him on his right, listening to him, smiling and nodding and applauding the excellence of his composition, pleased by Jim Kilbride, no longer the petty clerk.

He came almost to believe that the Listener really existed. At times he would come to a stop and turn to his right, meaning to explain a point he thought might be obscure, and for just a second he would be shocked to find that no one was there. But then he would remember, and laugh at his foolishness, and walk on, continuing to speak.

Slowly the Listener took on dimension. Slowly it became a woman, and then a young woman, who listened attentively and appreciatively to what he had to say. She still had no appearance, no particular hair color, shape of face, no voice, but he did give her a name. Doreen. Doreen Palmer, the woman he had never met, had always wanted to meet.

She grew more rapidly, once begun. He realized one day that she had honey-colored hair, rather long, and that it waved back gracefully from her head when the breeze blew across the island from the sea. It came to him that she had blue eyes, round and intelligent and possessing great depths, deeper even than the ocean. He understood that she was four inches shorter than he, five foot three, and that she had a sensuous but not overly voluptuous body and dressed in a white gown and green sandals. He knew that she was in love with him, because he was brave and strong and interesting.

But he still wasn't completely mad, not yet. Not until the day he first heard her voice.

It was a beautiful voice, clear and full and caressing. He had said, "A man alone is only half a man," and she replied, "You aren't alone."

In the first honeymoon of his insanity, life was buoyant and sweet. Over and over he recited the completed chapters of his book to her, and from time to time she would interrupt to tell him how fine it was, to raise her head and kiss him, with her honey-colored hair falling about her shoulders, to squeeze his hand and tell him that she loved him. They never talked about his life before he had come to the island, the incandescent office and the ruled and rigid ledgers.

They walked together, and he showed her the island, every grain of sand, every branch of every tree, and how he kept the fire going because he only had the eight matches. And when the infrequent storms came, whipping the island in their insensate rages, she huddled close to him in the lean-to he had built, her blond hair soft against his cheek, her breath warm against his neck, and they would wait out the storm together, their arms clasped tightly around each other, their eyes staring at the glittering fire, hoping and hoping that it wouldn't be blown out.

Twice it was, and he had to use precious matches to start it going again. But they reassured each other both times, saying that next time the fire would be more fully protected and would not go out.

One day, as he was talking to her, reciting the last chapter he had so far finished of the book, she said, "You haven't written any more in a long while. Not since I first came here."

He stopped, his train of thought broken, and realized that what she had said was true. He told her, "I will start the next chapter today."

"I love you," she answered.

But he couldn't seem to get the next chapter started. He didn't want to start another chapter, really. What he wanted to do was recite for her the chapters he had already completed.

She insisted that he start a new chapter, and for the first time since she had come to join him he left her. He walked away, to the other end of the island, and sat there staring out at the ocean.

She came to him after a while and begged his forgiveness. She pleaded with him to recite the earlier chapters of the book once more, and finally he took her in his arms and forgave her.

But she brought the subject up again, and then again, and yet again, each time more sternly, until finally one day he snapped at her, "Don't nag me!" and she burst into tears.

They were getting on each other's nerves, he realized that, and he slowly came also to realize that Doreen was behaving more and more like his mother, the only woman he had ever really known. She was possessive, as his mother had been, never letting him alone for a minute, never letting him go off by himself so he could think in peace. And she was demanding, as his mother had been, insisting that he show ambition, that he return to work on the book. He almost felt she wanted him to be just a clerk again.

They argued violently, and one day he slapped her, as he had never dared to do to his mother. She looked shocked, and then she wept, and he apologized, kissing her hands, kissing her cheek where the red mark of his hand stood out like fire against her skin, running his fingers through the softness of her hair, and she told him, in a subdued voice, that she forgave him.

But things were never again the same between them. She became more and more shrewish, more and more demanding, more and more like his mother. She had even started to look something like his mother, a much younger version of his mother, particularly around the eyes, which had grown harder and less blue, and in the voice, which was higher now and more harsh.

He began to brood, to be secretive, to keep his thoughts to himself and not speak to her for hours at a time. And when she would interrupt his thoughts, either to touch his hand gently as she had used to do or — more often now — to complain that he wasn't doing any work on his book, he would think of her as an interloper, an invader, a stranger. Bitterly he would snap at her to leave him alone, stay away from him, leave him in peace. But she would never leave.

He wasn't sure when the thought of murder first came into his mind, but once there it stayed. He tried to ignore it, tried to tell himself he wasn't the type of person who committed murder, he was a bookkeeper, small and mild and silent, a calm and passive man.

But he wasn't that at all, any more. He was an adventurer

now, a roamer of the sea, a dweller in the middle of the Pacific, tanned and husky, envied by all the poor and pathetic bookkeepers in all the incandescent offices in the world. And he was, he knew, quite capable of murder.

Day and night he thought about it, sitting before the tiny fire, staring into its flames and thinking about the death of Doreen, while she, not knowing his thoughts, not knowing how dangerous her actions were, continued to nag him, continued to demand that he work on the book. She took to watching the fire, snapping at him to bring more bark, more wood, not to let the fire go out as he had done the last two times, and he raged at the unfairness of the charge. The storms had put the fire out, not he. But, she answered, the storm wouldn't have put the fire out had he paid it the proper attention.

At last he could stand it no longer. In their earlier and happier days they had often gone swimming together, staying near shore for fear of sharks and other dangerous animals that might be out in the deeper water. They hadn't swum together for a long time now, but one day casually and cunningly, he suggested they take up the practice again.

She agreed at once, and they stripped together and ran into the water, laughing and splashing one another as though they were still lovers and still delighted with one another. He ducked her, as he had done in the old days and she came up laughing and sputtering. He ducked her again, and this time he held her under.

She fought him, but he felt the new muscles in his arms grow taut, and he held her in a terrible grip, keeping her under till her struggles grew feebler and feebler, until finally they subsided. Then he released her, and watched the ebb and flow of the waves carry her body out to sea, the honey-blond hair swaying in the water, the blue eyes closed, the soft body lying limp in the water. He stumbled back to the beach, shaken and exhausted, and collapsed on the sand.

Now he was alone. Truly alone.

By the next day he was already feeling the first touches of remorse. Her voice came back to him, and her face, and he remembered the happiness of their early days together. He picked over the broken bones of all their arguments, and now he could see so clearly the times when he too had been in the wrong. He thought back and he could see now that he had treated her unfairly, that he had always thought only of himself. She had wanted him to finish the book not for her sake but for his. He had been short-tempered and brutal, and it had been his fault that the arguments had grown, that they had come to detest each other so much.

He thought about how readily and how happily she had agreed to go swimming with him, and he knew that she had taken it as a sign of their reconciliation.

As these thoughts came to him, he felt horrible anguish and remorse. She had been the only woman who had ever returned his love, who had ever seen more in him than a little man stooped over ledgers in a hushed office, and he had destroyed her.

He whispered her name, but she was gone, she was dead, and he had killed her. He sprawled on the sand and wept.

In the following weeks, although he still missed her terribly, he did grow resigned to the loss. He felt that something dramatic and of massive import had moved through his life, changing him forever. His conscience pained him for the murder he had committed, but it was a sweet pain.

Five months later he was rescued. A small boat came to the island from a bulging gray steamer, and the sailors helped him as he climbed clumsily aboard. They brought him to the steamer, and helped him up the Jacob's ladder to the deck, and fed him, and gave him a place to sleep, and when he was refreshed they brought him before the captain.

The captain, a small gray man in faded clothing, motioned to him to sit down in the chair near his desk. He said, "How long were you on the island?"

"I don't know."

"You were alone?" asked the captain gently. "All the time?"

"No," he said. "There was a woman with me. Doreen Palmer."

The captain was surprised. "Where is she?"

"She's dead." All at once he started to weep, and the whole story came out. "We fought, we got on each other's nerves, and I murdered her. I drowned her and her body was washed out to sea."

The captain stared at him, not knowing what to do or say, and finally decided to do nothing but simply to turn the rescued man over to the authorities when they reached Seattle.

The Seattle police listened first to the captain's statement, and then they talked to Jim Kilbride. He admitted the murder at once, saying that his conscience had troubled him ever since. He spoke logically and sensibly, answering all their questions, filling in the details of his life on the island and the crime he had committed, and it never occurred to anyone that he might be mad. A stenographer typed his confession and he signed it.

Old office friends visited him in jail, and looked at him with new interest. They had never known him, not really. He smiled and accepted their awe.

He was given a fair trial, with court-appointed counsel, and was found guilty of first-degree murder. He was calm and dignified throughout the trial, and no one could believe that he had once been an insignificant clerk. He was sentenced to die in the gas chamber and was duly executed.

YOU PUT ON
SOME WEIGHT

He was out, and it felt great. His name was Charles Lambaski, alias Charlie Lane, alias Chuck Lewis, alias Jack Kent, and he'd just done four and a half of a ten-year bit for armed assault.

Prison life had agreed with him in a way, filling him out, so that at thirty-two he looked a bare twenty-five. He was just over six feet tall, and weighed a hundred seventy-eight, very little of it fat. His face was square, with a jutting jaw and a square chunk of nose and wide-set eyes beneath heavy straight brows. His black hair was in a prison crewcut, but pretty soon he'd have a wave back in it and it would be the way it used to be. Everything would be the way it used to be.

He was on a train, coming from the prison into Grand Central. They'd given him the ticket and a suit of clothes and ten bucks and the name of a parole officer he was supposed to go see. The parole officer's name had gone out the window the minute the train was under way, and Charlie had sat back and let his mind drift backward four and a half years. It was as though all those years had never been. It wasn't four and a half years ago, it was yesterday, and he'd had a bad dream last night about picking up a two-bit assault rap. And now the dream was over, and he was on his way back. It was great.

When the train reached Grand Central, Charlie walked off, no suitcase, and took a cab downtown to the old stamping grounds. The cabby complained about breaking the ten, but he did it. Then Charlie walked into the diner on the corner.

The counterman was new. He looked at Charlie and said, "Yessir?"

"Wally around?"

42

"Who's looking for him?"

"Charlie Lambaski."

"I'll take a look."

Charlie sat down at the counter. It felt funny, having to tell the counterman who he was. Four and a half years ago everybody had known Charlie Lambaski. But there was no sweat. Most people would remember him. And the new people would learn the name fast.

Wally came out from the kitchen, a short round guy in a dirty white apron, looking more like the assistant cook than the owner. His round face was wrinkled into a big smile, and he said, "Charlie! Good old Charlie!" And he pumped Charlie's hand.

"Good to see you, Wally."

Wally looked him over critically. "You're looking good, Charlie," he said. "You put on some weight."

"A few pounds," Charlie admitted.

"You want your bankbook?"

"Yeah. I'm flat."

"Come on to the kitchen."

Charlie followed the short man into the kitchen, and waited while Wally fiddled with the dials of the small safe over in the corner. Wally got the safe open, took the bankbook out, slammed the safe, and handed the bankbook to Charlie. "There you are, just like you left it. Only with interest. I brought it around to the bank every once in a while and they put the interest in."

Charlie looked in the bankbook. Over six grand. Great. Enough to live on until he got back in the groove. "Thanks for holding it," he said.

"Anything for a pal," said Wally. "Want a cup of coffee?"

"No, thanks. I got a lot to do."

"Sure thing."

Charlie started away, then turned back. "Andy at the same place?"

"No, he moved about two years ago. Wait a second, I'll write the new address down for you."

Charlie waited, then took the slip of paper, thanked Wally again, and left the diner. He grabbed a cab, read the address to the driver, and then sat back and thought about Andy.

Andy had been his partner. They'd worked together almost all the time, doing jobs for Corsi, who was mixed up in a little bit of everything, so that their jobs weren't too closely defined. One time they'd be collecting from a narcotics retailer who was behind in his payments. Another time they'd be helping organize some small downtown union. Another time they'd be discouraging some clown who thought he could muscle into Corsi's territory. It was a varied and interesting job, without a lot of dull desk work, and except for the rare solo gig like the one he'd been picked up on, it had always been him and Andy all the way.

It was going to be like that again. Charlie was looking forward to it, getting into the old groove. First he'd check in with Andy, maybe stay at his place for a day or two until he got squared away, then find an apartment somewhere and let Corsi know he was available for the payroll again. Back to the old life, sweet and easy.

Andy lived on 47th Street, way over on the west side. Charlie was surprised at how rundown the neighborhood was; Andy's old place had been a lot better. Down the street there was the 16th Precinct, which Charlie remembered from a couple pickups in his youth. It was next to a grammar school, which was maybe a good idea.

Charlie went into the building. There was no elevator, so he climbed the stairs to Andy's third-floor apartment. He pushed the buzzer, and after a minute Andy opened the door, stared at Charlie for a second, and then broke into a big smile, shouting, "Charlie!" He stepped back, throwing the door wide open. "Come on in, you old son of a gun!"

Charlie walked in, grinning back at his partner. Andy hadn't changed a bit. He still looked seventeen, was still wiry, underweight. He was only five foot seven, and most guys thought he was a shrimp and nothing much to worry about, until they tangled with him.

Andy closed the door and they stood in the small crowded living room and looked at one another. Andy said, "Charlie, you old son of a gun."

"Hiya, Andy," said Charlie.

"Let me look at you," said Andy. "You put on some weight, boy."

"A little."

Andy said, "Sit down, sit down. Want a beer?"

"Yeah, I would. I haven't had a beer in four and a half years."

"I'll bring you two. Sit down, I'll be right back."

Andy hurried away to the kitchen, and Charlie looked at the living room. It was full of cheap furniture, overstuffed armchairs and a huge sofa and seven or eight end tables and a bunch of table lamps and floor lamps, like a corner of the Salvation Army store. It was a funny kind of place for Andy to be living in.

Andy came back with the beer, gave one to Charlie, then sat across from him and said, "Boy, it sure brings up old times, Charlie, seeing you again."

"Here's to old times," said Charlie.

"Right."

Charlie tasted the beer and it was great, cool and delicious, tickling his throat. He remembered all the nights in stir, dreaming about a cold can of beer and one thing and another.

Andy was saying, "What are your plans, Charlie?"

"Take it easy for a few days," Charlie told him. "Then get back into the old groove. Think Corsi'll put me back on the payroll?"

Andy looked surprised. "Didn't you see Corsi upstate?"

"Upstate? You mean in the pen?"

"Sure. He went up about a year ago. There was some big stink about unions, there was Congressmen all over the place, and Corsi wound up in the big house."

"I didn't know about it. Who's taking over while he's gone?"

"I don't know who's running things now. I guess the combine's pretty well broken up."

"Aren't you working any more?"

Andy laughed. "You been out of touch, Charlie. I quit the racket over two years ago. When I got married."

Charlie stared at him. "Married?"

"Sure. It was due, Charlie. I had to settle down some time. It's a good thing I did, or maybe them Congressmen would have been breathing down my neck, too."

"Do I know her?"

"I don't think so. Her name's Mary. It used to be Mary Paulzak."

Charlie shook his head. "I don't think I know her."

"She's out shopping now, over to the A&P on Ninth. She'll be back in a little while." He got to his feet. "Come on, I'll show you something."

Charlie followed him through the apartment to a bedroom. Andy opened the door and stood aside for Charlie to look in. Andy's face was grinning and proud.

Charlie looked in. There was a crib in there, and a kid in the crib. He was sound asleep.

"It's a girl," Andy whispered. "Her name's Linda."

"That's great," said Charlie.

They walked back to the living room and Andy said, "Another beer?"

"No, I really gotta get going. I still got to find a place to live."

"Stick around and meet the little woman."

"I'll come back," Charlie told him. "In a day or two."

"You really got to rush?"

"I'm flat. I got to get to the bank before it closes."

"Okay, then. I'll see you later, Charlie."

"Sure."

"I'm in the phone book. Give me a ring when you're settled."

"Sure."

"I work the four-till-midnight shift, so I'm not home evenings. Except Tuesday and Wednesday."

"What are you doing now?"

"I drive a cab."

"Oh. Well, I'll see you around."

"Sure thing, Charlie. It was great to see you again, boy."

"It was great to see you, too, Andy."

Charlie went downstairs and outside to the pavement. He looked both ways, but he didn't see any cabs, so he started to walk. He went by the police station and the grammar school, and he felt kind of empty. This wasn't the way he'd figured it.

He got a cab after a while and went over to the bank. He took five hundred out of the account, bought a copy of the *Times*, and went apartment-hunting. He found a pretty good place, up in the Seventies, on the east side. There was a self-service elevator. He was on the fifth floor, a two-room apartment with a private bath and a kitchenette, and windows looking out from the bedroom to the back of the apartment buildings on the next street over.

There was a fire escape back there, and he was glad. Fire escapes made good exits when there were people you didn't like at the front door.

He left the apartment, after paying the landlord two months' rent, and walked down to the drugstore on the corner. He called the phone company and arranged to have a telephone put in, then called a couple of people he knew, girls, but strangers answered the phone each time, telling him he had a wrong number, there was no one there by that name.

It was getting late. He had dinner in a restaurant and then went down to Corsi's office. Usually, in the old days, the office didn't open till seven or eight o'clock at night, and there were guys coming in or going out until one or two in the morning. The office was in a crummy little building on Lafayette Street, way down, so Charlie took another cab. He thought for a second when he climbed in that the driver was Andy, but it wasn't.

There was nobody at the office. The lettering on the door said MYRON GREENBLATT, *Import-Export.* He left the building and walked over a block to Manny's where the guys used to hang out all the time.

Manny was still there, behind the bar, looking as though he hadn't come out from there since the last time Charlie'd seen him. He was exactly the same, short, bald, with a bullet head and no neck and thick pale lips that never smiled. He saw Charlie and said, "Hi. You're back."

"I'm back," said Charlie. There were four or five guys draped on the bar, but he didn't know any of them. "Beer," he said.

Manny gave him the beer, gave him change for the five Charlie put on the bar, and said, "Haven't seen you around for a while."

"Four and a half years." Charlie told him.

"That long? You look good. You put on some weight."

"Some. Where's all the guys?"

"The old bunch? Gone. Here and there. Up the river. Married. Moved on."

"Nobody's left?"

"I guess not." Manny shrugged. "Every once in a while I see a face from the old days. Like you, tonight."

"What happened?"

Manny shrugged again. "Some of the guys quit, got married, went to work. Some of them got hooked in that big Congressional investigation. Then we had a clean-up campaign and some of them moved out of town. Off to Chicago or Dallas or St. Louis or Reno or somewhere. New people came in. Things change fast."

"Who's running the bookies now?"

"Beats me. It's a different kind of crowd comes in here now. The cops took to watching the place."

A name came to Charlie. He said, "Sally Morrisey around?"

Manny shook his head. "She don't hustle no more. She's married."

"Married?"

"I heard a guy say they make the best kind of wife."

"Yeah, sure."

"You want another beer?"

"No. I — I got some people to see."

"I'll see you around," said Manny.

"Sure thing," said Charlie.

He left the bar and walked along, aimlessly, trying to remember names and faces and people. Somebody had to still be around, somebody who could fill him in, tell him who the boss was now, where to find him, how to get back into the old groove.

A prowl car slid to a stop beside him and a cop got out of the right-hand door. He said, "Okay, buddy, hold on a minute."

Charlie stopped and looked at him. He knew the cop, but he couldn't remember the name.

The cop said, "Charlie Lambaski!" and he looked pleased.

"Hi," said Charlie.

"When'd you get out?"

"Just today."

The cop looked him over. "Jail must have agreed with you," he said. "You put on some weight."

"Yeah," said Charlie.

"You walked across the street against the DON'T WALK sign back there," said the cop. "That's why I stopped you."

"I didn't notice it. I'm sorry."

"I understand. You haven't seen any signs like that for a while."

"Yeah."

"Okay, Charlie, just a warning. We got an anti-jay-walking campaign on. If I felt like being tough, that walk could cost you two bucks."

"I'll watch it from now on," Charlie told him.

"You do that. You got any plans yet, Charlie?"

"Not yet," said Charlie. "I'm just getting moved in."

"You better stay away from the old crowd," the cop said. "You don't want to get mixed up with them again."

"I won't," said Charlie.

"Learned your lesson, huh?"

"Sure."

"Okay, Charlie. See you around. I hope you make out good."

"Thanks."

The cop got back into the prowl car, and Charlie went on

walking. At the next corner he waited till the light turned green, and then crossed. After a while he took a taxi home. For just a second the driver looked like Andy.

Charlie went into his apartment but didn't turn on any lights. He walked through into the bedroom and lay down on the bed, kicked off his shoes and lit a cigarette. He felt around on the dresser beside the bed until he found an ashtray, then rested the ashtray on his chest and smoked and thought. Around him he could hear sounds. Strange sounds, non-prison sounds.

A baby was crying somewhere, and somewhere else a woman was screaming at her husband. The baby and the woman were both pretty far away and he could just hear them. Somebody else, a little closer, had a television set on and he could hear the audience laughing every once in a while.

Upstairs, people moved around and he heard the floor creak and crack under them as they walked. After a while he heard a door slam up there, and then there wasn't any more moving around.

He put the cigarette out, and returned the ashtray to the dresser. He put his hands behind his head and stared up at the dark ceiling, and thought.

Nothing was the way he'd expected. Nothing was working out right. He felt lost, for some reason. Lost and lonely.

There was a sound at the window beside his bed. Charlie froze and listened, and somebody was moving around out there on the fire escape. He heard the window slide slowly open, and then the shade fluttered as somebody raised it from outside.

Charlie moved swiftly and silently off the bed. In his socks, he moved around the room and stood against the wall beside the window. All of a sudden he felt good. He didn't know yet

51

what was up, but he didn't feel lost any more.

A form came through the window, cautiously but not too quietly. Charlie considered letting him have it, but then decided to wait. There might be more than one of them.

There was. A voice from outside whispered, "All clear?"

"All clear," the guy inside said.

Then the second one came in, and closed the window behind him. Charlie waited until the window was closed all the way, but the shade still up, so he could see them both in the pale light from outside, and then he stepped forward and thumped them both, twice each, cold and efficient the way he used to do it. They both went down, and neither of them tried to get up.

Charlie pulled the shade all the way down to the windowsill and then walked over by the door and turned the light on. He took a look at his catch.

Kids, that's all. They were both about seventeen, dressed in black jackets and dark blue levis. One of them was out cold and the other one was sitting up with a dazed expression on his face.

Charlie said to the one who was sitting up, "Wake your buddy. Slap his face."

The sitting-up one slapped the other one's face a couple of times, and then that one sat up too. They blinked up at Charlie, both scared and both trying not to show it.

Charlie said, "You kids taking a night course in burglary?"

They didn't say anything.

"If you aren't," Charlie told them, "you ought to. You two couldn't break into Macy's on bargain day without getting picked up."

One of the kids finally spoke up, saying, "You gonna call the cops?"

"For what? You two? You didn't do anything, just gave me

a little exercise, that's all. Just go home and forget this second-story dodge, you don't know the first thing about it."

The other kid looked defensive. "So what do *you* know about it?"

"I've forgotten more than you'll ever learn." Charlie pulled over a chair and sat facing them. "Look," he said. "When the lights are out, that don't mean there's nobody home. What you do, you scratch at the window like a cat. You do it two or three times. If nobody shows up, *then* you take a chance and open the window. Just a little bit. Then you listen. You listen for breathing, meaning somebody's in the room, asleep. You listen for somebody talking somewhere else in the apartment. You make sure the joint is empty *before* you go in. You got that?"

They nodded, slowly, wide-eyed.

Suddenly, Charlie had an idea. He got to his feet and pushed the chair back against the wall. He felt good now, he felt fine. The old tingling across his shoulders was there again, like when he and Andy were on their way to a job in the old days. Everything was going to be okay after all.

"Listen," he said to the kids. "The people upstairs just went out. Come on, we'll go up the fire escape, I'll show you how it's done. Just a dry run. We don't want to pull any jobs around here, this is headquarters and we don't want any cops in the building. Come on."

He started toward the window, then stopped and looked back at the kids. They were still sitting on the floor, and in their eyes was awe and admiration and respect.

He said, "You with me?"

They scrambled to their feet. "We're with you," they said.

THE CURIOUS FACTS
PRECEDING MY EXECUTION

I'm not sure when it was, exactly, that I knew I must murder Janice. Oh, I'd been thinking of it off and on for months, but I don't remember at what precise moment these idle daydreams hardened into cold and determined resolution.

Perhaps it was the day the mailman brought me the bill for a mink coat of which I had never until that moment heard. When I asked my darling if I might at least *see* this coat for which I was expected to shell out two thousand dollars, one fifth of a year's wages, she confessed prettily that she no longer had it. Shortly after its purchase, while coming home from the city after an exhausting shopping spree along Fifth Avenue, she had lost the dear thing on the train.

Or perhaps it was even earlier than that. Perhaps it was the evening I returned to our midtown apartment, wearied from my labors in the advertising vineyard, and learned that in my absence Janice had managed somehow to buy a house in Connecticut. No more were we to be pallid Manhattanites. It was the invigorating air of the ranch-style developments for us. Besides, it would improve my health — if not my disposition — for me to arise an hour earlier each morning and sprint for the railroad train.

Or perhaps it was much later, after the move from the city and after the lost mink coat and after Lord knows what else. Perhaps it was the evening when, while poring over our financial records, I discovered that in the last year we had spent more in bank fines than for electricity. When I pointed this out to Janice she replied that the fault was clearly mine, since I didn't put enough money into the account to cover the money she wanted to take out.

Or perhaps it wasn't really Janice at all, not finally. Perhaps the catalyst was Karen.

What shall I say of Karen? I had finally received the promotion which made it at least possible for me to feel optimistic about catching up with Janice's spending, and with this promotion had come my own office and my own secretary, and that secretary was Karen.

It was the old story. At home, a wife who was a constant source of frustration and annoyance. At the office, a charming and intelligent — not to say lovely — secretary, with whom one felt one could talk, with whom one could relax. I took to spending evenings in town, telling Janice I had to work late at the office while actually I was with Karen, and the inevitable happened. We fell in love.

But ours could not be a dark and furtive office romance. Karen was too honest, too gentle, too *good* for such a relationship. I knew I had to free myself of Janice and marry Karen, for the sake of everyone's happiness.

I did consider divorce, at first. There was no doubt in my mind that Janice would grant me one, since divorce is quite fashionable in our circle and Janice would wish always to be in fashion, but as I thought about it I saw that there was a problem, and the name of the problem was alimony.

I might legally disencumber myself of Janice as a wife, but it seemed clear to me that I would continue to be responsible for her support. And I understood only too well Janice's insatiable need for money. Statisticians claim that eighty-five per cent of American expenditures are made by women, but Janice beat those statistics cold. Over the course of our marriage I would venture to say that she had, month by month, never permitted her spending of my salary to fall much below one hundred and ten per cent.

It was practically impossible already for me to support both Janice and myself. Add Karen to my responsibilities, and I would be in debtor's prison within six months.

No, divorce was out, and for a while the problem seemed insoluble. But then Janice bought a speedy little foreign car — one of her few purchases I had no objection to — and I waited hopefully for her to demolish the auto and herself on the Merritt Parkway, but nothing ever came of it. Those cars are mawkishly ugly, but they are also exasperatingly safe.

Still, my mind had been turned to a perhaps more productive area of speculation. Could Janice expire? Nothing but grim Death itself, obviously, would ever stop her spending, but where were she and grim D. likely to meet?

Nowhere. Our home was brick outside, plaster and linoleum and plastic inside; not too much likelihood of a good flash fire. The trains to and from the city had their derailments and so on from time to time, but the accidents were almost invariably minor and never on Ladies' Day. The possibility of a jetliner falling out of the sky and landing on Janice was a bit too remote to be counted on. As for disease, Janice was so healthy that most doctors suspected we were Socialists.

At long last I had to accept the truth: it was up to me. If you want a thing done right — or at all — you must do it yourself.

This conviction grew in me, becoming stronger and stronger, until at last I dared broach the subject to Karen. She was, at first, shocked and appalled, but as I talked on, reasoning with her, explaining why it would never be possible for us to wed while Janice still lived, she too began to accept the inevitable.

Once accepted, the only questions left to answer were *when* and *how*. I had four types of murder from which to choose:

a) murder made to look like an accident
b) murder made to look like suicide
c) murder made to look like natural death
d) murder made to look like murder

I ruled out a) accident at once. I had daydreamed for months of possible accidents which might befall Janice, and had finally come to realize that they were all unlikely. And if they were unlikely even to me, who passionately desired that Janice should have herself an accident, how much more un-likely would they seem to the police?

As for b) suicide, there were far too many of Janice's sub-urban friends who would be delighted to volunteer the infor-mation that Janice was happy as a lark — and about as bright — and that she had absolutely no reason in the world to want to kill herself.

As for c) natural death, I knew far too little about medicine to want to try and outwit the coroner at his own game.

Which left d) murder. Murder, that is, made to look like murder. I planned accordingly.

My opportunity came, after a number of false starts, on a Wednesday in late March. On the Thursday and Friday of that week there was to be an important meeting in Chicago, concerning a new ad campaign for one of our most important accounts, and I was scheduled to attend. All I had to do was arrange for Karen to accompany me — an easy matter to jus-tify — and the stage was set.

Here was the plan: I had two tickets on the three P.M. train Wednesday for Chicago, due to arrive in that city at eight-forty the following morning. (Our explanation for trav-eling by train rather than by plane, should we need an expla-nation, was that I could get some preliminary paperwork done on the train, which would have been impossible in the

tubular movie houses which airplanes have lately become.)
At any rate, Karen was to take this train, carrying both our
tickets. We would leave the ad agency together at noon, os-
tensibly headed for Grand Central, lunch, and the train. But
while Karen went to Grand Central, I would hurry uptown to
the 125th Street station, where there was a twelve fifty-five
train for my portion of Connecticut. I would arrive at my
town at two-ten, wearing false mustache, horn-rimmed
glasses, and the kind of hat and topcoat I never wear.

Our mortgaged paradise was a good twenty blocks from
the station. I would walk this distance, shoot Janice with the
.32 revolver I had picked up second-hand on the lower East
Side two weeks before, ransack the house, take the
five-oh-two back to the city, go to a movie, take the twelve
forty-five plane for Chicago, arrive at three-forty A.M., and
be at the railroad station when Karen's train pulled in at
eighty-forty. We would both turn in our return-trip tickets,
claiming we had decided to go back to New York by plane.
This would necessitate my filling out and signing a railroad
company form; an extra little bit of evidence.

It was foolproof. And after a decent period of mourning, I
would marry my Karen and live happily — and solvently —
ever after.

The day arrived. After breakfast I told Janice I would see
her on the following Monday, and I took my suitcase with me
to the office. Karen and I left at twelve, and the plan went
promptly into effect. Karen took both our suitcases with her
to Grand Central and I headed immediately uptown, stop-
ping off only to buy a hat and topcoat. I caught the train at
125th Street and, in its swaying men's room, I donned the
horn-rimmed glasses and the mustache.

The train arrived barely five minutes late, and I found the
station virtually deserted at this time of day; even the news-

stand was shut down. I saw no one I knew in the twenty-block walk to the house, striding along with the pistol an unaccustomed weight in my pocket. I arrived at the house, saw the little foreign car in the driveway, which meant Janice was at home, and let myself in the front door with my key.

Janice was seated in the living room, on the unpaid-for new sofa, reading a slick women's magazine and being instructed, no doubt, in some new way to make money disappear.

At first she didn't recognize me. Then I removed the hat and glasses and she exclaimed, "Why, Freddie! I thought you were going to Chicago!"

"And so I am," I told her. I redonned the hat and glasses, and moved over to close the picture-window drapes.

She said, "Whatever are you doing with that mustache? You look terrible with a mustache."

I turned to face her, and withdrew the pistol from my pocket. "Walk out to the kitchen, Janice," I said. I planned to make it seem as though a burglar had come in the back way, been surprised by Janice in the kitchen, and he had shot her.

She blinked at the gun, then stared wide-eyed at my face. "Freddie, what on earth —"

"Walk out to the kitchen, Janice," I repeated.

"Freddie," she said petulantly, "if this is your idea of a joke —"

"I'm not joking!" I said fiercely.

All at once her eyes lit up and she clapped her hands together childishly and she cried, "Oh, you old dear!"

"What?"

"You did get the washer-dryer after all!" And she leaped to her feet and hobble-trotted out to the kitchen, her high heels going *clack-clack* on the linoleum. Even then, in the last seconds of her life, her only thought was of adding yet another artifact to the mound of possessions she had already heaped high about her.

I followed her to the kitchen, where she was turning, puzzled, to say, "There isn't any washer-dryer —"

I shot from the hip. Naturally, I missed, and the bullet perforated a dirty pot on the stove. I abandoned cowboy-style forthwith, aimed more carefully, and the second shot cut her down in midstream.

Three seconds of silence. They were followed by the sudden *brrriinnnggg* of the front doorbell, the sound box for which was on the kitchen wall three feet from my head.

I jumped, and then froze, not knowing what to do. My first instinct was to stay frozen and wait for whoever it was to go away. But then I remembered Janice's little car in the driveway, advertising her presence. If there were no answer to the doorbell the visitor might become alarmed, might call for help from the neighbors or the police, and I would never manage to avoid detection.

So I had to go to the door. Disguised as I was, I should be able to fool any of Janice's friends, none of whom knew me that well anyway. I would say I was the family doctor, that Janice was sick in bed and could see no one.

The bell rang again while I was still thinking, and the second burst unfroze me. Putting the gun away in my pocket, I hurried through the living room and stopped at the front door. I took a deep breath, steeled myself, and eased the door open an inch.

Peering out, I saw what was obviously a door-to-door salesman standing on the welcome mat. He carried a tan briefcase and wore a slender gray suit, a white shirt, a blue tie, and a smile containing sixty-four gleaming teeth. He said, "*Good* afternoon, sir. Is the lady of the house at home?"

"She's sick," I said, remembering to make my voice

deeper and hoarser than usual.

"Well, sir," he bubbled, "perhaps I could talk to you for just a moment."

"Not interested," I told him. "Sorry."

"Oh, but I'm sure you will be, sir. My company has something of interest to every parent —"

"I am not a parent."

"Oh." His smile faltered, but came back redoubled. "But my company isn't of interest only to parents, of course. Briefly, I represent the Encyclopedia Universicana, and I'm not actually a salesman. We are making a preliminary campaign in this area —"

"I'm sorry," I said firmly. "I'm not interested."

"But you haven't heard the best part," he said urgently.

"No," I said, and slammed the door, reflecting that Janice would have bought the Encyclopedia Universicana, and that I had dispatched her just in time.

But I had to get on with the plan. I would now ransack the house, emptying bureau drawers onto the floor, hurling clothing around in closets, and so forth. Then, when it was time, I would leave for my train.

I turned toward the bedrooms, and the phone rang.

Once again I froze. To answer or not to answer? If I did, if I didn't — I finally decided I should, and would be again the family doctor.

I picked up the receiver, said hello, and a falsely hearty female voice chirped, "Magill Communications Survey calling. Is your television set on, sir?"

I stood there with the phone to my ear.

"Sir?"

"No," I said, and I hung up.

Doggedly, I turned again toward the bedroom, and this time I reached it. Opening a bureau drawer, I tossed its entire contents on the scatter rug. I didn't have to worry about fingerprints, of course, since my fingerprints were quite naturally all over everything. The police would simply assume that the burglar, being a professional, had known enough to wear gloves.

I was working on the third drawer, having pocketed three pairs of earrings and an old watch for realism's sake, when the doorbell rang.

I sighed, plodded wearily to the living room, and opened the door the usual inch.

A short stout woman, smiling like an idiot, said, "*He*llo, there! I'm Mrs. Turner, from over on Marigold Lane? I'm selling chances for our new car raffle at the United Protestant Church."

"I don't want any raffles," I said.

"New *car* raffle," she said.

"I don't want any cars," I said. I shut the door. Then I opened it again. "I have a car," I said. And closed the door again.

On the way back to the bedroom, the echo of that conversation returned to me and it seemed to me I hadn't been very coherent. Could I be more nervous than I'd thought?

No matter. In little more than an hour I would leave here and catch the train for New York.

I lit two cigarettes, got annoyed, stubbed one out, and went back to work. I finished the bureau and the one drawer in the vanity table and was about to start on the closet when the phone rang.

I had never before realized just how shrill, just how *grating,* that telephone bell actually was. And how long each ring was. And what a little space of time there was between rings. Why, it rang three times before I so much as took a step, and it managed to get in one more jarring *dreeeeep* for good measure as I hurried down the hall to the living room.

I picked up the receiver and a male voice said in my ear, "Hello, Andy?"

"Andy?"

He said it again. "Hello, Andy?"

Something was wrong. I said, "Who?"

He said, "Andy."

I said, "Wrong number," and gently hung up.

The doorbell clanged.

I jumped, knocking the phone off its stand onto the floor. I scooped it up, fumbling, and the doorbell *spanged* again.

I raced across the room, and forgetting all caution hurled the door open wide.

The man outside was gray-haired, portly, and quite dignified. He wore a conservative suit and carried a black briefcase. He smiled upon me and said, "Has Mr. Wheet been by yet?"

"Who?"

"Mr. Wheet," he said. "Hasn't he been here?"

"No one by that name here," I said. "Wrong number."

"Well, then," said the portly man, "I suppose I'll just have to talk to you myself." And before I knew what was going on he had slipped past me and was standing in the living room, looking around with a great display of admiration and murmuring, "Lovely, lovely. A really lovely room."

"Now, see here —" I began.

"Sampson," said the portly man, extending a firm plump hand. "Encyclopedia Universicana. Little woman at home?"

"She's sick," I said, ignoring the hand. "I was just fixing some broth for her. Chicken broth. Perhaps some other —"

"I see," said the portly man. He frowned as though thinking things over, and then smiled and said, "Well sir, you go right ahead. That'll give me a chance to set the presentation up."

With that, he sat himself down on the sofa, right where Janice had been when I first came in. I opened my mouth, but he opened his briefcase faster, dove in, and emerged with a double handful of paper. Sheets and sheets of paper, all standard typewriter size, all gaily colored in green and blue, prominently featuring photographs of receding rows of books. SAVE! roared some of the sheets of paper in block print. FREE! screamed others, in red. TRIAL OFFER! shrieked still more, in rainbow hues

Portly Mr. Sampson leaned far forward, puffing a bit and began to arrange his papers in rows upon the rug, just in front of his pointed-toe, highly polished black shoes. "Our program," he said, smiling at me, and lowered his head to distribute more sheets of paper over the floor.

I stared at him. Not five feet from where he was sitting my late wife lay sprawled upon the kitchen floor. In the bedroom chaos was the order of the day. In just under an hour I would be leaving here to catch my train back to the city. I would leave the pistol — wiped clean — in some litter basket in town, knowing full well some enterprising soul would shortly pick it out again, and that by the time the police got hold of it, if they ever did, it would have committed any number of crimes past this current one. And then I would fly to Chicago and see Karen. Lovely Karen. Dear darling Karen.

And this miserable man was trying to sell me encyclopedias!

I opened my mouth. Quite calmly I said, "Get out."

He looked up at me, smiling quizzically. "Eh?"

"Get out," I said.

The smile flickered. "But — you haven't seen —"

"Get out!" I repeated, this time a bit louder. I pointed at the door, my forearm upsetting a table lamp. "Get out! Just — just — just get out!"

The miserable creature began to sputter: "Well, but — see here —"

"GET OUT!"

I dashed forward and grabbed all his papers, crumpling them this way and that, gathering them in my arms and hurried with them to the front door. In turning the knob I dropped a lot of them, but the remainder I hurled outside, and they fluttered leaflike to the lawn. I kicked at those that had fallen around my feet, and turned to glare at Mr. Sampson as he scuttled from the house. He wanted to bluster, but he was a bit too startled and afraid of me to say anything.

I slammed the door after him and took a deep breath, telling myself I must be calm. I lit a cigarette. I lit another cigarette. Irritably I stubbed the first one in a handy ashtray and lit a third. *"Tcha!"* I cried, and mashed them all out, and stormed back to the bedroom, where I tore into the closet with genuine pleasure. Once the closet was a hopeless wreck I ripped the covers from the bed and dumped the mattress on the floor. Then I stood back, breathing hard, to survey my handiwork.

And the doorbell rang.

"If that is Mr. Sampson," I muttered to myself, "by heaven I'll —"

It rang again. We had an incredibly loud doorbell in that house. Odd I'd never noticed it before.

It rang a third time as I was on my way to answer, and I almost shouted at it to shut up, but managed to bring myself under control by the time I reached the door. I even remembered to open it no more than an inch.

A tiny girl in a green uniform stood looking up at me; she bore a box of cookies.

Life, I reflected at that moment, is unkind and cruel. I

said, "We already bought some, little girl," and softly closed the door.

And the telephone screamed.

I leaned against the door and let my nerves do whatever they wanted. But I knew I couldn't stay there; the phone would only make that noise again. And again. And again and again and again until finally I would have to give up and answer it. The only sensible move would be to answer it right away. Then it wouldn't make that noise any more.

A good plan. I was full of good plans. I went over and picked up the phone.

"Hiya, neighbor!" shouted a male voice in my ear. "This is Dan O'Toole, of WINK. Can you Top That Mop?"

"What?"

"This is the grand new radio game everybody's talking about, neighbor. If you can Top That —"

I suppose he kept on talking. I don't know. I hung up.

I caught myself about to light a cigarette, and made myself stop. I also forced myself to be calm, to think rationally, to consider the circumstances. The house, except for my own ragged breathing, was blessedly silent.

With waning fervor I studied once more the tableau I was leaving for the police. The dead woman in the kitchen, and the ransacked house. All that remained was to fix the back door to make it look as though the burglar had forced his way in.

It seemed as though my plan should work perfectly well. It really did seem that way.

Slowly I trudged out to the kitchen. For some reason I no longer believed in my plan, but was merely going through the motions because there was nothing else to do. All of life was involved in a great conspiracy against me, and I didn't know why. Could every day be like this in the suburbs? Was it possible that Janice's reckless spending had simply been a form of escape, a kind of sublimated satisfaction in lieu of biting people like Mr. Sampson and Top That Mop?

At the back door I paused, listening for doorbells and phone bells and church bells and jingle bells, but there was only silence. So I opened the door, and a short round woman was standing there, her finger halfway to the bell button. She was our next-door neighbor, she wore a flour-stained apron, and she had an empty cup in her other hand.

I gaped at her. She looked at me in puzzled surprise, and then her gaze moved beyond me and came to rest on something behind me, at floor level. Her eyes widened. She screamed and let go of the empty cup and went dashing away.

I went rigid. I stared at the cup, watching it in helpless fascination. It seemed to hang there in midair for the longest while, long after its owner had run completely out of sight, and then, quite slowly at first, it began to fall. It fell faster, and faster, and at long last it splattered itself with a terrible crash on the patio cement.

And when that cup splattered, so did I. I went all limp, and sat down with a thud on the kitchen floor.

And there I sat, waiting. I sat waiting for the census taker and the mailman with a Special Delivery letter, for the laundry man and the Railway Express driver, for the man from the cleaners, a horde of Boy Scouts on a paper drive, a political candidate, five wrong numbers, the paper boy, the police, the milkman, a lady collecting for a worthy charity, a call from the tax assessor's office, a young man working his way through college selling magazines . . .

GOOD NIGHT, GOOD NIGHT

Pain.

Pain in his chest, and in his stomach, and in his legs. And a girl singing to him, her voice too loud. And darkness, with shifting blue-gray forms in the distance.

I'm Don Denton, he thought. I've hurt myself.

How? How have I hurt myself?

But the girl was singing too loudly, so it was impossible to think. He felt himself falling away again, blacking out again, and with sudden terror he knew he wasn't fading into sleep, he was fading into death.

He had to wake up! Open the eyes, force the eyes open, *make* the eyes open. Listen to that damn loud girl, *listen* to her, concentrate on the words of the song, force the mind to get to work again.

Good night, good night,
We turn out every light;
The party's done, the night's begun,
Good night my love, good night.

It was dark, blue-gray dark, and his eyelids were terribly heavy. He forced them up, wanting to see, wondering why the singing girl and the strange blue-gray dark.

Oh. The television set. All the lights in the room were off, and the doors closed, and the shades drawn against the nightglow of the city. Only the television set lit the room, with pale and shifting blues.

As he watched, the girl came to the end of her song and

bowed to thunderous applause. And then he saw *himself*, striding into view across the stage, smiling and clapping his hands together, and memory at last came flooding back.

He was Don Denton. This was Wednesday night, between the hours of eight and nine. On the television screen was appearing *The Don Denton Variety Show*, taped that afternoon.

The Don Denton Variety Show was, in television jargon, live-on-tape. The show he was now watching was not a kinescope of a previously presented program, nor was it a motion picture utilizing the cutting and editing techniques of film. Since it was neither, since it had been run through just as though it actually were going on the air at the time it had been performed, it was a "live" show, even though it had actually been recorded on videotape three hours before airtime. Union requirements and other factors made it cheaper and more feasible to do the show between five and six than between eight and nine.

Denton watched all his own shows, not because he was an egotist — though he was — but out of a professional need to study his own product, to be sure it did not deteriorate and, if possible, to see how it might be improved.

Tonight, after finishing the show, he had had dinner at the Athens Room and then had come home to watch the show. He was alone in the apartment, of course; he never permitted anyone else to be in the place while he watched one of his shows. He had come home, changed into slacks and sport shirt and slippers, made himself a drink, flicked on the television set, and settled himself in the chair with the specially built right arm. The arm of this chair was a miniature desk, with two small drawers in the side and a flat wooden work space on top, where he rested his notebook.

Across the room the eight o'clock commercials had flickered across the television screen, and then the opening credits of *The Don Denton Variety Show* had come on. He had watched and listened in approval as his name was mentioned by the announcer and appeared on the screen three times, and then the fanfare had blared forth, the camera had trained itself on the empty curtain-faced stage, and through a part in the curtain had come the tiny blue-white image of himself, in response to a great wave of applause.

He had frowned. Too much applause? The studio audience's efforts were — jargon again — "technically augmented" in the control booth, and the augmentation tonight might have been just a little too enthusiastic. He had made a note of it.

The image of himself on the television screen had smiled and spoken and cracked a joke. Sitting in his chair at home, Don Denton had nodded approvingly. Then the image had introduced a girl singer, and Denton had turned over the pad to doodle awhile on its back. And then —

Yes. Now that memory came back, too, and he understood how he had been hurt. The apartment door, off there to his right, had suddenly opened, he remembered that now, and he . . .

He turned toward it, annoyed. The show was on, damn it, he was not to be disturbed. They all knew that, knew better than to come here between eight and nine on a Wednesday night.

The only light came from the hall, from behind the intruder, so that he — or she — was in silhouette, features blacked out. It was January outside, so the intruder was encased in a bulky overcoat; Denton couldn't even be sure whether it was a man or a woman.

He half rose from the chair, frowning in anger. "What the hell do you —"

Then there was a yellow-white flash from the center of the silhouetted figure, and the beginning of a thunderclap, and silence.

Until he heard the girl again, singing too loudly.

He'd been shot! Someone — *who?* — had come in here and shot him!

He sat slumped in the chair, trying to figure out where in his body the bullet might be and the probable extent of the damage. His legs ached with a throbbing numbness. There was a clammy weight in his stomach, pressing him down, nauseating him. But the bullet wasn't there, nor in his legs. Higher it was, higher, higher . . .

There!

Inside the chest, high on the right side, a burning core, a tiny center of heat and pain radiating out to the rest of his body. There it was, still within him, and he knew it was a bad wound, a terribly bad wound . . .

A crowd applauded, and he was startled; he'd been slipping away again. He focused his eyes with some difficulty and saw himself again on the television screen, just stepping backward out of sight as the comic came out — "It's a funny thing about these new cars . . ." — And just to the right of the television set was the telephone on its stand.

He had to get help. The bullet was still in his chest, it was a terribly bad wound, he had to get help. He had to stand; he had to walk across the room to the telephone; he had to call for help.

He moved his right arm, and the arm seemed far away, the hand a million miles away, pushing through thick water. He tried to lean forward, and the pain buffeted him, slapping him back into the seat. He gripped the chair arms with hands that were a million miles away; he slowly pulled himself forward, grimacing against the pain and the effort.

But his legs just wouldn't work. He was paralyzed below the waist, completely, nothing but his arms and his head were still working. He was dying, good God, he was dying, death was creeping slowly upward through his body. He had to get help before death reached his heart.

He tugged himself forward, and the pain lashed him again and his mouth stretched open in what should have been a scream. But no sound came out, only a strained rush of air. He couldn't make a sound.

The television set laughed with a thousand voices.

He looked again at the screen, the comic leering there. "Please," he whispered.

" 'That's all right,' she says," the comic answered. " 'I got an extra engine in the trunk!' "

The television set roared.

Bowing, bowing on the screen, the comic winked at the dying man, laughed and waved and ran away.

Then the unwounded image of himself came back, tiny and colorless but whole and sound, breathing and laughing alive and sure, shouting, "That was great, Andy, great!" The image grinned up at him from the screen, asked him, "Wasn't it?"

"Please," he whispered.

"Who do you suppose we have next?" the image asked him, twinkling. "Who?"

Who? Who had done this? He had to know who had done this, who had shot him, who had tried to murder him.

He couldn't think. A busy spider scurried across his brain, trailing gray threads of fuzzy silk, webbing him in, slurring his thoughts.

No! He had to know *who!*

A key. There was a clear thought; a key, it had to be someone with a key. Remembering, thinking back, he seemed to hear again the tiny click of a key just before the door had swung open.

They had to have a key; he remembered locking the door. He always locked the door. This was New York, this was Manhattan, one always locked doors.

There were only four people in the world who had keys to this apartment, other than Denton himself, only four people in the world.

Nancy. His wife, from whom he was separated but not divorced.

Herb Martin, the chief writer for *The Don Denton Variety Show.*

Morry Stoneman, his business manager.

Eddie Blake, the stooge-straightman-second comic of the show.

It had to be one of the four. They all knew he'd be here, alone, watching the show. And they were the ones with keys.

One of those four. He let the remembered faces and names of the four circle in his mind — Nancy and Herb and Morris and Eddie — while he tried to figure out which one of them would have tried to kill him.

And then he closed his eyes and almost gave himself up to death. Because it could have been any one of them. They all hated his guts, all four of them, hated him enough to be the one who had come here tonight to kill him.

Bitter, bitter, that was the most bitter moment of his life, to know that of four of the people closest to him hated him enough to want to see him dead.

His own voice said, "Oh, come now, Professor."

He opened his eyes, terrified. He'd almost faded away there, he'd almost passed out, and to pass out was surely to die. He could no longer feel anything below the knee, and his fingers were now numb and separate. Death. Death creeping in from his extremities.

No. He had to stay alive. He had to fool them, all four of them. He had somehow to stay alive. Keep thinking, that was it, keep the mind active, fight away the darkness.

Think about the four of them. Which had done this thing?

"*Gott im Himmel,*" cried a gruff voice, and the augmented laughter dutifully followed on its heels.

Denton strained to see the television screen. Eddie Blake was there now, doing that miserable Professor routine of his. Denton watched, and wondered. Could it have been him?

Eddie Blake stood in the doorway of the dressing room. "You wanted to see me, Don?"

Denton, sitting before the bulb-flanked mirror as he removed his make-up, didn't bother to look away from his own reflection. "Come on in, Eddie," he said softly. "Close the door."

"Right," said Eddie. He stepped inside, shut the door, and stood there awkwardly waiting, a tow-headed hook-nosed wide-mouthed little comic with a long thin frame and enough nervous mannerisms for twenty people.

Denton made him wait until he'd finished cleaning his face of make-up. The time was a little after six, just after the taping of the show. Denton wasn't happy with the way it had gone today, and the more he thought about it the more irritated he was getting. He spun around finally and studied Eddie with a discontented frown. Eddie was still in the Professor costume, still in make-up, his left hand fidgeting at his side. Once, years ago, he'd been in an automobile accident, leaving his right arm weak and nearly useless.

"You were lousy tonight, Eddie," Denton said calmly. "I can't remember when you've been worse."

Eddie flushed, his face working, trying to hide the quick

anger. He didn't say a word.

Denton lit a cigarette, more slowly than necessary, and when it was going he said, "You back on the sauce, Eddie?"

"You know better than that, Don," Eddie said indignantly.

"Maybe you just weren't thinking about the show tonight," Denton suggested. "Maybe you were saving yourself for that Boston date."

"I did my best, Don," Eddie insisted. "I worked my tail off."

"This show comes first, Eddie," Denton told him. He studied the comic coldly. "Where would you be without this show, Eddie?"

Eddie didn't answer. He didn't have to; they both knew what it was. The answer was *nowhere*. Eddie was basically a straight man, a stooge, a second banana, and he'd spent years either as an unsuccessful single or second man to a string of second-rates. It was *The Don Denton Variety Show* that had finally given him his break, gained him exposure to a large national audience, and allowed him to develop routines of his own like the Professor bit. One of the results was outside jobs like the Boston night-club gig coming up this weekend.

"This show comes first, Eddie," Denton repeated. "You don't do anything else anywhere until you're doing your job on this show."

"Don, I —"

"Now, in your contract it says I've got to approve any outside booking you take on."

"Don, you aren't going to —"

"I've been pretty lax about that," Denton went on, smoothly overriding Eddie's protests. "But now I see what the result is. You start doing second-rate work here, saving yourself for your other jobs."

"Don, listen —"

"I think," Denton said, "you better cut out all other jobs until you get up to form here." He nodded. "Okay, Eddie, that's all. See you at rehearsal Friday morning." He turned back to the mirror, started unbuttoning his shirt.

Behind him Eddie fidgeted, ashen-faced. "Don," he said. "Listen, Don, you don't mean it."

Denton didn't bother answering.

"Don, look, you don't have to do this, all you have to do is tell me —"

"I just told you," said Denton.

"Don — listen, listen, what about Boston?"

"What about Boston?"

"I've got a date there this weekend, I —"

"No you don't."

"Don, for God's sake —"

"You'll be rehearsing all weekend. You won't have time to go to Boston."

"Don, the booking's already been made!"

"So what?"

Eddie's left hand darted and fidgeted, playing the buttons of his shirt like a clarinet. His eyes were wide and hopeless. "Don't do this, Don," he begged. "For God's sake, don't do this."

"You've done it to yourself."

"You dirty louse, *you're* the one who was off tonight! Just because *you* can't get a laugh that doesn't come off tape —"

"Stop right there." Denton was on his feet now, and stood glaring until Eddie blinked and swallowed and looked away. Denton said, "Don't forget the contract, Eddie, don't you ever forget it. It's still got four and a half years to run. And I can always throw you off the show, cut off your pay, and hold you to the contract. I can keep you from making a nickel, Eddie boy, and don't you forget it. Unless you'd like to wash dishes for your dough."

Eddie retreated to the door, weak and mutinous and frightened. "Don't push it, Don," he said, his voice trembling. "Don't push it too far."

"X plus Y," said the heavily accented voice on the television set, "iz somezing un-prro-*nounz*-able!"

Denton blinked, trying to keep his eyes in focus. His sight kept blurring. He stared at the grinning little Professor figure on the screen. Eddie Blake? Could it have been Eddie Blake?

There was a way Eddie might figure it. With Denton in his grave the contract between them would be no longer a problem. And who would be the most likely immediate replacement for Denton on the show? Why, Eddie Blake, of course, who already knew the show cold, knew the people, and was associated with the show in the public mind. Denton's death might be, in Eddie's eyes, the stepping stone to top banana.

But could he have done it? Eddie Blake? That weak, ineffectual, fidgety little nothing?

There were new voices coming from the TV now. He stared, trying to make out the picture, and finally saw it was the commercial. A husband and wife, a happy and devoted couple, and the secret of their successful marriage was . . . their brand of instant coffee.

Successful marriage. He thought of Nancy. And of the writer, Herb Martin.

"I want a divorce, Don."

He paused in his eating. "No."

The three of them were at the table together in the Athens Room, Denton and Nancy and Herb. Nancy had said, this afternoon, that she wanted to talk to him about something important, and he had said it would have to wait until after the show. He didn't want to be upset by domestic scenes just before airtime.

Herb now said, "I don't see what good it does you, Don. You obviously don't love Nancy, and she just as obviously doesn't love you. You aren't living together. So what's the sense of it?"

Denton looked sourly at Herb and pointed his fork at Nancy. "She's mine," he said. "No matter what, she's still mine. It'll take a better man than you, buddy, to take anything of mine away from me."

"I can get a divorce without your consent," Nancy said. She was a lovely girl, oval face framed by long blond hair. "I can go to Nevada —"

"If there's any divorce," Denton interrupted, "and there won't be — but if there was one *I'd* be the plaintiff. And I wouldn't even have to leave the state. Adultery will do very nicely. And the co-respondent just incidentally used to be a Commie."

Herb said, "That's getting old-hat, Don. How long you think you can use that threat?"

"For as long as there's a blacklist, baby," Denton told him.

"Things are different now. The blacklist doesn't mean what it used to."

"You think *so*? You want to *test* that theory?"

"Nineteen thirty-eight —"

"Baby, it doesn't matter *when* you were a Commie, you know that. Now, basically I like you, Herb, I think you write some fine stuff. I'd hate to see you thrown out of the industry just —"

"Why won't you let us *alone*?" wailed Nancy, and diners at nearby tables looked curiously around.

Denton patted his lips with the napkin and got to his feet. "You've asked your question," he said, "and I've given my answer."

"Do me a favor," said Herb. "On your way home, get run over by a cab."

"Don't joke with him, Herb," Nancy said, putting her hand on the waiter's arm.

"Who's joking?" said Herb grimly.

"All joking aside, friends," his voice said, "Dan and Ann are one of the finest dance teams in the country."

Slumped in the chair, Denton stared desperately at himself on the screen. That little self there on the screen, he could talk, he could move around, he could laugh and clap his palms together. He was alive, and content, and not hurt.

Who? Who? *Who?* Herb? Nancy? Both of them together?

He tried to think back, tried to visualize that silhouetted figure again, tried to see in memory whether it had been a man or a woman. But he couldn't tell; it had been only a bulky shape inside an overcoat, only a black shape outlined against the hall light. Inside the overcoat it could have been as thin as Eddie, as shapely as Nancy, as muscular as Herb, as fat as Morry Stoneman.

Morry Stoneman?

Dan and Ann, one of the poorest dance teams in the country, were stumbling through their act before the cameras. Backstage, fat Morry Stoneman was dabbing at his forehead with a handkerchief and saying, "They looked good, Don, honest to God they did. They got all kinds of rave notices on the Coast —"

"They're stumblebums," Denton told him coldly. He glanced out at Dan and Ann. "And I do mean stumble."

"You approved the act, Don. You gave it the okay."

"On your say-so, Morry. Or is it *my* fault?"

Morry hesitated, dabbing his face with the handkerchief, looking everywhere but at Denton. "No, Don," he said finally. "It isn't your fault."

"How much, Morry?"

Morry's face became a white round O of injured innocence. "Don, you don't think —"

"How much are they giving you, Morry?"

The white round O collapsed, and Morry mumbled, "Five."

"Okay. We take that off your cut."

"They got rave notices on the Coast, Don, I swear to God they did. I can show you the clips."

Denton brushed that aside, said, "That's five hundred more on the IOU's."

"That's what I was thinking of." Morry's left hand held the handkerchief, dab-dab-dabbing at his forehead, while his right hand clutched at Denton's sleeve. "All I was trying to do," he said urgently, "was promote some extra cash so I can start paying off. You want that money back, don't you?"

"So you can thumb your nose and walk out on me? That'll be the day, Morry. I want you around."

"Listen, would I walk out on you? Don, I —"

"That's right," said Denton. "You haven't been trying to get next to that Lyle broad."

Injured innocence again. "Who told you a dumb thing like that, Don? I wouldn't —"

"You won't," Denton interrupted him. "The minute you quit me the IOU's become payable. So you can just forget Lisa Lyle."

Applause. It was time to go back and give Dan and Ann a few televised words of congratulation. Denton jabbed a thumb at the bowing, smiling dancers onstage. "Get them out of here," he said. "I don't want them around for the final bow." Then he trotted onstage, ignoring the expression on Morry's face.

He found the right camera, and beamed at it. "For our last act tonight . . ."

"For our last act tonight," the image on the screen told his dying likeness, "we have that wonderful new singer — she's getting her own show starting in March, you know — *Lisa Lyle!*"

Denton watched his blue-and-white self, teeth gleaming, hands beating together. "She wants Morry," he whispered at that unhearing image. "And Morry wants her."

Morry? Was it Morry who'd shot him?

Who was it?

The space between himself and the television set seemed to blur and mist, as though a fog were rising there. He blinked and blinked and blinked, afraid it was death.

In the fog, then, he seemed to see them, the four who could have done this to him. Herb and Nancy, directly in front of him, arms around one another, studying him in somber triumph. Eddie Blake, off to the right, his left hand playing his shirt buttons with jittery fingers as he stared at Denton in tentative defiance. And Morry, behind the others and off to the left, stocky and unmoving, glaring his frustration and hate.

"Which one of you?" Denton whispered. Fighting back the pain in his chest, he strained forward toward them, demanding, willing them to speak, needing to know.

And they spoke. "When you are dead," said Nancy, "I can marry Herb."

"When you are dead," said Eddie, "it will be *The Eddie Blake Variety Show.*"

"When you are dead," said Herb, "so is that blacklist threat."

"When you are dead," said Morry, "so are those IOU's. I can make a mint with Lisa Lyle."

"Which one of you? Which one of you?"

The fog shifted and swam, the figures faded. Straining, he could once more make out that other figure, the black silhouette framed by the doorway, lit only from behind. He stared at the silhouette, needing to know, demanding to know which one it had been.

He searched the bulky shapeless outline, looking for something that would tell him. The remembered outline of the head, the ears, the neck, then the collar of the coat, the —

The ears.

He squinted, trying to see, trying to remember, and yes, the ears had been visible. Which reduced the four possibilities to three; Nancy had long blond hair that curled around her face and covered her ears. It couldn't have been Nancy.

Three. Now it was one of three, Herb or Eddie or Morry. But which one?

Height. That would help, if he could visualize the figure well enough, if he could see it in relation to the door frame, the height . . . Eddie and Herb were both tall, Morry was short. Probably Eddie even seemed taller than he was because he was so thin. But really he was —

Denton pulled himself back to awareness. His mind was beginning to wander, and he recognized that as a danger sign. He couldn't lose consciousness, he couldn't permit himself to give up awareness, not until he *knew*.

He stared at the outlined figure in the fog before his face, and slowly he forced himself to visualize the door frame around it again, and slowly he saw it clear, and the figure was tall.

Tall.

Eddie or Herb. Herb or Eddie.

It was those two, now, one or the other. He tried to super-impose the figures of each of them on the figure of the silhou-ette, but the bulky coat ruined that. It was impossible, there was nothing left to distinguish it, make it any more one person than another.

And death was creeping closer, moving in like the fog, creeping across his shoulders and down among his ribs, up from his legs to touch his stomach with icy fingers. He had to know soon.

He tried to see it all again, in the mist between himself and the television set, seeing it like a run-through for the show, seeing every step in all its detail. The door opening, the black figure standing there, the bright flash —

From the figure's *right* side!

"Herb!" he shouted.

It couldn't have been Eddie. Eddie was left-handed, that crippled right hand of his would never have been able to lift the gun or squeeze the trigger. It had been Herb.

With his shout — his whispered shout — the fog faded completely away from before his eyes, the outlined figure was gone. Sight and sound returned, and he heard Lisa Lyle singing her song. It was the last number of the show. Almost nine o'clock; he'd been sitting here wounded now for nearly an hour.

Lisa Lyle finished, and there was thunderously augmented applause, and he saw himself come striding into camera range. He saw that whole and walking self, that strong and smiling self come out and wave at the audience in the theater and at home, wave at Don Denton lying in his chair.

He stared at that tiny image of himself. That was *him!* Him, at six o'clock, with two hours left before the bullet, and that self could somehow change this, could somehow keep what had and was happening from being true.

Dream and reality, desire and fact, need and truth, all shifted and mingled confusedly in his mind. He was barely real himself. He was dying faster now, becoming less and less real, and the image on the television screen was almost all that was left of him.

That image had to be warned. "It's Herb!" Denton called. "It's Herb!" Whispering it at that tiny blue-gray self across the room. Reality was going, like the lights of a city flicking out one by one, and the darkness was spreading in. "Be careful! It's Herb!"

"That's about all the show there is, folks," answered his image.

"Don't go home! Listen! It's Herb!"

"I certainly hope you've enjoyed yourself," said the image, smiling at him.

"Stay away!" screamed Denton.

The image waved a careless hand, as though to tell Denton not to be silly, there was nothing to worry about, nothing at all. "We'll be seeing you!"

He had to get away, he had to live, he had to warn himself not to come here tonight. There was that image, the *real* Don Denton, in the television set, and right beside the set was the telephone.

"Help me!" shrieked Denton. "Call! Call! Help me!" And it seemed to him as though it should be the easiest thing in the world for that real image of himself to reach over and pick up the telephone and call for help.

But instead, the image merely waved and cried, "Good night!" The blind and stupid image of himself in the box, blowing a kiss at the dying man in the chair.

"Help me!" Denton screamed, but the words were buried by a bubbling up of blood, filling his throat.

The image receded, down and down, growing smaller and ever smaller as the boom camera was raised toward the ceiling. "Love you! Love you!" cried the tiny doomed image to the dead man in the chair. "Good night! Good night!"

THE RISK
PROFESSION

Mr. Henderson called me into his office my third day back on Earth. That was a day and a half later than I'd expected. Roving claims investigators for Tangier Mutual Insurance Corporation don't usually get to spend more than thirty-six consecutive hours at home base.

Henderson was jovial but stern. That meant he was happy with the job I'd just completed, and that he was pretty sure I'd find some crooked shenanigans on this next assignment. That didn't please me. I'm basically a plain-living type, and I hate complications. I almost wished for a second that I was back on Fire and Theft in Greater New York. But I knew better than that. As a roving claims investigator, I avoided the more stultifying paperwork inherent in this line of work and had the additional luxury of an expense account nobody ever questioned.

It made working for a living almost worthwhile.

When I was settled in the chair beside his desk, Henderson said, "That was good work you did on Luna, Ged. Saved the company a pretty pence."

I smiled modestly and said, "Thank you, sir." And reflected to myself for the thousandth time that the company could do worse than split that saving with the guy who'd made it possible. Me, in other words.

"Got a tricky one this time, Ged," said my boss. He had done his back-patting, now we got down to business. He peered keenly at me, or at least as keenly as a round-faced, tiny-eyed fat man *can* peer. "What do you know about the Risk Profession Retirement Plan?" he asked me.

"I've heard of it," I said truthfully. "That's about all."

He nodded. "Most of the policies are sold off-planet of course. It's a form of insurance for non-insurables. Spaceship crews, asteroid prospectors, people like that."

"I see," I said unhappily. I knew right away this meant I was going to have to go off-Earth again. I'm a one-gee boy all the way. Gravity changes get me in the solar plexus. I get g-sick at the drop of an elevator.

"Here's the way it works," he went on, either not noticing my sad face or choosing to ignore it. "The client pays a monthly premium. He can be as far ahead or as far behind in his payments as he wants — the policy has no lapse clause — just so he's all paid up by the Target Date. The Target Date is a retirement age, forty-five or above, chosen by the client himself. After the Target Date he stops paying premiums, and we begin to pay him a monthly retirement check, the amount determined by the amount paid into the policy, his age at retiring, and so on. Clear?"

I nodded, looking for the gimmick that made this a paying proposition for good old Tangier Mutual.

"The Double R-P — that's what we call it around the office here — assures the client that he won't be reduced to panhandling in his old age, should his other retirement plans fall through. For Belt prospectors, of course, this means the big strike, which may be one in a hundred find. For the man who never does make that big strike, this is something to fall back on. He can come home to Earth and retire, with a guaranteed income for the rest of his life."

I nodded again, like a good company man.

"Of course," said Henderson, emphasizing this point with an upraised chubby finger, "these men are still uninsurables. This is a retirement plan only, not an insurance policy. There is no beneficiary other than the client himself."

And there was the gimmick. I knew a little something of the actuarial statistics concerning uninsurables, particularly Belt prospectors. Not many of them lived to be forty-five, and the few who would survive the Belt and come home to collect the retirement wouldn't last more than a year or two. A man who's spent the last twenty or thirty years on low-gee asteroids just shrivels up after a while when he tries to live on Earth.

It needed a company like Tangier Mutual to dream up a racket like that. The term "uninsurables" to most insurance companies means those people whose jobs or habitats make them too likely as prospects for obituaries. To Tangier Mutual, uninsurables are people who have money the company can't get at.

"Now," said Henderson importantly, "we come to the problem at hand." He ruffled his up-to-now-neat In basket and finally found the folder he wanted. He studied the blank exterior of this folder for a few seconds, pursing his lips at it, and said, "One of our clients under the Double R-P was a man named Jafe McCann."

"Was?" I echoed.

He squinted at me, then nodded at my sharpness. "That's right, he's dead." He sighed heavily and tapped the folder with all those pudgy fingers. "Normally," he said, "that would be the end of it. File closed. However, this time there are complications."

Naturally. Otherwise, he wouldn't be telling *me* about it. But Henderson couldn't be rushed, and I knew it. I kept the alert look on my face and thought of other things, while waiting for him to get to the point.

"Two weeks after Jafe McCann's death," Henderson said, "we received a cash-return form on his policy."

"A cash-return form?" I'd never heard of such a thing. It

didn't sound like anything Tangier Mutual would have anything to do with. We *never* return cash.

"It's something special in this case," he explained. "You see, this isn't an insurance policy, it's a retirement plan, and the client can withdraw from the retirement plan at any time, and have seventy-five per cent of his paid-up premiums returned to him. It's, uh, the law in plans such as this."

"Oh," I said. That explained it. A law that had snuck through the World Finance Code Commission while the insurance lobby wasn't looking.

"But you see the point," said Henderson. "This cash-return form arrived two weeks after the client's death."

"You said there weren't any beneficiaries," I pointed out.

"Of course. But the form was sent in by the man's partner. one Ab Karpin. McCann left a handwritten will bequeathing all his possessions to Karpin. Since, according to Karpin, this was done before McCann's death, the premium money cannot be considered part of the policy, but as part of McCann's cash-on-hand. And Karpin wants it."

"It can't be that much, can it?" Not enough, I was hoping, to make it worth the company's while to send me to the asteroids.

"McCann died," Henderson said ponderously, "at the age of fifty-six. He took out the policy at the age of thirty-four, with retirement at age sixty and monthly payments of fifty credits. Figure it out for yourself."

I did, and came up with a figure of thirteen thousand two hundred credits. Seventy-five per cent of that would be nine thousand nine hundred credits. Call it ten thousand.

I had to admit it; it was worth the trip.

"I see," I said sadly.

"Now," said Henderson, "the conditions — the circumstances — of McCann's death are somewhat suspicious. And so is the cash-return form itself."

"There's a chance it's a forgery?"

"One would think so. But our handwriting experts have worn themselves out with that form, comparing it with every other single scrap of McCann's writing they can find. And their conclusion is that not only is it genuinely McCann's handwriting, but it is McCann's handwriting at age fifty-six."

"So McCann must have written it," I said. "Under duress, do you think?"

"I have no idea," said Henderson complacently. "That's what you're supposed to find out. Oh, there's just one thing more."

I looked alert.

"McCann and Karpin," he said, "had been partners — unincorporated, of course — for the last fifteen years. They'd found small rare-metal deposits now and again, but never that one big strike all the Belt prospectors spend their lives looking for. Not until the day before McCann died."

"Ah hah," I said. "And McCann's death?"

"Accidental."

"Sure. What proof?"

"None. The body is lost in space. And law is rare that far out."

"So all we've got is Karpin's word for how McCann died, is that it?"

"That's all we have," Henderson agreed. "So far."

"And now you want me to go on out there and find out what's cooking, and see if I can maybe save the company ten C's."

"Exactly," said Henderson.

The copter took me to the spaceport west of Cairo, and there I boarded the good ship *Demeter* for Luna City and points Out. By the time we got to Atronics City, in the asteroid belt, my insides and I had come to a shaky kind of agreement; as long as I didn't try to eat, my stomach would leave me alone.

Atronics City is as depressing as a Turkish bath with all the lights on. It stands on a chunk of rock a couple of miles thick and looks like nothing so much as a welder's practice range.

On the outside, Atronics City is a derby-shaped dome of nickel-iron, black and dirty-looking, and on the inside it looks just as bad, four levels of Basic Life Maintenance. There's the top level, directly under the dome, with parking area for scooters and tuggers, plus office shacks for Assayer, Entry Authority, Industry Troopers, and so on. Below that, the levels have been burned into the bowels of the planetoid, level two being the Atronics plant, level three shopping and entertainment area, and level four housing. All of these levels have one thing in common: square corners, painted olive-drab. It's like being in the middle of a stack of jerry cans.

At any rate, this was as far as *Demeter* would take me. Now, while the ship went on to Ludlum City and Chemisant City and the other asteroid business towns, my two suitcases and I dribbled down by elevator to my hostelry on level four. And I do mean dribbled. An elevator ride on a low-gravity planetoid is well worth avoiding, if you ask me. The elevator manages to sink faster than you do because rather than being lowered down it's being pulled down. Which means the suitcases have to be lashed down and the passengers have to hold tight to the hand-grips and in all it's a bad experience.

But we did get down to level four, and off I went with my suitcases and the operator's directions. The suitcases weighed half an ounce each out here, and I felt not much heavier myself. Every time I raised a foot I was sure I was about to go sailing into a wall. Local citizens eased by me, their feet occasionally touching the iron pavement as they soared along, and I gave them all dirty looks.

Level four was nothing but walls and windows. The iron floor went among these walls and windows in a straight line, bisecting other "streets" at perfect right angles, and the iron ceiling sixteen feet up was lined with a double row of fluorescent tubes. I was beginning to feel claustrophobic already.

The Chalmers Hotel — named for an Atronics vice-president — had received my advance registration, which was nice. I was shown to a second-floor room — nothing on level four had more than two stories — and was left to unpack my suitcases as best I could.

I had decided to spend a day or two at Atronics City before taking a scooter out to Ab Karpin's claim. Atronics City had been Karpin's and McCann's home base. All of McCann's premium payments had been mailed from here, and the normal mailing address for both of them was CPO Atronics City.

I wanted to know as much as possible about Ab Karpin before I went out to see him. And Atronics City seemed like the best place to get my information.

But not today. Today my stomach was very unhappy, and my head was on sympathy strike. Today I was going to spend my time exclusively in bed, trying not to float up to the ceiling.

The Mapping & Registry Office, it seemed to me the next day, was the best place to start. This was where prospectors filed their claims, but it was a lot more than that. The waiting room of M&R was the unofficial club of the asteroid prospectors. This was where they met with one another, talked together, and made and dissolved their transient partnerships.

In this way, Karpin and McCann were unusual. They had maintained their partnership for fifteen years. That was about sixty times longer than most such arrangements lasted.

Searching the asteroid chunks for rare and valuable metals is basically pretty lonely work, and it's inevitable that the prospectors will every once in a while get hungry for human company and decide to try a team operation. But at the same time work like this attracts people who don't get along very well with human company. So the partnerships come and go, and the hatreds flare and are forgotten, and the normal prospecting partnership lasts an average of three months.

The Mapping & Registry Office occupied a good-sized shack over near the dome wall on level one. I pushed open the door and went in, finding the waiting room cozy and surprisingly large, large enough to comfortably hold the six maroon sofas scattered here and there on the pale green carpet. There were only six prospectors here at the moment, chatting together in two groups of three, and they all looked alike. Grizzled, ageless, watery-eyed, their clothing clean but baggy. I passed them and went on to the desk at the far end, behind which sat a young man in official gray, slowly turning the crank of a microfilm reader.

He looked up at my approach. I flashed my company identification and asked to speak to the manager. He went away, came back, and ushered me into an office which managed to be Spartan and sumptuous at the same time. The walls had been plastic-painted in textured brown, the iron floor had been lushly carpeted in gray, and the desk had been covered with a simulated wood coating.

The manager — a man named Teaking — went well with the office. His face and hands were spare and lean but his uniform was immaculate, covered with every curlicue the regulations allowed. He welcomed me politely but curiously, and I said, "I wonder if you know a prospector named Ab Karpin?"

"Karpin? Of course. He and old Jafe McCann — pity about McCann. I hear he got killed."

"Yes, he did."

"And that's what you're here for, eh? I didn't know the Belt boys could get insurance."

"It isn't exactly that," I said. "This concerns a retirement plan, and — well, the details don't matter. I was hoping you could give me some background on Karpin. And on McCann, too, for that matter."

He grinned a bit. "You saw the men sitting outside?"

I nodded.

"Then you've seen Karpin and McCann. Exactly the same. It doesn't matter if a man's thirty or sixty or what. It doesn't matter what he was like before he came out here. If he's been here a few years, he looks exactly like the bunch you saw outside there."

"That's appearance," I said. "What I was looking for was personality."

"Same thing," he said. "All of them. Close-mouthed, anti-social, fiercely independent, incurably romantic, always convinced that the big strike is just a piece of rock away. McCann, now, he was a bit more realistic than most. He'd be the one I'd expect to take out a retirement policy. A real pence-pincher, that one, though I shouldn't say it as he's dead. But that's the way he was. Brighter than most Belt boys when it came to money matters. I've seen him haggle over a new piece of equipment for their scooter, or some repair work, or some such thing, and he was a wonder to watch."

"And Karpin?" I asked him.

"A prospector," he said, as though that answered my question. "Same as everybody else. Not as sharp as McCann when it came to money. That's why all the money stuff in the partnership was handled by McCann. But Karpin was one of the sharpest boys in the business when it came to mineralogy. He knew rocks you and I never heard of, and most times he knew them by sight. Almost all of the Belt boys are college grads — you've got to know what you're looking for out here and what it looks like when you've found it — but Karpin has practically all of them beat. He's *sharp*."

"Sounds like a good team," I said.

"I guess that's why they stayed together so long," he said. "They complemented each other." He leaned forward, the inevitable prelude to a confidential remark. "I'll tell you something off the record, mister," he said. "Those two were smarter than they knew. Their partnership was never legalized, it was never anything more than a piece of paper. And there's a bunch of fellas around here mighty unhappy about that today. Jafe McCann is the one who handled all the money matters, like I said. He's got IOU's all over town."

"And they can't collect from Karpin?"

He nodded. "Jafe McCann died just a bit too soon. He was sharp and cheap, but he was honest. If he'd lived, he would have repaid all his debts, I'm sure of it. And if this strike they made is as good as I hear, he would have been able to repay them with no trouble at all."

I nodded, somewhat impatiently. I had the feeling by now that I was talking to a man who was one of those who had a Jafe McCann IOU in his pocket. "How long has it been since you've seen Karpin?" I asked him, wondering what Karpin's attitude and expression were now that his partner was dead.

"Oh, Lord, not for a couple of months," he said. "Not since they went out together the last time and made that strike."

"Didn't Karpin come in to make his claim?"

"Not here. Over to Chemisant City. That was the nearest M&R to the strike."

"Oh." That was a pity. I would have liked to have known if there had been a change of any kind in Karpin since his partner's death. "I'll tell you what the situation is," I said with a false air of truthfulness. "We have some misgivings about McCann's death. Not suspicions, exactly, just misgivings. The timing is what bothers us."

"You mean, because it happened just after the strike?"

"That's it," I answered frankly.

He shook his head. "I wouldn't get too excited about that, if I were you," he said. "It wouldn't be the first time it's happened. A man makes the big strike after all, and he gets so excited he forgets himself for a minute and gets careless. And you only have to be careless once out here."

"That may be it," I said. I got to my feet, knowing I'd picked up all there was from this man. "Thanks a lot for your cooperation," I said.

"Any time," he said. He stood and shook hands with me.

I went back out through the chatting prospectors and crossed the echoing cavern that was level one, aiming to rent myself a scooter.

I don't like rockets. They're noisy as the dickens, they steer hard and drive erratically, and you can never carry what *I* would consider a safe emergency excess of fuel. Nothing like the big steady-g interplanetary liners. On those I feel almost human.

The appearance of the scooter I was shown at the rental agency didn't do much to raise my opinion of this mode of transportation. The thing was a good ten years old, the paint scraped and scratched all over its egg-shaped, originally green-colored body, and the windshield — a silly term, really, for the front window of a craft that spends most of its time out where there isn't any wind — was scratched and pockmarked to the point of translucency by years of exposure to the asteroidal dust.

The rental agent was a sharp-nosed, thin-faced type who displayed this refugee from a melting vat without a blush and still didn't blush when he told me the charges. Twenty credits a day, plus fuel.

I paid without a murmur — it was the company's money, not mine — and paid an additional ten credits for the rental of a suit to go with it. I worked my way awkwardly into the suit, and clambered into the driver's seat of the relic. I attached the suit to the ship in all the necessary places, and the agent closed and spun the door.

Most of the black paint had worn off the handles of the controls, and insulation peeked through rips in the plastic siding here and there. I wondered if the thing had any slow leaks and supposed fatalistically that it had. The agent waved at me, stony-faced, the conveyor belt trundled me outside the dome, and I kicked the weary rocket into life.

The scooter had a tendency to roll to the right. If I hadn't kept fighting it back, it would have soon worked up a dandy little spin. I was spending so much time juggling with the controls that I practically missed a couple of my beacon rocks, and that would have been just too bad. If I'd gotten off the course I had carefully outlined for myself, I'd never have found my bearings again, and I would have just floated around amid the scenery until some passer-by took pity and towed me back home.

But I managed to avoid getting lost, which surprised me, and after four nerve-racking hours I finally spotted the yellow-painted X of a registered claim on a half-mile-thick chunk of rock dead ahead. As I got closer, I spied a scooter parked near the X, and beside it an inflated portable dome. The scooter was somewhat larger than mine, but no newer and probably even less safe. The dome was varicolored from repeated patching.

This is where I would find Karpin, sitting on his property while waiting for the sale to go through. Prospectors like Karpin are free-lance men, working for no particular company. They register their claims in their own names, and then sell the rights to whichever company shows up with the most attractive offer. There's a lot of paperwork to such a sale, and it's all handled by the company. While waiting, the smart prospector sits on his claim and makes sure nobody chips off a part of it for himself, a stunt that still happens now and again. It doesn't take too much concentrated explosive to make two rocks out of one rock, and a man's claim is only the rock with his X on it.

I set the scooter down next to the other one, and flicked the toggle for the air pumps, then put on the fishbowl and went about unattaching the suit from the ship. When the red light flashed on and off, I spun the door, opened it, and stepped out onto the rock, moving very cautiously.

I clumped across the crude X to Karpin's dome. The dome had no viewports at all, so I wasn't sure Karpin was aware of my presence. I rapped my metal glove on the metal outer door of the lock, and then I was sure.

But it took him long enough to open up. I had just about decided he'd joined his partner in the long sleep when the door cracked open an inch. I pushed it open and stepped into the lock, ducking my head.

When the red light high on the left-hand wall clicked off, I rapped on the inner door. It promptly opened, I stepped through and removed the fishbowl.

Karpin stood in the middle of the room, a small revolver in

his hand. "Shut the door," he said.

I obeyed, moving slowly. I didn't want that gun to go off by mistake.

"Who are you?" Karpin demanded. The M&R man had been right. Ab Karpin was a dead ringer for all those other prospectors I'd seen back at Atronics City. Short and skinny and grizzled and ageless. He could have been forty, and he could have been ninety, but he was probably somewhere the other side of fifty. His hair was black and limp and thinning, ruffled in little wisps across his wrinkled pate. His forehead and cheeks were lined like a plowed field, and were much the same color. His eyes were wide apart and small, so deep-set beneath shaggy brows that they seemed black. His mouth was thin, almost lipless. The hand holding the revolver was nothing but bones and blue veins covered with taut skin.

He was wearing a dirty undershirt and an old pair of trousers that had been cut off raggedly just above his knobby knees. Faded slippers were on his feet. He had good reason for dressing that way, the temperature inside the dome must have been nearly ninety degrees. The dome wasn't reflecting away the sun's heat as well as it had when it was young.

I looked at Karpin, and despite the revolver and the tense expression on his face, he was the least dangerous-looking man I'd ever run across. All at once, the idea that this anti-social old geezer had the drive or the imagination to murder his partner seemed ridiculous.

Apparently I spent too much time looking him over, because he said again, "Who are you?" And this time he motioned impatiently with the revolver.

"Stanton," I told him. "Ged Stanton, Tangier Mutual Insurance. I have identification, but it's in my pants pocket, down inside this suit."

"Get it," he said. "And move slow."

"Right you are."

I moved slow, as per directions, and peeled out of the suit, then reached into my trouser pocket and took out my ID clip. I flipped it open and showed him the card bearing my signature and picture and right thumbprint and the name of the company I represented, and he nodded, satisfied, and tossed the revolver over onto his bed. "I got to be careful," he said. "I got a big claim here."

"I know that," I told him. "Congratulations for it."

"Thanks," he said, but he still looked peevish. "You're here about Jafe's insurance, right?"

"That I am."

"Don't want to pay up, I suppose. That doesn't surprise me."

Blunt old men irritate me. "Well," I said, "we do have to investigate."

"Sure," he said. "You want some coffee?"

"Thank you."

"You can sit in that chair there. That was Jafe's."

I settled gingerly in the cloth-and-plastic foldaway chair he'd pointed at, and he went over to the kitchen area of the dome to start coffee. I took the opportunity to look the dome over. It was the first portable dome I'd ever been inside of.

It was all one room, roughly circular, with a diameter of about fifteen feet. The sides went straight up for the first seven feet, then curved gradually inward to form the roof. At the center of the dome, the ceiling was about twelve feet high.

The floor of the room was simply the asteroidal rock surface, not completely level and smooth. There were two chairs and a table to the right of the entry lock, two foldaway cots around the wall beyond them, the kitchen area next, and a cluttered storage area around on the other side. There was a heater standing alone in the center of the room, but it certainly wasn't needed now. Sweat was already trickling down the back of my neck and down my forehead into my eyebrows. I peeled off my shirt and used it to wipe sweat from my face. "Warm in here," I said.

"You get used to it," he muttered, which I found hard to believe.

He brought over the coffee, and I tasted it. It was rotten, as bitter as this old hermit's soul, but I said, "Good coffee. Thanks a lot."

"I like it strong," he said.

I looked around at the room again. "All the comforts of home, eh? Pretty ingenious arrangement."

"Sure," he said sourly. "How about getting to the point, mister?"

There's only one way to handle a blunt old man. Be blunt right back. "I'll tell you how it is," I said. "The company isn't accusing you of anything, but it has to be sure everything's on the up and up before it pays out any ten thousand credits. And your partner just happening to fill out that cash-return form just before he died — well, you've got to admit it is a funny kind of coincidence."

"How so?" He slurped coffee, and glowered at me over the cup. "We made this strike here," he said. "We knew it was the big one. Jafe had that insurance policy of his in case he never did make the big strike. As soon as we knew this was the big one, he said, 'I guess I don't need that retirement now,' and sat right down and wrote out the cash-return. Then we opened a bottle of liquor and celebrated, and he got himself killed."

The way Karpin said it, it sounded smooth and natural. *Too* smooth and natural. "How did this accident happen anyway?" I asked him.

"I'm not one hundred per cent sure of that myself," he said. "I was pretty well drunk by that time. But he put on his suit and said he was going out to paint the X. He was falling all over himself, and I tried to tell him it could wait till we'd had some sleep, but he wouldn't pay any attention to me."

"So he went out," I said.

He nodded. "He went out first. After a couple minutes I got lonesome in here, so I suited up and went out after him. It happened just as I was going out the lock, and I just barely got a glimpse of what happened."

He attacked the coffee again, noisily, and I prompted him, saying, "What did happen, Mr. Karpin?"

"Well, he was capering around out there, waving the paint tube and such. There's a lot of sharp rock sticking out around here. Just as I got outside, he lost his balance and kicked out, and scraped right into some of that rock and punctured his suit."

"I thought the body was lost," I said.

He nodded. "It was. The last thing in life Jafe ever did was try to shove himself away from those rocks. That, and the force of air coming out of that puncture for the first second or two, was enough to throw him up off the surface. It threw him up too high, and he never got back down."

My doubt must have showed in my face, because he added, "Mister, there isn't enough gravity on this place to shoot craps with."

He was right. As we talked, I kept finding myself holding unnecessarily tight to the arms of the chair. I kept having the feeling I was going to float out of the chair and hover around up at the top of the dome if I were to let go. It was silly of course — there was *some* gravity on that planetoid, after all — but I just don't seem to get used to low-gee.

Nevertheless, I still had some more questions. "Didn't

102

you try to get his body back? Couldn't you have reached him?"

"I tried to, mister," he said. "Old Jafe McCann was my partner for fifteen years. But I was drunk, and that's a fact. And I was afraid to go jumping up in the air, for fear *I'd* go floating away, too."

"Frankly," I said, "I'm no expert on low gravity and asteroids. But wouldn't McCann's body just go into orbit around this rock? I mean, it wouldn't simply go floating off into space, would it?"

"It sure would," he said. "There's a lot of other rocks out here, too, mister, and a lot of them are bigger than this one and have a lot more gravity pull. I don't suppose there's a navigator in the business who could have computed Jafe's course in advance. He floated up, and then he floated back over the dome here and seemed to hover for a couple minutes, and then he just floated out and away. His isn't the only body circling around the sun with all these rocks, you know."

I chewed a lip and thought it all over. I didn't know enough about asteroid gravity or the conditions out here to be able to say for sure whether Karpin's story was true or not. Up to this point, I couldn't attack the problem on a fact basis. I had to depend on *feeling* now, the hunches and instincts of eight years in this job, hearing some people tell lies and other people tell the truth.

And my instinct said Ab Karpin was lying in his teeth. That dramatic little touch about McCann's body hovering over the dome before disappearing into the void, that sounded more like the embellishment of fiction than the circumstance of truth. And the string of coincidences were just too much. McCann just coincidentally happens to die right after he and his partner make the big strike. He happens to write out the cash-return form just before dying. And his body just happens to float away, so nobody can look at it and check Karpin's story.

But no matter what my instinct said, the story was smooth. It was smooth as glass, and there was no place for me to get a grip on it.

What now? There wasn't any hole in Karpin's story, at least none that I could see. I had to break his story somehow, and in order to do that I had to do some nosing around on this planetoid. I couldn't know in advance what I was looking for, I could only look. I'd know it when I found it. It would be something that conflicted with Karpin's story.

And for that, I had to be sure the story was complete. "You said McCann had gone out to paint the X," I said. "Did he paint it?"

Karpin shook his head. "He never got a chance. He spent all his time dancing, up till he went and killed himself."

"So you painted it yourself."

He nodded.

"And then you went on into Atronics City and registered your claim, is that the story?"

"No. Chemisant City was closer than Atronics City right then, so I went there. Just after Jafe's death, and everything— I didn't feel like being alone any more than I had to."

"You said Chemisant City was closer to you *then*," I said. "Isn't it now?"

"Things move around a lot out here, mister," he said. "Right now Chemisant City's almost twice as far from here as Atronics City. In about three days it'll start swinging in closer again. Things keep shifting around out here."

"So I've noticed," I said. "When you took off to go to Chemisant City, didn't you make a try for your partner's body then?"

He shook his head. "He was long out of sight by then," he

said. "That was ten, eleven hours later, when I took off."

"Why's that? All you had to do was paint the X and take off."

"Mister, I told you. I was drunk. I was falling down drunk, and when I saw I couldn't get at Jafe, and he was dead anyway, I came back in here and slept it off. Maybe if I'd been sober I would have taken the scooter and gone after him, but I was *drunk.*"

"I see." And there just weren't any more questions I could think of to ask, not right now. So I said, "I've just had a shaky four-hour ride coming out here. Mind if I stick around awhile before going back?"

"Help yourself," he said in a pretty poor attempt at genial hospitality. "You can sleep over, if you want."

"Fine," I said. "I think I'd like that."

"You wouldn't happen to play cribbage, would you?" he asked, with the first real sign of animation I'd seen in him yet.

"I learn fast," I told him.

"Okay," he said. "I'll teach you." And he produced a filthy deck of cards and taught me.

After losing nine straight games of cribbage I quit, and got to my feet. I was at my most casual as I stretched and said, "Okay if I wander around outside for a while? I've never been on an asteroid like this before. I mean, a little one like this. I've just been to the company cities up to now."

"Go right ahead," he said. "I've got some polishing and patching to do, anyway." He made his voice sound easy and innocent, but I noticed his eyes were alert and wary, watching me as I struggled back into my suit.

I didn't bother to put my shirt back on first, and that was a mistake. The temperature inside an atmosphere suit is a steady sixty-eight degrees. That had never seemed particularly chilly before, but after the heat of that dome, it seemed cold as a blizzard inside the suit.

I went on out through the air-lock, and moved as briskly as possible in the cumbersome suit while the sweat chilled on my back and face, and I accepted the glum conviction that one thing I was going to get out of this trip for sure was a nasty head cold.

I went over to the X first, and stood looking at it. It was just an X, that's all, shakily scrawled in yellow paint, with the initials "J-A" scrawled much smaller beside it.

I left the X and clumped away. The horizon was practically at arm's length, so it didn't take long for the dome to be out of sight. And then I clumped more slowly, studying the surface of the asteroid.

What I was looking for was a grave. I believed that Karpin was lying, that he had murdered his partner. And I didn't believe that Jafe McCann's body had floated off into space. I was convinced that his body was still somewhere on this asteroid. Karpin had been forced to concoct a story about the body being lost because the appearance of the body would prove somehow that it had been murder and not accident. I was convinced of that, and now all I had to do was prove it.

But that asteroid was a pretty unlikely place for a grave. That wasn't dirt I was walking on, it was rock, solid metallic rock. You don't dig a grave in solid rock, not with a shovel. You maybe can do it with dynamite, but that won't work too well if your object is to keep anybody from seeing that the hole has been made. Dirt can be patted down. Blown-up rock looks like blown-up rock, and that's all there is to it.

I considered crevices and fissures in the surface, some cranny large enough for Karpin to have stuffed the body into. But I didn't find any of these either as I plodded along, being sure to keep one magneted boot always in contact with the ground.

Karpin and McCann had set their dome up at just about the only really level spot on that entire planetoid. The rest of it was nothing but jagged rock, and it wasn't easy traveling at all, maneuvering around with magnets on my boots and a bulky atmosphere suit cramping my movements.

And then I stopped and looked out at space and cursed myself for a ring-tailed baboon. McCann's body might be anywhere in the Solar System, anywhere at all, but there was one place I could be sure it wasn't, and that place was this asteroid. No, Karpin had not blown a grave or stuffed the body into a fissure in the ground. Why not? Because this chunk of rock was valuable, that's why not. Because Karpin was in the process of selling it to one of the major companies, and that company would come along and chop this chunk of rock to pieces, getting the valuable metal out, and McCann's body would turn up in the first week of operations if Karpin were stupid enough to bury it here.

Ten hours between McCann's death and Karpin's departure for Chemisant City. He'd admitted that already. And I was willing to bet he'd spent at least part of that time carrying McCann's body to some other asteroid, one he was sure was nothing but worthless rock. If that were true, it meant the mortal remains of Jafe McCann were now somewhere — *anywhere* — in the Asteroid Belt. Even if I assumed that the body had been hidden on an asteroid somewhere between here and Chemisant City — which wasn't necessarily so — that wouldn't help at all. The relative positions of planetoids in the Belt just keep on shifting. A small chunk of rock that was between here and Chemisant City a few weeks ago — it could be almost anywhere in the Belt right now.

The body, that was the main item. I'd more or less

counted on finding it somehow. At the moment I couldn't think of any other angle for attacking Karpin's story.

As I clopped morosely back to the dome, I nibbled at Karpin's story in my mind. For instance, why go to Chemisant City? It was closer, he said, but it couldn't have been closer by more than a couple of hours. The way I understood it, Karpin was well known back on Atronics City — it was the normal base of operations for him and his partner — and he didn't know a soul at Chemisant City. Did it make sense for him to go somewhere he wasn't known after his partner's death, even if it *was* an hour closer? No, it made a lot more sense for a man in that situation to go where he's known, go someplace where he has friends who'll sympathize with him and help him over the shock of losing a partner of fifteen years' standing, even if going there does mean traveling an hour longer.

And there was always the cash-return form. That was what I was here about in the first place. It just didn't make sense for McCann to have held up his celebration while he filled out a form that he wouldn't be able to mail until he got back to Atronics City. And yet the company's handwriting experts were convinced that it wasn't a forgery, and I could pretty well take their word for it.

Mulling these things over as I tramped back toward the dome, I suddenly heard a distant bell ringing way back in my head. The glimmering of an idea, not an idea yet but just the hint of one. I wasn't sure where it led, even if it led anywhere at all, but I was going to find out.

Karpin opened the doors for me. By the time I'd stripped off the suit he was back to work. He was cleaning the single unit which was his combination stove and refrigerator and sink and garbage disposal.

I looked around the dome again, and I had to admit that a lot of ingenuity had gone into the manufacture and design of this dome and its contents. The dome itself, when deflated, folded down into an oblong box three feet by one foot by one foot. The lock itself, of course, folded separately, into another box somewhat smaller than that.

As for the gear inside the dome, it was functional and collapsible, and there wasn't a single item there that wasn't needed. There were the two chairs and the two cots and the table, all of them foldaway. There was that fantastic combination job Karpin was cleaning right now, and that had dimensions of four feet by three feet by three feet. The clutter of gear over to the left wasn't as much of a clutter as it looked. There was a Geiger counter, an automatic spectrograph, two atmosphere suits, a torsion densiometer, a core-cutting drill, a few small hammers and picks, two spare air tanks, boxes of food concentrate, a paint tube, a doorless jimmy-john, and two small metal boxes about eight inches cube. These last were undoubtedly Karpin's and McCann's pouches, where they kept whatever letters, money, address books, or other small bits of possessions they owned. Back of this mound of gear, against the wall, stood the air reconditioner, humming quietly to itself.

In this small enclosed space there was everything a man needed to keep himself alive. Everything except human company. And if you didn't need human company, then you had everything. Just on the other side of that dome there was a million miles of death, in a million possible ways. On this side of the dome, life was cozy, if somewhat Spartan and very hot.

I knew for sure I was going to get a head cold. My body had adjusted to the sixty-eight degrees inside the suit, finally, and now was very annoyed to find the temperature shooting up to ninety again.

Since Karpin didn't seem inclined to talk, and I would rather spend my time thinking than talking anyway, I took a hint from him and did some cleaning. I'd noticed a smeared spot about nose-level on the faceplate of my fishbowl, and now was as good a time as any to get rid of it. It had a tendency to make my eyes cross.

My shirt was sodden and wrinkled by this time anyway, having first been used to wipe sweat from my face and later been rolled into a ball and left on the chair when I went outside, so I used it for a cleaning rag, buffing like mad the silvered surface of the faceplate. Faceplates are silvered, not so the man inside can look out and no one else can look in, but in order to keep some of the more violent rays of the sun from getting through to the face.

I buffed for a while, and then I put the fishbowl on my head and looked through it. The spot was gone, so I went over and reattached it to the rest of the suit, and then settled back in my chair again and lit a cigarette.

Karpin spoke up. "Wish you wouldn't smoke. Makes it tough on the conditioner."

"Oh," I said. "Sorry." So I just sat, thinking morosely about nonforged cash-return forms, and coincidences, and likely spots to hide a body in the Asteroid Belt.

Where would one dispose of a body in the asteroids? I went back through my thinking on that topic, and I found holes big enough to drive Karpin's claim through. This idea of leaving the body on some worthless chunk of rock, for instance. If Karpin had killed his partner — and I was dead sure he had — he'd planned it carefully and he wouldn't be leaving anything to chance. Now, an asteroid isn't worthless to a prospector until that prospector has landed on it and tested it. *Karpin* might know that such-and-such an asteroid was nothing but worthless stone, but the guy who stops there and finds McCann's body might *not* know it.

No, Karpin wouldn't leave that to chance. He would get rid of that body, and he would do it in such a way that nobody would *ever* find it.

How? Not by leaving it on a worthless asteroid, and not by just pushing it off into space. The distance between asteroids is large, but so's the travel. McCann's body, floating around in the blackness, might just be found by somebody.

And that, so far as I could see, eliminated the possibilities. McCann's body was in the Belt. I'd eliminated both the asteroids themselves and the space around the asteroids as hiding places. What was left?

The sun, of course.

I thought that over for a while, rather surprised at myself for having noticed the possibility. Now, let's say Karpin attaches a small rocket to McCann's body, stuffed into its atmosphere suit. He sets the rocket going, and off goes McCann. Not that he aims it toward the sun, that wouldn't work well at all. Instead of falling into the sun, the body would simply take up a long elliptical orbit *around* the sun, and would come back to the asteroids every few hundred years. No, he would aim McCann *back*, in the direction opposite to the direction of rotation of the asteroids. He would, in essence, slow McCann's body down, make it practically stop in relation to the motion of the asteroids. And then it would simply *fall* into the sun.

None of my ideas, it seemed, were happy ones. If McCann's body were even at this moment falling toward the sun, it was just as useful to me as if it were on some other asteroid.

But wait a second. Karpin and McCann had worked with the minimum of equipment, I'd already noticed that. They didn't have extras of anything, and they certainly wouldn't have extra rockets. Except for one fast trip to Chemisant City

— when he had neither the time nor the excuse to buy a jato rocket — Karpin had spent all of his time since McCann's death right here on this planetoid.

So that killed that idea.

While I was hunting around for some other idea, Karpin spoke up again, for the first time in maybe twenty minutes. "You think I killed him, don't you?" he said, not looking around from his cleaning job.

I considered my answer. There was no reason at all to be overly polite to this sour old buzzard, but at the same time I am naturally the soft-spoken type. "We aren't sure," I said. "We just think there are some odd items to be explained."

"Such as what?" he demanded.

"Such as the timing of McCann's cash-return form."

"I already explained that," he said.

"I know. You've explained everything."

"He wrote it out himself," the old man insisted. He put down his cleaning cloth and turned to face me. "I suppose your company checked the handwriting already, and Jafe McCann is the one who wrote that form."

He was so blasted sure of himself. "It would seem that way," I said.

"What other odd items you worried about?" he asked me, in a rusty attempt at sarcasm.

"Well," I said, "there's this business of going to Chemisant City. It would have made more sense for you to go to Atronics City, where you were known."

"Chemisant was closer," he said. He shook a finger at me. "That company of yours thinks it can cheat me out of my money," he said. "Well, it can't. I know my rights. That money belongs to me."

"I guess you're doing pretty well without McCann," I said.

His angry expression was replaced by one of bewilderment. "What do you mean?"

"They told me back at Atronics City," I explained, "that McCann was the money expert and you were the metals expert, and that's why McCann handled all your buying on credit and stuff like that. Looks as though you've got a pretty keen eye for money yourself."

"I know what's mine," he mumbled, and turned away. He went back to scrubbing the stove coils again.

I stared at his back. Something had happened just then, and I wasn't sure what. He'd just been starting to warm up to a tirade against the dirty insurance company, and all of a sudden he'd folded up and shut up like a clam.

And then I saw it. Or at least I saw part of it. I saw how that cash-return form fit in, and how it made perfect sense.

Now all I needed was proof of murder. Preferably a body. I had the rest of it. Then I could pack the old geezer back to Atronics City and get proof for the part I'd already figured out.

I'd like that. I'd like getting back to Atronics City, and having this all straightened out, and then taking the very next liner straight back to Earth. More immediately, I'd like getting out of this heat and back into the cool sixty-eight degrees of —

And then it hit me. The whole thing hit me, and I just sat there and stared. They did not carry extras, Karpin and McCann, they did not carry one item of equipment more than they needed.

I sat there and looked at the place where the dead body was hidden, and I said, "Well, I'll be a son of a gun!"

He turned and looked at me, and then he followed the direction of my gaze, and he saw what I was staring at, and he made a jump across the room at the revolver lying on the cot.

That's what saved me. He moved too fast, jerked his muscles too hard, and went sailing up and over the cot and ricocheted off the dome wall. And that gave me plenty of time to get up from the chair, moving more cautiously than he had, and get my hands on the revolver before he could get himself squared away again.

I straightened with the gun in my hand and looked into a face white with frustration and rage. "Okay, Mr. McCann," I said. "It's all over."

He knew I had him, but he tried not to show it. "What are you talking about? McCann's dead."

"Sure he is," I said. "Jafe McCann was the money-minded part of the team. He was the one who signed for all the loans and all the equipment bought on credit. With this big strike in, Jafe McCann was the one who'd have to pay all that money."

"You're babbling," he snapped, but the words were hollow.

"You weren't satisfied with half a loaf," I said. "You should have been. But you wanted every penny you could get your hands on, and you wanted to pay out just as little money as you possibly could. So when you killed Ab Karpin, you saw a way to kill your debts as well. You'd *become* Ab Karpin, and it would be Jafe McCann who was dead, and the debts dead with him."

"That's a lie," he said, his voice getting shrill. "*I'm* Ab Karpin, and I've got papers to prove it."

"Sure. Papers you stole from a dead man. And you might have gotten away with it, too. But you just couldn't leave well enough alone, could you? Not satisfied with having the whole claim to yourself, you switched identities with your victim to avoid your debts. And not satisfied with *that,* you filled out a cash-return form and tried to collect your money as your own heir. *That's* why you had to go to Chemisant City, where nobody would recognize Ab Karpin or Jafe McCann, rather than to Atronics City, where you were well known."

"You don't want to make too many wild accusations," he shouted, his voice shaking. "You don't want to go around accusing people of things you can't prove."

"I can prove it," I told him. "I can prove everything I've said. As to who you are, there's no problem. All I have to do is bring you back to Atronics City. There'll be plenty of people there to identify you. And as to proving you murdered Ab Karpin, I think his body will be proof enough, don't you?"

McCann watched me as I backed slowly around the room to the mound of gear. The partners had no extra equipment, no extra equipment at all. I looked down at the two atmosphere suits lying side by side on the metallic rock floor.

Two atmosphere suits. The dead man was supposed to be in one of those, floating out in space somewhere. He was in the suit, right enough, I was sure of that, but he wasn't floating anywhere.

A space suit is a perfect place to hide a body, for as long as it has to be hid. The silvered faceplate keeps you from seeing inside, and the suit is, naturally, a sealed atmosphere. A body can rot away to ashes inside a space suit, and you'll never notice a thing on the outside.

I'd had the right idea after all. McCann had planned to get rid of Karpin's body by attaching a rocket to it, slowing it down, and letting it fall into the sun. But he hadn't had an opportunity yet to go buy a rocket. He couldn't go to Atronics City, where he could have bought the rocket on credit, and he couldn't go to Chemisant City until the claim sale went through and he had some money to spend. And in the meantime, Karpin's body was perfectly safe, sealed away inside his atmosphere suit.

And it would have been safe, too, if McCann hadn't been just a little bit too greedy. He could kill his partner and get away with it; policemen on the Belt are even farther apart than the asteroids. He could swindle his creditors and get away with it; they had no way of checking up and no reason to suspect a switch in identities. But when he tried to get his own money back from Tangier Mutual Insurance, *that's* when he made his mistake.

I studied the two atmosphere suits, at the same time managing to keep a wary eye on Jafe McCann, standing rigid and silent across the room. Which one of those suits contained the body of Ab Karpin?

The one with the new patch on the chest, of course. As I'd guessed, McCann had shot him, and that's why he had the problem of disposing of the body in the first place.

I prodded that suit with my toe. "He's in there, isn't he?"

"You're crazy."

"Think I should open it up and check? It's been almost a month, you know. I imagine he's pretty ripe by now."

I reached down to the neck-fastenings on the fishbowl, and McCann finally moved. His arms jerked up, and he cried, "Don't! He's in there, he's in there! For God's sake, don't open it up!"

I relaxed. Mission accomplished. "Crawl into your suit, little man," I said. "We've got ourselves a trip to make, the three of us."

Henderson, as usual, was jovial but stern. "You did a fine job up there, Ged," he said with false familiarity. "Really brilliant work."

"Thank you very much," I said. I was holding the last piece of news for a minute or two, relishing it.

"But you brought McCann in over a week ago. I don't see

why you had to stay up at Atronics City at all after that, much less ten days."

I sat back in the chair and negligently crossed my legs. "I just thought I'd take a little vacation," I said carelessly, and lit a cigarette. I flicked ashes in the general direction of the ashtray on Henderson's desk. Some of them made it.

"A vacation?" he echoed, eyes widening. Henderson was a company man, a *real* company man. A vacation for him was purgatory, it was separation from a loved one. "I don't believe you have a vacation coming," he said frostily, "for at least six-months."

"That's what you think, Henry," I said.

All he could do at that was blink.

I went on, enjoying myself hugely. "I don't like this company," I said. "And I don't like this job. And I don't like you. And from now on, I've decided, it's going to be vacation all the time."

"Ged," he said, his voice faint, "what's the matter with you? Don't you feel well?"

"I feel well," I told him. "I feel fine. Now I'll tell you why I spent an extra ten days at Atronics City. McCann made and registered the big strike, right?"

Henderson nodded blankly, apparently not trusting himself to speak.

"Wrong," I said cheerfully. "McCann went to Chemisant City and filled out all the forms required for registering a claim. But every place he was supposed to sign his name he wrote *Ab Karpin* instead. Jafe McCann *never did make a legal registration of his claim.*"

Henderson just looked fish-eyed.

"So," I went on, "as soon as I turned McCann over to the law at Atronics City, I went and registered that claim myself. And then I waited around for ten days until the company finished the paperwork involved in buying that claim from me. And then I came straight back here, just to say goodbye to you. Wasn't that nice?"

He didn't move.

"Goodbye," I said.

NEVER SHAKE A
FAMILY TREE

Actually, I was never so surprised in my life, and I seventy-three my last birthday and eleven times a grandmother and twice a great-grandmother. But never in my life did I see the like, and that's the truth.

It all began with my interest in genealogy, which I got from Mrs. Ernestine Simpson, a widow I met at Bay Arbor, in Florida, when I went there three summers ago. I certainly didn't like Florida — far too expensive, if you ask me, and far too bright, and with just too many mosquitoes and other insects to be believed — but I wouldn't say the trip was a total loss, since it did interest me in genealogical research, which is certainly a wonderful hobby, as well as being very valuable, what with one thing and another.

Actually, my genealogical researches have been valuable in more ways than one, since they have also been instrumental in my meeting some very pleasant ladies and gentlemen, although some of them only by postal, and of course it was through this hobby that I met Mr. Gerald Fowlkes in the first place.

But I'm getting far ahead of my story, and ought to begin at the beginning, except that I'm blessed if I know where the beginning actually is. In one way of looking at things, the beginning is my introduction to genealogy through Mrs. Ernestine Simpson, who has since passed on, but in another way the beginning is really almost two hundred years ago, and in still another way the story doesn't really begin until the first time I came across the name of Euphemia Barber.

Well. Actually, I suppose, I ought to begin by explaining

just what genealogical research is. It is the study of one's family tree. One checks marriage and birth and death records, searches old family Bibles and talks to various members of one's family, and one gradually builds up a family tree, showing who fathered whom and what year, and when so-and-so got married, and when so-and-so died, and so on. It's really fascinating work, and there are any number of amateur genealogical societies throughout the country, and when one has one's family tree built up for as far as one wants — seven generations, or nine generations, or however long one wants — then it is possible to write this all up in a folder and bequeath it to the local library, and then there is a *record* of one's family for all time to come, and I for one think that's important and valuable to have even if my youngest boy, Tom, does laugh at it and say it's just a silly hobby. Well, it *isn't* a silly hobby. After all, I found evidence of murder that way, didn't I?

So, actually, I suppose the whole thing really begins when I first came across the name of Euphemia Barber. Euphemia Barber was John Anderson's second wife. John Anderson was born in Goochland County, Virginia, in 1754. He married Ethel Rita Mary Rayborn in 1777, just around the time of the Revolution, and they had seven children, which wasn't at all strange for that time, though large families have, I notice, gone out of style today, and I for one think it's a shame.

At any rate, it was John and Ethel Anderson's third child, a girl named Prudence, who is in my direct line on my mother's father's side, so of course I had them in my family tree. But then, in going through Appomattox County records — Goochland County being now a part of Appomattox, and no longer a separate county of its own — I came across the name of Euphemia Barber. It seems that Ethel Anderson died in 1793, in giving birth to her eighth child — who also died —

and three years later, 1796, John Anderson remarried, this time marrying a widow named Euphemia Barber. At that time he was forty-two years of age, and her age was given as thirty-nine.

Of course, Euphemia Barber was not at all in my direct line, being John Anderson's second wife, but I was interested to some extent in her pedigree as well, wanting to add her parents' names and her place of birth to my family chart, and also because there were some Barbers fairly distantly related on my father's mother's side, and I was wondering if this Euphemia might be kin to them. But the records were very incomplete, and all I could learn was that Euphemia Barber was not a native of Virginia, and had apparently only been in the area for a year or two when she married John Anderson. Shortly after John's death in 1798, two years after their marriage, she sold the Anderson farm, which was apparently a somewhat prosperous location, and moved away again. So that I had neither birth nor death records on her, nor any record of her first husband, whose last name had apparently been Barber, but only the one lone record of her marriage to my great-great-great-great-great-grandfather on my mother's father's side.

Actually, there was no reason for me to pursue the question further, since Euphemia Barber wasn't in my direct line anyway, but I had worked diligently and, I think, well, on my family tree, and had it almost complete back nine generations, and there was really very little left to do with it, so I was glad to do some tracking down.

Which is why I included Euphemia Barber in my next entry in the *Genealogical Exchange*. Now, I suppose I ought to explain what the *Genealogical Exchange* is. There are any number of people throughout the country who are amateur genealogists, concerned primarily with their own family trees, but of course family trees do interlock, and any one of these people is liable to know about just the one record which has been eluding some other searcher for months. And so there are magazines devoted to the exchanging of such information, for nominal fees. In the last few years I had picked up all sorts of valuable leads in this way. And so my entry in the summer issue of the *Genealogical Exchange* read:

BUCKLEY, Mrs. Henrietta Rhodes, 119 A Newbury St., Boston, Mass. Xch data on Rhodes, Anderson, Richards, Pryor, Marshall, Lord. Want any info Euphemia Barber, m. John Anderson, Va. 1796.

Well. The *Genealogical Exchange* had been helpful to me in the past, but I never received anywhere near the response caused by Euphemia Barber. And the first response of all came from Mr. Gerald Fowlkes.

It was a scant two days after I received my own copy of the summer issue of the *Exchange*. I was still poring over it myself, looking for people who might be linked to various branches of my family tree, when the telephone rang. Actually, I suppose I was somewhat irked at being taken from my studies, and perhaps I sounded a bit impatient when I answered the phone.

If so, the gentleman at the other end gave no sign of it. His voice was most pleasant, quite deep and masculine, and he said, "May I speak, please, with Mrs. Henrietta Buckley?"

"This is Mrs. Buckley," I told him.

"Ah," he said. "Forgive my telephoning, please, Mrs. Buckley. We have never met. But I noticed your entry in the current issue of the *Genealogical Exchange* —"

"Oh?" I was immediately excited, all thought of impatience gone. This was surely the fastest reply I'd ever had to date.

"Yes," he said. "I noticed the reference to Euphemia Barber. I do believe that may be Euphemia Stover who married Jason Barber in Savannah, Georgia, in 1791. Jason Barber is in my direct line, on my mother's side. Jason and Euphemia had only the one child, Abner, and I am descended from him."

"Well," I said. "You certainly do seem to have complete information."

"Oh, yes," he said. "My own family chart is almost complete. For twelve generations, that is. I'm not sure whether I'll try to go back farther than that or not. The English records before 1600 are so incomplete, you know."

"Yes, of course," I said. I was, I admit, taken aback. Twelve generations! Surely that was the most ambitious family tree I had ever heard of, though I had read sometimes of people who had carried particular branches back as many as fifteen generations. But to actually be speaking to a person who had traced his entire family back twelve generations!

"Perhaps," he said, "it would be possible for us to meet, and I could give you the information I have on Euphemia Barber. There are also some Marshalls in one branch of my family; perhaps I can be of help to you there, as well." He laughed, a deep and pleasant sound, which reminded me of my late husband, Edward, when he was most particularly pleased. "And, of course," he said, "there is always the chance that you may have some information on the Marshalls which can help me."

"I think that would be very nice," I said, and so I invited him to come to the apartment the very next afternoon.

At one point the next day, perhaps half an hour before Gerald Fowlkes was to arrive, I stopped my puttering around to take stock of myself and to realize that if ever there were an indication of second childhood taking over, my thoughts and actions preparatory to Mr. Fowlkes' arrival were certainly it. I had been rushing hither and thither, dusting, rearranging, polishing, pausing incessantly to look in the mirror and touch my hair with fluttering fingers, all as though I were a flighty teenager before her very first date. "Henrietta," I told myself sharply, "you are seventy-three years old, and all that nonsense is well behind you now. Eleven times a grandmother, and just look at how you carry on!"

But poor Edward had been dead and gone these past nine years, my brothers and sisters were all in their graves, and as for my children, all but Tom, the youngest, were thousands of miles away, living their own lives — as of course they should and only occasionally remembering to write a duty letter to Mother. And I am much too aware of the dangers of the clinging mother to force my presence too often upon Tom and his family. So I am very much alone, except of course for my friends in the various church activities and for those I have met, albeit only by postal, through my genealogical research.

So it *was* pleasant to be visited by a charming gentleman caller, and particularly so when that gentleman shared my own particular interests.

And Mr. Gerald Fowlkes, on his arrival, was surely no disappointment. He looked to be no more than fifty-five years of age, though he swore to sixty-two, and had a fine shock of gray hair above a strong and kindly face. He dressed very well, with that combination of expense and breeding so little found these days, when the well-bred seem invariably to be poor and the well-to-do seem invariably to be horribly plebeian. His manner was refined and gentlemanly, what we used to call courtly, and he had some very nice things to say about the appearance of my living room.

Actually, I make no unusual claims as a housekeeper. Living alone, and with quite a comfortable income having been left me by Edward, it is no problem at all to choose tasteful furnishings and keep them neat. (Besides, I had scrubbed the apartment from top to bottom in preparation for Mr. Fowlkes' visit.)

He had brought his pedigree along, and what a really beautiful job he had done. Pedigree charts, photostats of all sorts of records, a running history typed very neatly on bond paper and inserted in a loose-leaf notebook all in all, the kind of careful, planned, well-thought-out perfection so unsuccessfully striven for by all amateur genealogists

From Mr. Fowlkes, I got the missing information on Euphemia Barber. She was born in 1765, in Salem, Massachusetts, the fourth child of seven born to John and Alicia Stover. She married Jason Barber in Savannah in 1791. Jason, a well-to-do merchant, passed on in 1794 shortly after the birth of their first child, Abner. Abner was brought up by his paternal grandparents, and Euphemia moved away from Savannah. As I already knew, she had then gone to Virginia, where she had married John Anderson. After that, Mr. Fowlkes had no record of her, until her death in Cincinnati, Ohio, in 1852. She was buried as Euphemia Stover Barber, apparently not having used the Anderson name after John Anderson's death.

This done, we went on to compare family histories and discover an Alan Marshall of Liverpool, England, around 1680, common to both trees. I was able to give Mr. Fowlkes Alan Marshall's birth date. And then the specific purpose of our meeting was finished. I offered tea and cakes, it then being four-thirty in the afternoon, and Mr. Fowlkes graciously accepted.

Before leaving, Mr. Fowlkes asked me to accompany him to a concert on Friday evening, and I very readily agreed. And so began the strangest three months of my entire life.

It didn't take me long to realize that I was being courted. Actually, I couldn't believe it at first. After all, at *my* age! But I myself did know some very nice couples who had married late in life — a widow and a widower, both lonely, sharing interests, and deciding to lighten their remaining years together — and looked at in that light it wasn't at all as ridiculous as it might appear at first.

Actually, I had expected my son Tom to laugh at the idea, and to dislike Mr. Fowlkes instantly upon meeting him. I suppose various fictional works that I have read had given me this expectation. So I was most pleasantly surprised when Tom and Mr. Fowlkes got along famously together from their very first meeting, and even more surprised when Tom came to me and told me Mr. Fowlkes had asked him if he would have any objection to his, Mr. Fowlkes', asking for my hand in matrimony. Tom said he had no objection at all, but actually thought it a wonderful idea, for he knew that both Mr. Fowlkes and myself were rather lonely, with nothing but our genealogical hobbies to occupy our minds.

As to Mr. Fowlkes' background, he very early gave me his entire history. He came from a fairly well-to-do family in up-state New York, and was himself now retired from his business, which had been a stock brokerage in Albany. He was a widower these last six years, and his first marriage had not been blessed with any children, so that he was completely alone in the world.

The next three months were certainly active ones. Mr. Fowlkes — Gerald — squired me everywhere, to concerts and to museums and even, after we had come to know one another well enough, to the theater. He was at all times most polite and thoughtful, and there was scarcely a day went by but what we were together.

During this entire time, of course, my own genealogical

researches came to an absolute standstill. I was much too busy, and my mind was much too full of Gerald, for me to concern myself with family members who were long since gone to their rewards. Promising leads from the *Genealogical Exchange* were not followed up, for I didn't write a single letter. And though I did receive many in the *Exchange*, they all went unopened into a cubbyhole in my desk. And so the matter stayed while the courtship progressed.

After three months Gerald at last proposed. "I am not a young man, Henrietta," he said. "Nor a particularly handsome man" — though he most certainly was very handsome, indeed — "nor even a very rich man, although I do have sufficient funds for my declining years. And I have little to offer you, Henrietta, save my own self, whatever poor companionship I can give you, and the assurance that I will be ever at your side."

What a beautiful proposal! After being nine years a widow, and never expecting even in fanciful daydreams to be once more a wife, what a beautiful proposal and from what a charming gentleman!

I agreed at once, of course, and telephoned Tom the good news that very minute. Tom and his wife, Estelle, had a dinner party for us, and then we made our own plans. We would be married three weeks hence. A short time? Yes, of course, it was, but there was really no reason to wait. And, we could honeymoon in Washington D.C., where my oldest boy, Roger, has quite a responsible position with the State Department. After which, we would return to Boston and take up our residence in a lovely old home on Beacon Hill, which was then for sale and which we would jointly purchase.

Ah, the plans! The preparations! How newly filled were my so-recently empty days!

I spent most of the last week closing my apartment on

Newbury Street. The furnishings would be moved to our new home by Tom, while Gerald and I were in Washington. But, of course, there was ever so much packing to be done, and I got at it with a will.

And so at last I came to my desk, and my genealogical researches lying as I had left them. I sat down at the desk, somewhat weary, for it was late afternoon and I had been hard at work since sunup, and I decided to spend a short while getting my papers into order before packing them away. And so I opened the mail which had accumulated over the last three months.

There were twenty-three letters. Twelve asked for information on various family names mentioned in my entry in the *Exchange*, five offered to give me information, and six concerned Euphemia Barber. It was, after all, Euphemia Barber who had brought Gerald and me together in the first place, and so I took time out to read these letters.

And so came the shock. I read the six letters, and then I simply sat limp at the desk, staring into space, and watched the monstrous pattern as it grew in my mind. For there was no question of the truth, no question at all.

Consider: Before starting the letters, this is what I knew of Euphemia Barber: She had been born Euphemia Stover in Salem, Massachusetts, in 1765. In 1791 she married Jason Barber, a widower of Savannah, Georgia. Jason died two years later, in 1793, of a stomach upset. Three years later Euphemia appeared in Virginia and married John Anderson, also a widower. John Anderson died two years thereafter, in 1798, of stomach upset. In both cases Euphemia sold her late husband's property and moved on.

And here is what the letters added to that, in chronological order:

From Mrs. Winnie Mae Cuthbert, Dallas, Texas:

Euphemia Barber, in 1800, two years after John Anderson's death, appeared in Harrisburg, Pennsylvania, and married one Andrew Cuthbert, a widower and a prosperous feed merchant. Andrew died in 1801, of a stomach upset. The widow sold his store, and moved on.

From Miss Ethel Sutton, Louisville, Kentucky: Euphemia Barber, in 1804, married Samuel Nicholson of Louisville, a widower and a well-to-do tobacco farmer. Samuel Nicholson passed on in 1807, of a stomach upset. The widow sold his farm, and moved on.

From Mrs. Isabelle Padgett, Concord, California: In 1808 Euphemia Barber married Thomas Norton, then Mayor of Dover, New Jersey, and a widower. In 1809 Thomas Norton died of a stomach upset.

From Mrs. Luella Miller, Bicknell, Utah: Euphemia Barber married Jonas Miller, a wealthy shipowner of Portsmouth, New Hampshire, a widower, in 1811. The same year Jonas Miller died of a stomach upset. The widow sold his property, and moved on.

From Mrs. Lola Hopkins, Vancouver, Washington: In 1813, in southern Indiana, Euphemia Barber married Edward Hopkins, a widower and a farmer. Edward Hopkins died in 1816, of a stomach upset. The widow sold the farm, and moved on.

From Mr. Roy Cumbie, Kansas City, Missouri: In 1819 Euphemia Barber married Stanley Thatcher of Kansas City, Missouri, a river barge owner and a widower. Stanley Thatcher died, of a stomach upset, in 1821. The widow sold his property, and moved on.

The evidence was clear, and complete. The intervals of time without dates could mean that there had been other widowers who had succumbed to Euphemia Barber's fatal charms, and whose descendants did not number among themselves an amateur genealogist. Who could tell just how many husbands Euphemia had murdered? For murder it quite clearly was, brutal murder, for profit. I had evidence of eight murders, and who knew but what there were eight more, or eighteen more? Who could tell, at this late date, just how many times Euphemia Barber had murdered for profit, and had never been caught?

Such a woman is inconceivable. Her husbands were always widowers, sure to be lonely, sure to be susceptible to a wily woman. She preyed on widowers, and left them all, a widow.

Gerald.

The thought came to me, and I pushed it firmly away. It couldn't possibly be true; it couldn't possibly have a single grain of truth.

But what did I know of Gerald Fowlkes, other than what he had told me? And wasn't I a widow, lonely and susceptible? And wasn't I financially well off?

Like father, like son, they say. Could it be also, like great-great-great-great-great-grandmother, like great-great-great-great-great-grandson?

What a thought! It came to me that there must be any number of widows in the country, like myself, who were interested in tracing their family trees. Women who had a bit of money and leisure, whose children were grown and gone out into the world to live their own lives, and who filled some of the empty hours with the hobby of genealogy. An unscrupulous man, preying on well-to-do widows, could find no better introduction than a common interest in genealogy.

What a terrible thought to have about Gerald! And yet I couldn't push it from my mind, and at last I decided that the only thing I could possibly do was try to substantiate the autobiography he had given me, for if he had told the truth about himself, then he could surely not be a beast of the type I was imagining.

A stockbroker, he had claimed to have been in Albany, New York. I at once telephoned an old friend of my first husband's, who was himself a Boston stockbroker, and asked him if it would be possible for him to find out if there had been, at any time in the last fifteen or twenty years, an Albany stockbroker named Gerald Fowlkes. He said he could do so with ease, using some sort of directory he had, and would call me back. He did so, with the shattering news that no such individual was listed!

Still I refused to believe. Donning my coat and hat, I left the apartment at once and went directly to the telephone company, where, after an incredible number of white lies concerning genealogical research, I at last persuaded someone to search for an old Albany, New York, telephone book. I knew that the main office of the company kept books for other major cities, as a convenience for the public, but I wasn't sure they would have any from past years. Nor was the clerk I talked to, but at last she did go and search, and came back finally with the 1946 telephone book from Albany, dusty and somewhat ripped, but still intact, with both the normal listings and the yellow pages.

No Gerald Fowlkes was listed in the white pages, or in the yellow pages under Stocks & Bonds.

So. It was true. And I could see exactly what Gerald's method was. Whenever he was ready to find another victim, he searched one or another of the genealogical magazines until he found someone who shared one of his own past relations. He then proceeded to effect a meeting with that person, found out quickly enough whether or not the intended victim was a widow, of the proper age range, and with the properly large bank account, and then the courtship began.

I imagined that this was the first time he had made the mistake of using Euphemia Barber as the go-between. And I doubted that he even realized he was following in Euphemia's footsteps. Certainly, none of the six people who had written to me about Euphemia could possibly guess, knowing only of the one marriage and death, what Euphemia's role in life had actually been.

And what was I to do now? In the taxi, on the way back to my apartment, I sat huddled in a corner, and tried to think.

For this *was* a severe shock, and a terrible disappointment. And how could I face Tom, or my other children, or any of my friends, to whom I had already written the glad news of my impending marriage? And how could I return to the drabness of my days before Gerald had come to bring me gaiety and companionship and courtly grace?

Could I even call the police? I was sufficiently convinced myself, but could I possibly convince anyone else?

All at once, I made my decision. And, having made it, I immediately felt ten years younger, ten pounds lighter, and quite a bit less foolish. For, I might as well admit, in addition to everything else, this had been a terrible blow to my pride.

But the decision was made, and I returned to my apartment cheerful and happy.

And so we were married.

Married? Of course. Why not?

Because he will try to murder me? Well, of course, he *will* try to murder me. As a matter of fact, he has already tried, half a dozen times.

But Gerald is working at a terrible disadvantage. For he cannot murder me in any way that looks like murder. It must appear to be a natural death, or, at the very worst, an accident. Which means that he must be devious, and he must plot and plan, and never come at me openly to do me in.

And there is the source of his disadvantage. For I am fore-warned, and forewarned is forearmed.

But what, really, do I have to lose? At seventy-three, how many days on this earth do I have left? And how *rich* life is these days! How rich compared to my life before Gerald came into it! Spiced with the thrill of danger, the excitement of cat and mouse, the intricate moves and countermoves of the most fascinating game of all.

And, of course, a pleasant and charming husband. Gerald *has* to be pleasant and charming. He can never disagree with me, at least not very forcefully, for he can't afford the danger of my leaving him. Nor can he afford to believe that I suspect him. I have never spoken of the matter to him, and so far as he is concerned I know nothing. We go to concerts and museums and the theater together. Gerald is attentive and gentlemanly, quite the best sort of companion at all times.

Of course, I can't allow him to feed me breakfast in bed, as he would so love to do. No, I told him, I was an old-fashioned woman, and believed that cooking was a woman's job, and so I won't let him near the kitchen. Poor Gerald!

And we don't take trips, no matter how much he suggests them.

And we've closed off the second story of our home, since, I pointed out that the first floor was certainly spacious enough for just the two of us, and I felt I was getting a little old for climbing stairs. He could do nothing, of course, but agree.

And, in the meantime, I have found another hobby, though of course Gerald knows nothing of it. Through discreet inquiries, and careful perusal of past issues of the various genealogical magazines, and the use of the family names in Gerald's family tree, I am gradually compiling another sort of tree. Not a family tree, no. One might facetiously call it a

hanging tree. It is a list of Gerald's wives. It is in with my genealogical files, which I have willed to the Boston library.
Should Gerald manage to catch me after all, what a surprise is
in store for the librarian who sorts out those files of mine! Not
as big a surprise as the one in store for Gerald, of course.

Ah, here comes Gerald now, in the automobile he bought
last week. He's going to ask me again to go for a ride with
him.

But I shan't go.

THE MOTHER OF INVENTION
IS WORTH A POUND OF CURE

Margo rolled over on her side. "Let's discuss morality," she said.

How I mistrusted her! Feigning unconcern, I adjusted a pillow against the head board and said, "Morality? Such as."

"Such as you, dear Roderick. Light me a cigarette."

I lit two, gave her one, and put the ashtray on the sheet between us. Once, for fun, I'd put the cold glass ashtray on her bare stomach, and without batting an eye she'd mashed the burning end of her cigarette against my leg. That was before I'd known her so well, before I'd learned to be wary.

"Morality," she said thoughtfully, blowing smoke and considering the sound of the word. "What do you think of morality, Roderick?"

She called me by my full name that way whenever she wanted to tease or provoke me, but I refused to rise to the bait. "Morality," I said, trying for the light touch, "I think morality is good."

"Do you? And do you think that *you* are moral, Roderick? Are you a moral man?"

"About average."

"Is that so? Roderick, I am a married woman."

"I'm aware of that."

"What we are doing together with disgusting frequency, Roderick, is called adultery. You know the word?"

"I've heard it mentioned."

"It's immoral."

"And illegal," I said, still trying for the light touch, "but unless you get pregnant it's hardly fattening."

"If you commit adultery, Roderick, you are no longer moral."

"Morality in moderation," I said. "Everything in moderation. Except sex, of course."

"Stop that, I'm talking."

I shifted position. "Sorry."

"There is no such thing," she said, looking very serious, "as morality in moderation, that was a very stupid joke."

"My apologies."

"One is either moral, or one is immoral. Sinful, or pure. Once you sin, there is no longer any question; you are immoral. Commit one sin, and it's the same as though you've committed them all."

"Is this your own theology?"

"Theology has nothing to do with it, I'm discussing morals. Once you do something immoral, *knowing* it to be immoral, and do it anyway for whatever reason, there's nothing more to be said for you."

"And you," I said. "It takes two to tangle."

She raised her head and offered me a wintry smile. "I'm aware of that, Roderick," she said. "I make no pretension to be moral."

"Good."

"Being capable of one immorality," she went on, "I now know I am capable of *any* immorality. Whatever I want, whatever I need, whatever is necessary." She smiled again, as before. "But what about you?"

"Me?"

"You have never struck me," she said, "as the introspective type. I suspect you have never spent a quiet evening thinking about your relationship to common morality."

"The lady wins a cigar."

"The gentleman loses."

"Loses what?"

She rolled over, sat up, flicked ashes into the tray. "That depends," she said.

"On what?"

"On how stupid you are."

"Oh, very stupid."

"I know. But *too* stupid?" She raised her head all at once, and looked full at me. Such a striking face, with its prominent cheekbones, its cold blue eyes, its hungry mouth; a barbaric beauty, more erotic than I can say. "Can you," she said, "accept the real-life implications of the philosophical truth I have just described? Once you fall from grace, you must be prepared to perform *any* immoral action, as required. Do you know why?"

"I imagine you're about to ten me."

"Yes, I am." So serious, so intent. "The only reason," she said, "to refuse to perform an immoral act, other than self-interest, is the claim that you are moral and such an act is foreign to your nature. If, on the other hand, an immoral act is presented to you as being advantageous to you, and if you have performed other immoral acts in the past, then you can have no objection, no defense, no acceptable reason for saying no. Do you agree with me?"

I would have agreed with anything she said. "Yes," I said.

"Good." She put her cigarette out — in the ashtray, happily — and got up from the bed. "Get dressed," she said. "Charles will be home in an hour."

"Is that it?" I said. "Conversation finished?"

"What more is there to say? You agree that an immoral person cannot refuse to perform any immoral act, except from the argument of self-interest. That says it all."

I said, "I thought you were leading up to something."

She laughed. "You're such a fool, Roderick. Get up from there now."

"I want to take a shower." I loved their walk-in shower, all blue tile.

But she said, "No, not tonight. Just get dressed and get out of here."

Too bad. But with her mood so cruel and changeable, it was perhaps just as well to be leaving. I got out of bed and dressed myself.

Always she gave me a five-dollar bill for cabfare. Yes, and when we were out together she'd hand me a twenty-dollar bill to pay a twelve-dollar restaurant tab, and we would never speak of the change. Margo was hardly the first woman with whom I'd developed such a relationship, but she was by far the youngest and most attractive. At first I'd been amazed that she should require this sort of arrangement, but later on I came to understand: her personality was too savage to put up with unless one softened it with cash.

Tonight, however, the five-dollar bill did not put in its usual appearance. Instead she said, "After four months of you, Roderick, I am sorry to have to tell you your services will no longer be required."

"I beg your pardon?"

She smiled. "You're being laid off," she said.

"Margo . . ."

"Now, dear." She put her hand on my arm. "Don't say anything, it will only be stupid."

"But —"

"Before you go," she said, "I have something to show you. Come along."

I followed her, baffled and more than a little worried, to her office, a small quaint room off the kitchen, containing a desk at which she sat while paying bills and a long sofa on which — because I am who I am — I had always craved to make love to Margo and on which — because she is who she is — my craving had never been satisfied. Motioning at this sofa now, she said, "Sit down while I find it."

I sat down. To my left was the view of the river and, beyond it, Long Island City and all the decaying borough of Queens. Far below us, out of sight because so close to the building, was FDR Drive, a race course for taxicabs. A gentle breeze came through the window, redolent of the smells of Queens and the sounds of Manhattan.

Margo was rummaging through her desk. "I wonder," she said, as though distracted, hardly thinking what she was saying, "what will ever become of you, Roderick."

I knew her by now. She was never distracted, never less than totally aware of what she was saying. It had been, in fact, a sad blow to what might be called my professional pride that I never *could* manage to offer her total distraction. Now, therefore, I understood that she was rummaging through the desk merely for effect, and that what she was saying was both calculated and important. I listened, searching for the hook, and said nothing.

"You're getting older," she went on. "In a few years your value on the open market will begin to dip. As it is, you'll never again find anyone as" — she smiled at me — "interesting to work for as me."

This was all true, bitterly true, and it was a mark of her cruelty that she would drag it into the open at the same time she was firing me. I kept my face blank and my mouth shut.

Now at last she came up with an envelope, legal-size, which she handed me with a flourish, saying, "Read that. I think you'll find it interesting."

Within the envelope was a single sheet of paper, written on in Margo's small, thin, economical hand, and addressed To

Whom It May Concern. The body of the letter was as follows:

> I, Margo Ewing, freely and honestly admit that I murdered my husband, Charles.
>
> I killed him because I could no longer stand to live with him, but he would never give me grounds to divorce him and I could less stand to live without his money.
>
> No one else, and particularly no other man, was involved.
>
> I am writing this confession because, I am surprised to learn, I have a conscience. I never thought I would feel remorse at having murdered Charles, but that is exactly what I feel. I cannot go on carrying this burden alone.
>
> I shot Charles three times with a small automatic he bought me once as a Christmas present, a .25 caliber of Star make. After I killed him I wiped off the fingerprints and threw the gun into the Central Park lake, from about the middle of the footbridge and to the downtown side.
>
> Immediately afterward, I began to regret what I had done.
>
> (Mrs.) Margo Ewing

I looked up from this amazing document and stared at Margo, who was watching me as a scientist might watch a rabbit he has just injected full of germs. I said, I whispered, "You've murdered Charles?"

"What?" She gave a scornful laugh. "What a fool! Of course not!"

"But this . . . this . . ."

She opened a drawer of the desk, pulled something from it, and tossed it into my lap. I started, and it fell to the floor: her little .25 caliber automatic. She said, "There. It isn't in Central Park lake, is it?"

"I don't — I don't . . ."

"You don't understand. They'll engrave that on your tombstone, Roderick." She smiled, and shook her head at me like an indulgent teacher, and got to her feet. "I'm going out," she said. "Charles will be here in half an hour."

"What do you want from me, Margo? For God's sake, say it out plain."

"Do I really have to?" She studied me a moment, and then sighed, and nodded. "Yes, I see I do."

"My mind?" I said, somewhat waspishly, "is not as devious as yours."

"God knows. Roderick, I have given you my confession of murder, and the murder weapon. If Charles were to die, Roderick, in the appropriate manner, do you know what you could do?"

I shook my head.

"You could *blackmail* me!"

"I could what?"

"Roderick, you would have the evidence that could hang me. You could blackmail me, you could live comfortably the rest of your life." She smiled, frostily. "I confess I'd rather have you as a blackmailer the rest of my life than Charles as a husband. Because, dear Roderick, I know you would keep your demands within reason." The smile got colder and colder, colder and colder. "Wouldn't you?"

Her meaning had become staggeringly clear. "You, you want me to . . ."

"I don't *want* you to do anything," she said quickly. And then added, "Do you know, no man has ever refused me anything I wanted, not ever. Most of the time I don't even have to ask, it's just done for me. I wonder what I would do if a man ever did refuse."

I said, "You've planned this, haven't you? For months.

That's why you took me on, isn't it?"

"You silly fool," she said, "did you really think I had to pay anyone? I suffered the humiliation of your moronic misunderstanding because it was necessary, but I can tell you now that I detested paying you for your services very nearly as much as I detested accepting the services I was paying for."

Now, that stung. I said, "I never got any complaints."

"Really? Roderick, I must be off. Charles will be home any minute —"

"Wait," I said.

"Wait? Wait for what?"

"I want to think —"

She laughed. "This is hardly the time to break new ground," she said.

I had no time to listen to her, nor to respond. I had to decide what to do.

Kill the husband? Follow it through, follow it through, what if I actually did kill Charles Ewing, even though I'd never killed anyone before and am among the most squeamish of men? Having killed him, I am now supposed to blackmail Margo for the rest of my life.

Oh? Blackmail Margo? Me? Vie with her in the evil duel of wits which is what blackmail is? She'd have the confession in her hands and me in my grave in six months.

Then what? Refuse? Should I be the first man in Margo's career to refuse her something she wanted?

Margo looked at me. "Well?" she said.

Twenty minutes have passed. I've waited for you to come home, Charles, and now at last you're here, and I've told you everything. I'm sorry I had to keep this little gun pointed at you all the while, but without it I hardly think you'd have agreed to listen to me.

No. I thought not.

I expect you hate me now for having cuckolded you, but that doesn't matter. The horn I have placed on your forehead is a feather compared to the more weighty problems of the moment.

Margo's confession, by the by, is in the envelope on the table beside you. Ill wait, if you'd care to read it and verify my tale.

Am I going to obey Margo's command? Is it my intention to murder you?

Well. I had thought, at first, of an alternate solution, one both complex and satisfactory. If you'll look once more at the confession. Charles, you'll see that, read a certain way, it could also be construed as a suicide note. Do you follow me?

Of course. I would hit Margo on the head with something hard — the butt of this little gun, say — and wait for you to come home, as I have. Whereupon I would shoot you — if Margo was to have committed suicide in remorse at having murdered you, it followed that you would have to be murdered — then throw Margo out the window, hurry to Central Park to rid myself of the gun, and be safe from both of you forever.

In her office, behind her as she sat at the desk, I raised the gun above her . . .

And couldn't do it.

No. I am too weak a creature for such blood-letting. Margo, in her talk of morality, forgot one thing: cowardice is far stronger a moral force than conscience. And if I could not kill her, whom I hate and fear, how less likely that I could kill you.

No, Charles, you won't die at my hand. But perhaps you will die at someone's — and I at Margo's — if you yourself do not take the offensive.

This is my solution: just as Margo flung me at your head, I now fling you at hers. You are, I believe, stronger than I and more likely to succeed. If you weren't, Margo would surely have dispatched you herself. I wish you, most earnestly, bon chance.

And now, if you'll excuse me, I must run.

SNIFF

Albert felt the sniffles first on Monday, which was Post Office Day, but he didn't worry about them very much. In his experience, the sniffles came and went with the changing of the seasons, never serious enough even to need a call on the family doctor; how should he have known that *these* sniffles were the harbinger of more than spring? There was no reason to think that this time . . .

Well. Monday, at any rate, was Post Office Day, as every Monday had been for well over a year now. Sniffles or no sniffles, Albert went through his normal Post Office Day routine just the same as ever. That is, at five minutes before noon he took a business-size white envelope from the top left drawer of his desk, placed it in the typewriter, and addressed it to himself, thusly:

Albert White
c/o General Delivery
Monequois, N.Y.

Then, after looking around cautiously to be absolutely certain Mr. Clement was nowhere in sight, he put a return address in the upper left-hand corner, like so:

After five days return to:
Bob Harrington
Monequois Herald-Statesman
Monequois, N.Y.

Finally, taking the envelope from the typewriter, Albert affixed a five-cent stamp to it from his middle desk drawer and tucked the still-empty envelope away in the inside pocket of his jacket. (It was one of his small but intense and very secret pleasures that Mr. Clement himself, all unknowing, was actually supplying the stamps to keep the system in operation.)

Typing the two addresses on the envelope had taken most of the final five minutes till noon, and putting his desk in order consumed the last several seconds, so that at exactly twelve o'clock Albert could stand, turn to the right, walk to the door, and leave the office for lunch, closing behind himself the door on which was painted the legend JASON CLEMENT, *Attorney-at-Law.*

His first stop, this and every Monday lunchtime, was in the Post Office, where he claimed the bulky white envelope waiting for him in General Delivery. "Here we are, Mr. White!" cried Tom the Postal Clerk, as usual. "The weekly scandal!"

Albert and Tom the Postal Clerk had come to know one another fairly well in the course of the last fifteen months, what with Albert dropping in every Monday for his General Delivery letter. In order to allay any suspicion that might have entered Tom the Postal Clerk's mind, Albert had early on explained that Bob Harrington, the well-known crusading reporter on the Monequois newspaper, had employed Albert as a sort of legman to check out leads and tips and confidential information that had been sent in by the newspaper's readers. "It's a part-time job," Albert had explained, "in addition to my regular work for Mr. Clement, and it's very hush-hush. That's why Bob sends me the material care of General Delivery. And why we make believe we don't even know one another."

Tom the Postal Clerk had grinned and winked and cried, "Mum's the word!"

But later on Tom the Postal Clerk apparently did some thinking, because one Monday he said to Albert, "Why is it you let this stuff sit around here so long? Almost a week, most times."

"I'm supposed to pick up mail on Monday," Albert answered, "no matter when Bob may send it out to me. If I were to come in here every day of the year it might cause suspicion."

"Oh, yeah," said Tom the Postal Clerk, and nodded wisely. But then he said, "You know, you don't want to miss. You see this up here in the corner, this 'After five days return to —' Well, that means exactly what it says. If you don't pick one of these up in the five days, well, that's it."

Albert said, "Would you really send it back?"

"Well, we'd have to," said Tom the Postal Clerk. "That's the regulations, Mr. White."

"I'm glad," said Albert. "I know Bob wouldn't want information like this sitting around too long. If I ever let a letter stay more than five days, you go ahead and *send* it back. Bob and I will both thank you."

"Check," said Tom the Postal Clerk.

"And you won't ever give one of these letters to somebody who *says* he's from me."

"Definitely not, Mr. White. It's you or nobody."

"I mean, even if you got a phone call from somebody who said he was me and he was sending a friend to pick up the letter in my place."

Tom the Postal Clerk winked and said, "I know what you're getting at, Mr. White. I know what you mean. And don't you worry. The U.S. Mails won't let you down. No one will ever get delivery on any of these letters but you or Mr.

Harrington, and that's guaranteed."

"I'm glad to hear that," Albert said, and meant every word of it.

In the months since then, Tom the Postal Clerk had had no more questions, and life had gone along sunnily. Of course, it was necessary these days for Albert to read Bob Harrington's column in the *Herald-Statesman*, since from time to time Tom the Postal Clerk would mention some one of the incredible scandals Bob Harrington was incessantly digging up and want to know if Albert had had anything to do with that particular case. In most instances, Albert said no, explaining that the majority of leads he was given turned out to be worthless. When he did from time to time admit that yes, such-and-such a ruined reputation or exposed misdeed had been a part of his undercover work for Bob Harrington, Tom the Postal Clerk beamed like a quiz-show winner. (Tom the Postal Clerk was obviously a born conspirator who had never — till now — found an outlet for his natural bent.)

Today, however, Tom the Postal Clerk had nothing undercover to talk about. Instead, he looked closely at Albert and said, "You got a cold, Mr. White?"

"It's just the sniffles," Albert said.

"You look sort of rheumy around the eyes."

"It's nothing," Albert said. "Just the sniffles."

"It's the season for it," said Tom the Postal Clerk.

Albert agreed it was the season for it, left the Post Office, and went to City Hall Luncheonette, where he told Sally the Waitress, "I think the roast beef today."

(Albert's wife, Elizabeth, would gladly have made a lunch for him, and Albert would gladly have eaten it, except that Mr. Clement did not believe that law clerks — even forty-year-old law clerks with steel-rim glasses and receding hairlines and expanding waistlines — should sit at their desks in their offices and eat sandwiches from a paper bag. Therefore the daily noontime walk to City Hall Luncheonette, which served food that was adequate without being as scrumptious as the menu claimed.)

While Sally the Waitress went off to order the roast beef, Albert walked back to the men's room to wash up and also to continue the normal routine of Post Office Day. He took from his right-side jacket pocket the letter which Tom the Postal Clerk had just given him, carefully ripped it open, and took from it the bulky wad of documents it contained. This package went into the fresh envelope he had just typed before leaving the office. He sealed the new envelope and returned it to his inner jacket pocket, then ripped the old envelope into very small pieces and flushed the pieces down the toilet. He then washed his hands, went out to sit at his normal table, and ate a passable lunch of peas, french fries, rye bread, coffee, and roast beef.

He had first stumbled across the originals of these documents eight years ago, one day when Mr. Clement was detained in court and Albert had required to know a certain fact which was on a certain piece of paper. With no ulterior motive he had searched Mr. Clement's desk, had noticed that one drawer seemed somewhat shorter than the others, had taken it out to look behind it, had seen the green metal box back there, had given in to curiosity, and within the green metal box had learned that Mr. Clement was very, very rich and had become so by grossly dishonest means.

Mr. Clement was an old man, a bony white-haired firebrand who still struck awe in those who met him. And not always merely awe; he carried a cane with a silver knob atop it, and had been known to flail away with it at persons who had been ungracious or rude to him in streets, buses, stores, or wherever he happened to be. His law business leaned heavily to estates and the affairs of small local corporations. The documents in the green metal box proved that Mr. Clement had stolen widely and viciously from these estates and corporations, had salted most of the money away in bank accounts under false names, and was now a millionaire several times over.

A confusing medley of thoughts had run through Albert's mind on finding these documents. First, he was stunned and disappointed to learn of Mr. Clement's perfidy; although the old man's irascibility had kept Albert from ever really liking him, he *had* respected and admired him, and now he was finding his respect and admiration to have been misplaced. Second, he was terrified at the thought of what Mr. Clement would do if he learned of Albert's discovery; surely these documents limned a man ruthless enough to stop at nothing if he thought exposure were near. And third — amazing himself — he thought of blackmail.

In those first kaleidoscopic moments, Albert White found himself yearning for things the existence of which he had hardly ever before noticed. Acapulco. Beautiful women. White dinner jackets. Sports cars. Highballs. Penthouses. Wouldn't Mr. Clement pay for all those things, in order to keep Albert's mouth shut?

Of course he would. If there were no *better* way to shut Albert's mouth. The thought of potential better ways made Albert shudder.

Still, he *wanted* all those things. Ease and luxury. Travel. Adventure. Sinning expensively. All that jazz.

At intervals over the next few months Albert snuck documents out of the green metal box and had them photostated. He continued until he had enough evidence to put Mr. Clement behind bars until the twenty-second century. He hid this evidence in the garage behind the little house he shared with his wife, Elizabeth, and for the next four years he didn't do a thing.

He needed a plan. He needed some way to arrange things so that the evidence would go to the authorities if anything happened to him, and also so that he could convince Mr. Clement that he had the evidence and the authorities would get it unless, and also so that Mr. Clement couldn't get his hands on it himself. A tall order. But four years Albert had no way to fill it.

But then he read a short story by a writer named Richard Hardwick, outlining the method Albert eventually came to use, with the documents mailed to himself c/o General Delivery and a crusading reporter for the return address. Albert promptly initiated the scheme himself, pruned his evidential documents down to manageable proportions, sent them circulating through the postal system, and saw that everything worked just as Hardwick had said it would.

Now all that was left was to approach Mr. Clement, detail the evidence and the precautions, arrange satisfactory terms, and sit back to enjoy evermore a life of luxury.

Uh huh.

The same day that Albert dropped the envelope into the mailbox for the very first time he also went to beard Mr. Clement in his den; that is, in his inner office. Albert knocked at the door before entering, as he had been taught years and years ago when he'd first obtained this employment, stepped inside, and said, "Mr. Clement?"

Mr. Clement raised his bony face, glared at Albert with his stony eyes, and said, "Yes, Albert? What is it?"

Albert said, "Those Duckworth leases. Do you want them this afternoon?"

"Naturally I want them this afternoon. I told you yesterday I would want them this afternoon."

"Yes, sir," said Albert, and retreated.

Back at his desk, he sat and blinked in some confusion at the far wall. He had opened his mouth, back there in Mr. Clement's office, with the full intention of saying "Mr. Clement, I know all." It had been with baffled consternation that he had heard himself say instead, "Those Duckworth leases." Besides the fact that he hadn't intended to say, "Those Duckworth leases," there was the additional fact that he had already known Mr. Clement would want the Duckworth leases this afternoon. Not only a wrong question, but a useless question as well.

"I was afraid of him, that's all," Albert told himself. "And there's no reason to be afraid. I do have the goods on him, and he doesn't dare touch me."

Later that same day Albert tried again. It was, as a matter of fact, when he brought the Duckworth leases in. He placed them on the desk, stood around a few seconds, then coughed hesitantly and said, "Mr. Clement?"

Mr. Clement glowered. "What is it this time?"

"I'm not feeling too well, Mr. Clement. I'd like to take the rest of the afternoon off, please."

"Have you typed the Wilcox papers?"

"No, sir, not yet."

"Type them up, and then you can go."

"Yes, sir. Thank you."

A saddened Albert left Mr. Clement's office, knowing he had failed again and knowing also there was no point his trying any more today; he'd only go on failing. So he merely typed the Wilcox papers, tidied his desk, and went home an hour early, explaining to Elizabeth that he'd felt a bit queasy at the office, which was perfectly true.

In the fifteen months that followed, Albert made frequent attempts to inform Mr. Clement that he was in the process of being blackmailed, but somehow or other when he opened his mouth it was always some other sentence that came out. Sometimes, at night, he practiced in front of a mirror, outlining the situation and his demands with admirable clarity and brevity. Other times he wrote the speeches out and set himself to memorize them, but the prepared speeches were always too verbose and unwieldy.

It was clear enough in his mind what he intended say. He would tell about his discovery and of the General Delivery scheme. He would explain his desire to travel, explain how he intended to remail the evidence every week to a new location — Cannes, Palm Beach, Victoria Falls — and point out that he would require a large and steady income to enable him to pick the evidence up each time within the five-day deadline. He would say that although he thought Elizabeth was perhaps too much of a homebody to fully enjoy the sort of life Albert intended leading from now on, he did still feel a certain fondness for her and would prefer to be able to think that she was being suitably provided for by Mr. Clement in his absence.

He *would* say all that. Some day. All hope, he believed, was not yet lost. The day would come when his courage was sufficiently high or his desire for the good life sufficiently strong, and on that day he would *do* it. The day, however, had not yet come.

In the meantime, the mailing and remailing of the blackmail letter had become a normal part of Albert's weekly routine, integrated into his orderly life as though there were nothing strange about it at all. Every Monday, on his way to lunch, he picked up the letter at General Delivery. Every Monday, in the washroom of the City Hall Luncheonette, he transferred the documents to the fresh envelope and flushed the used envelope away. Every Monday, on the way back to work from lunch, he dropped the letter into a handy mailbox.

(The letter would reach Tom the Postal Clerk on Tuesday. Wednesday would be day number one, Thursday number two, Friday three, Saturday four, Sunday no number, and Monday five, the end of the old cycle and beginning of the new.)

This particular Monday was no different from any other, except of course for the sniffles. Sally the Waitress commented on that, saying, as she delivered the roast beef, "You look like you're coming down with something, Mr. White."

"Just the sniffles," said Albert.

"Probably one of those twenty-four-hour bugs that's going around," she said.

Albert agreed with her diagnosis, ate his lunch, paid for it and left his usual twenty-five-cent tip, and walked on back to the office, making two stops on the way. The first was at the handy mailbox, where he dropped the evidence in for another round-trip through the postal system, and the second was at the Bizy Korner Stationery, where he bought a pocket packet of tissues for his sniffles.

He would have preferred to think that Sally the Waitress was right about the length of time these sniffles would be with him — the "twenty-four-hour bug" she had mentioned — but he rather doubted it. From past experience he knew that the sniffles lasted him approximately three days; he could look forward to runny nose and rheumy eyes until about Thursday, when it would surely begin to clear up.

Except that it didn't. Monday went by, uneventful after the remailing of the documents, Tuesday and Wednesday followed, and Thursday dawned clogged and stuffy, both in the outside world and in the interior of Albert's head. Albert wore his raincoat and rubbers, carried his umbrella, and snuffled his way through Thursday, going through an entire box of tissues in the office.

And Friday was even worse. Elizabeth, the kind of woman who looks most natural when wearing an apron and holding an apple pie, took one look at Albert on Friday morning and said, "Don't you even bother to get up. I'll call Mr. Clement and tell him you're too sick to go to work today."

And Albert was. He was too sick to go to work, too sick even to protest at having to stay in bed, and so utterly miserably sick that he even forgot all about the letter ticking away in General Delivery.

He remained just as sick, and just as oblivious, all through the weekend, spending most of his time in uneasy dozing, rising to a sitting position now and then in order to down some chicken broth or tea and toast, and then reclining at once to sleep some more.

About eleven o'clock Sunday night Albert awoke from a sound sleep with a vision of that envelope clear in his mind. It was as though he had dreamed it: the envelope, clean and clear, sitting fat and solitary in a pigeonhole, and a hand reaching out to take it, a hand that belonged to Bob Harrington, crusading reporter.

"Good heavens!" cried Albert. Elizabeth was sleeping in the guest bed while Albert was sick, and so didn't hear him. "I'd better be well tomorrow," he said aloud, laid his head back down on the pillow, and stayed awake quite a while, thinking about it.

But he wasn't well on the morrow. He was awakened Monday morning by the sound of rain beating on the bedroom window. He sat up, knew at once that he was as dizzy and weak as ever, and felt a real panic begin to slide over him like a blanket of fire. But he fought it down, if not quite out; he had, at all costs, to remain calm.

When Elizabeth came in to ask him what he wanted for breakfast, Albert said, "I've got to make a phone call."

"Who do you want me to call, dear?"

"No," said Albert firmly. "*I* have to make the call."

"Dear, I'll be happy to —"

Albert was seldom waspish, but when the mood was on him he could be insufferable. "What would make you happy," he now said, the sardonic ring in his voice muffled a bit by the blockage in his nose, "is of not the slightest interest to me. *I* must make a phone call, and all I ask of *you* is that you help me get to the living room."

Elizabeth protested, thinking to be kindly, but eventually she saw Albert was not going to be reasonable, and so she agreed. He was weak as a kitten, and leaned heavily on her as they made their way down the stairs to the first floor and into the living room. Albert sagged into the chair beside the phone and sat there panting a few minutes, done in by the exertion. Elizabeth meantime went to the kitchen to prepare, as she put it, "a nice poached egg."

"A nice poached egg," Albert muttered. He felt vile, he felt vicious. He had never been physically weaker in his life, and yet he had never felt before such violent desires to wreck furniture, shout, create havoc, beat people up. If only Mr. Clement had been here now, Albert would have told him what was what in jig time. He'd never *been* so mean.

Nor so weak. He could barely lift the phone book, and turning the pages was a real chore. Then, of course, he looked it up in the wrong place first; under "P" for "Post Office." Finding the number eventually in one of the subheadings under "US GOVT," Albert dialed it and said to the person who answered, "Let me talk to Tom, please."

"Tom who?"

"How do I know? Tom!"

"Mister, we got three Toms here. You want Tom Skylzowsky, you want —"

"Tom!" cried Albert. "At the General Delivery window!"

"Oh, you mean Tom Kennebunk. Hold on a minute."

Albert held on three minutes. At intervals he said, "Hello?" but received no answer. He thought of hanging up and dialing again, but he could hear voices in the background, which meant the receiver was still off the hook at the other end, which probably meant if he broke the connection and dialed again he'd get a busy signal.

His impatience was ultimately rewarded by the sound of Tom the Postal Clerk's voice saying, "Hello? You want me?"

"Hello, there, Tom," said Albert, striving for joviality. "It's me, Mr. White. Albert White, you know."

"Oh, yeah!" How are ya, Mr. White?"

"Well, that's just it, Tom, I'm not very good. As a matter of fact, I've been sick in bed all weekend, and —"

"Gee, that's too bad, Mr. White. That's what you were coming down with last week, I bet."

"Yes, it is. I was —"

"I knew it when I saw you. You remember? I said how you looked awful rheumy around the eyes, remember?"

"Well, you were right, Tom," said Albert, keeping a tight lid on his impatience. "But what I'm calling you about," he said, rushing on before Tom the Postal Clerk could produce any more medical reminiscences, "is the letter you've got for me."

"Let's see," said Tom the Postal Clerk. "Hold on." And before Albert could stop him, he'd *klunked* the phone down on a table somewhere and gone away.

As Albert sat in impotent rage, waiting for Tom the Chipper Moron to return, Elizabeth appeared with a steaming cup of tea, saying, "Drink this, dear. It'll help keep your strength up." She set it on the phone table and then just stood there, hands folded over her apron. Hesitantly, she said, "This must be awfully important."

It occurred to Albert then that sooner of later he was going to have to explain all this to Elizabeth. What the explanation would be he had as yet no idea; he only hoped it would occur to him before he had to use it. In the meantime, a somewhat more pleasant attitude on his part might serve as an adequate substitute. He fixed his features into an approximation of a smile, looked up and said, "Well you know, it's business. Something I had to get done to day. How's the poached egg coming?"

"Be ready in just a minute," she said, and went on back to the kitchen.

Tom the Postal Clerk returned a minute later, saying "Yep, you've got a letter, Mr. White. From you-know-who."

"Tom," said Albert, "now, listen carefully. I'm sick today, but I hope to be better by tomorrow. Hold on to the letter. Don't send it to Bob Harrington."

"Just a sec, Mr. White."

"Tom — !"

But he was gone again.

Elizabeth came in and pantomimed that the poached egg was ready, Albert nodded and made his smile face and waved his hand for Elizabeth to go away, and Tom the Postal Clerk came back once more, saying, "Say, there, Mr. White, we've had this letter since last Tuesday."

Elizabeth was still standing there. Albert said into the phone, "I'll be up and around in just a day or two." He waved violently for Elizabeth to go away.

"You better call Mr. Harrington," suggested Tom the Postal Clerk. "Tell him to send it out again as soon as it comes back."

"Tom, *hold* it for me!"

"I can't do that, Mr. White. You remember, we talked

about that once. You said yourself we should definitely send it back if you didn't pick it up in the five days."

"But I'm sick!" cried Albert. Elizabeth persisted in standing there, looking concerned for Albert's well-being when in point of obvious fact she was crazy to know what this phone call was all about.

Tom the Postal Clerk, with infuriating calm, said, "Mr. White, if you're sick you shouldn't be doing any undercover work anyway. Except under the bedcovers, eh? He he."

"Tom, you *know* me! You can recognize my voice, can't you?"

"Well, sure, Mr. White."

"The letter's addressed to *me,* isn't it?"

"Mr. White, Postal Regulations say —"

"Oh, *damn* Postal Regulations!"

Elizabeth looked shocked. The silence of Tom the Postal Clerk sounded shocked. Albert himself was a little shocked. He said, "I'm sorry, Tom, I didn't mean that, I'm a little upset and being sick and all —"

"It isn't the end of the world, Mr. White," Tom the Postal Clerk said, now obviously trying to help. "Mr. Harrington isn't going to fire you or anything, not if you're sick."

Albert, with a new idea created by Elizabeth's unending presence directly in front of him, said, "Tom, listen. Tom, I'm going to send my wife down to get the letter." It meant telling Elizabeth the truth, or at least an abridged version of the truth, but it could no longer be helped. "I'll have her bring identification from me, my driver's license or a note to you or something, and —"

"It just can't be done, Mr. White. Don't you remember, you told me that yourself, I should never give one of these letters to anybody but you in person, no matter what phone calls I got or anything like that."

Albert did remember that, damn it. But this was different! He said, "Tom, please. You don't understand."

"Mr. White, now, you made me give you my word —"

"Oh, shut *up!*" cried Albert, finally admitting to himself that he wasn't going to get anywhere, and slammed the phone into its cradle.

Elizabeth said, "Albert, what *is* this? I've never seen you act this way, not in all your life."

"Don't bother me now," said Albert grimly. "Just don't bother me now." He leafed through the phone book again, found the number of the Monequois *Herald-Statesman*, dialed it, and asked to speak to Bob Harrington. The switchboard girl said, "One moment, puh-leez."

In that moment Albert visualized how the conversation would go. He would tell a crusading reporter that a letter he had never mailed was going to be returned to him and would he please not open it? This, to a crusading reporter? Ask someone like Bob Harrington not to open a letter which has come to him via the most unusual and mysterious of methods? It would be like throwing a raw steak into a lion's cage and asking the lion please not to eat it.

Before the moment was up, Albert had cradled the receiver.

He shook his head sadly, back and forth. "I don't know what to do," he said. "I just don't know what to do."

Elizabeth said, "Shall I call Dr. Francis?"

Dr. Francis had been called on Friday, had prescribed over the phone, and had himself called the pharmacy to tell them what to deliver to the White household. It had been said, with some justice, that Dr. Francis wouldn't make a house call if the patient were his own wife. But Albert, suddenly aflame with a new idea, cried, "Yes! Call him! Tell him to get over here right away, it's an emergency! In the meantime," he added, more quietly, "I'll eat my poached egg."

Dr. Francis arrived about two that afternoon, shucked out of his sopping raincoat — it was the worst rainstorm of the spring season thus far — and said, in a disgruntled manner, "All right, let's see this emergency."

Albert had remained on the first floor, reclining on the living-room sofa and covered with blankets. Now he propped himself up and called, "Me, Doctor! In here!"

Dr. Francis came in and said, "You're a virus, aren't you? I prescribed for you last Friday."

"Doctor," said Albert urgently, "I absolutely have to go to the Post Office today. It's vital, a matter of life and death. I want you to give me something, a shot, whatever it is you do, something that will keep me going just long enough to get to the Post Office."

Dr. Frances frowned and said, "What's this?"

"I *have* to get there."

"You've been watching those TV spy thrillers," Dr. Francis told him. "There's no such thing as what you want. When you're sick, you're sick. Take the medicine I prescribed, stay in bed, you might be on your feet by the end of the week."

"But I've got to go there today!"

"Send your wife."

"YAAAAAHHHHHH!"

It was nothing but fury and frustration that kept Albert moving then. He came up off the sofa in a flurry of blankets, staggered out to the front hall, dragged his topcoat from the closet and put it on over his pajamas, slammed a hat on his head — he was wearing slipper socks on his feet — and headed for the front door. Elizabeth and Dr. Francis were both shouting things at him, but he didn't hear a word they said.

Two steps down the walk, Albert's slipper socks skidded on the wet pavement, his feet went out from under him, down he went in a flailing of arms and legs, and that's how he broke his collarbone

Elizabeth and Dr. Francis carried him up to his bed. And there, after Dr. Francis taped him, he stayed, silent and grouchy and mad at the world.

He was still there Wednesday afternoon when the phone rang and Elizabeth came to the door, an odd expression on her face, and said, "It's Mr. Clement, dear."

Fatalistically, Albert picked up the bedside phone, put it to his head and said, "Hello?"

Mr. Clement's voice grated on Albert's eardrum: "My plane leaves in a minute, you little sneak, but I wanted to talk to you first. I wanted you to know we're not done, you and I. I'll be back. I'll be back."

Click.

Albert hung up.

Elizabeth, still in the doorway, asked, "Dear?"

Albert opened his mouth. What to tell her? How to tell her? It was all so troubled and complicated.

"Dear? Is something wrong?"

"Yes," he said. And then, in a burst of irritation, "Can't you leave me alone? I've lost my job!"

DEVILISHLY

I said, "I believe I'll be the devil. That ought to be funny."

"Hilarious," said Doris, in that sardonic voice of hers. "Where *do* you think them up?"

"Well, after all," I said defensively, "it is appropriate. The scalawag son returns —"

"To cop his mama's sparklers," Doris finished.

"Just so. A Lucifer suit seems perfectly in keeping with the occasion. The most devilish guest at the costume ball, that's me."

"Subtle," said Doris. "That's what I love about you, how subtle you are. Why don't you just go as the Prodigal Son?"

I considered the idea, but shook my head. "No," I said. "The costume wouldn't be self-explanatory. But a bright red demon suit, now, with a long tail and a pitchfork —"

"Scrumptious," said Doris. "Pass the pickles."

I passed the pickles. I took a bite out of my pastrami sandwich, chewed it, swallowed it, and said, "You're so smart, what are *you* going to be?"

"I haven't decided yet. But nothing banal, darling, believe me. Nothing obvious. Something beautifully original."

"September Morn," I suggested.

"You *would* say something like that," she said. "Why don't you suggest Lady Godiva?"

I'd been about to. I ate some more pastrami sandwich instead.

Just before we finished lunch, Doris reached across the table and took my hand and said, "Don't mind me, Willy. You know I don't mean it as bad as it sounds —"

I did know that, and said so. "You're cleverer than I am," I said, "in some ways. But you love me all the same."

"Oh, you know I do," she said, and gave me an emotional smile, and squeezed my hand. "And I know you love me," she said.

"I should think so."

Yes, I should think so. I'd been disowned for loving Doris, disinherited, kicked out of the biggest house in this city. I threw over a multimillion-dollar inheritance for the love of Doris. Here was one wife who need never have doubts about her husband's affection.

The last five years, since I'd packed and moved out of the Piedmont estate, giving up any claim to the Piedmont soapflake fortune, had not been entirely easy ones. William Piedmont III could not, it goes without saying, do manual labor for his livelihood, but a liberal arts education at an Ivy League college had left me singularly unprepared for any sort of white-collar occupation. With work impossible, Doris and I had had to be fast on our toes and quick with our wits in order to maintain an income sufficient to our tastes.

But after the first year, when in essence we'd been learning our trades, life went along rather well. A bit of pocketpicking here, a touch of burglary there, a modest stock sale elsewhere, it all mounted up. And in rural parts of the country, especially in the South, the old badger game was still worth a small but reliable income.

Not that things went so well that I was prepared to forgive my dear family, however. Oh, no, definitely not. Aside from having turned me out to starve or worse, my nearest and dearest relatives had seen fit to be insulting about Doris, my only true love, merely because she had come from a poverty-stricken family with a scattering of police records among its members. The sting of that rejection was still with me, as sharp as ever, and had been with me constantly throughout these five years. To get back at my family, to somehow even the score with them, how I longed for the opportunity.

But it was impossible. I couldn't approach them, not on any pretext, and if I couldn't approach them, how could I get at them, how could I work my vengeance upon them? No, it was impossible.

Or, that is, *had* been impossible. Impossible until the happy day when I'd found, within a wallet my light fingers had lifted from its former owner, an invitation for two at the Piedmont estate. For a Mardi Gras, a masquerade ball. Prizes would be given.

Oh, yes. Prizes would be given.

The time was two weeks off. We had just come to town the day before I received the invitation — I returned once or twice a year to my native city, drawn back time and time again by the till now fruitless quest for revenge — and had engaged in only the barest minimum of pilfering and light larceny. It was safe to stay, so long as we avoided any part of town where my family might be and recognize me, and so long as we were careful not to pull any capers big enough to start a manhunt. We lived, in the meantime, on the fruits of others' hip pockets, and bided our time.

Now, during lunch at a deli three days before the big masquerade ball, it had come to me what costume I wanted to wear. Doris made fun of it, of course; one of the things I loved most about her was her unceasing war against the banal, the obvious, the trite. I had come from a family for whom banality was a philosophic concept, and it was by now impossible for me to change this style within myself, but I appreciated Doris's position and took a real pleasure in the way she punctured every cliché I launched.

On the other hand, I had still inherited a taste for the apparent, and was not about to give it up. The Lucifer suit, for instance; I thought of it, Doris punctured the triteness of the conception, I took pleasure in her barbed attack, and afterward I would take a different kind of pleasure in going right ahead and wearing the Lucifer suit.

I would call myself, generally, amiable. Yes, amiable. In my dealings with the world except for the single instance of my immediate family, toward whom I was implacably determined upon revenge — my normal, almost my only, reaction was of amiability.

Now, having reaffirmed our love for one another, we went ahead and finished our lunch. We left the deli, I jostled a stranger, and we walked four blocks to the costume shop I'd noticed earlier. With money from the stranger's wallet I put a deposit on a really stunning Satan outfit, tail and pitchfork and all. To Doris, I then said, "Well? Is there anything here you want? I might as well put a deposit for both costumes at once." The stranger had apparently been well-to-do; in any case, he carried a goodly amount of cash on his person.

But Doris shook her head, making a face. "I don't think so," she said. "I'll think of something. Something — different. Something original."

"I'm sure you will," I said.

But by Saturday afternoon, when I went out to the costumer's to pick up the suit, the idea had not as yet occurred to her. "I'll have something by the time you get back," she swore.

"Oh, yes, you will," I said disbelievingly. "You'll wind up going in an old sheet. The ghost of Christmas past."

"You'll see," she said.

And when I came back from the costumer's, my diablo uniform in a box under my arm, there was Doris dressed all in black, form-fitting black from head to foot. She looked as though she'd been dipped nude into a vat of black paint. The outfit included a skull-tight head covering like that worn by the Phantom and other masked heroes of the comics, which completely shielded everything but the lower part of her face. *That* was covered by a small square mirror she had somehow attached to the nose of her costume.

I looked at her, and found her very difficult to see. All that black — The only thing my eyes could really focus on was my own reflection in that little mirror.

I blinked several times, and said, "All right, I give up. What are you supposed to be?"

"You," she said from behind the mirror.

"Eh?"

"I'm going as you," she said. "Whoever I'm talking to, whoever is looking at me, that's who I am."

I looked at the mirror. I saw me.

I said, "Oh, come on, Doris, that's cheating. You have to *be* somebody."

"I am somebody," she said. "I'm you. Besides, this isn't really a bad outfit for burgling in, is it?"

I said, "Oh." I looked ruefully at the box containing my bright scarlet fiend suit, and belatedly I visualized what I was going to look like, flitting along through the darkened up-stairs halls.

There's no getting around it, Doris is *much* more imagina-tive than I am.

Well, it was too late to change. Besides, I still like the devil costume for other reasons. So when we arrived at my family's mansion a little after nine that evening, beneath my coat I was all encased in bright red, just as Doris under her coat was all in black.

There were no names on the invitations, of course, as that would have spoiled the fun of guessing who everybody was. I handed mine to Kibber, a villainous old servant whose continued employment had never ceased to amaze me, and Doris and I joined the colorful throng on the inside, in the main banquet room.

The room had been cleared of furnishings for the occasion, except for a row of settees along the wall opposite the French doors. The massive chandelier sparkled from a million facets, clever masks of various types were hung on the walls all around the room, and at the far end, on a raised platform, was the Irwin Sweets Society Ork, a bush league Guy Lombardo which played at all my parents' tax-deductible soirees. (This was business entertainment, *n'est-ce pas?*) And here and there in great clumps all around the room were massed the guests brightly bedecked, a riot of color, portraying everything from Long John Silver to the Last Leaf of Summer. A rabbit fox-trotted by with a fox. A mailman chatted with a mailbox.

Doris became the instant hit of the party. People kept coming up and asking her what she was supposed to be, and invariably she said, "You." Then the questioner would look blank for a second, finally get it, and collapse with delight.

I finally took her out onto the dance floor, where I murmured in her ear, "Once upon a time, it seems to me, you told me the first rule of the good burglar, as it had been passed on to you by your Dad. Do you remember what it was?"

"Be inconspicuous," she answered.

I said, "Uh huh."

"Smarty," she said, and stuck her thumb into my ribs.

A little later I danced with my sister Eugenie, who confessed, "I feel I must know who you are. It's right on the tip of my tongue. You're so familiar somehow."

Dear Eugenie. I was pleased to see she was as impenetrably stupid as ever.

I saw my brothers Jocko and Hubert from time to time, but didn't dance with them, and so could not be certain that they also had remained feeble-minded. Looking at them from a safe distance, however, I must say they *seemed* the same old bumblebrains. (I noticed them looking at me one time, but the perusal didn't last. Afterward I saw that they were staring at each guest in turn. Memorizing the costumes, I supposed.)

At ten-thirty I returned to Doris, where she stood surrounded by lusting males, and whispered in her ear, "It's time."

She made excuses to her new-found circle of friends and joined me in the hall. Down by the door, Kibber was still at his post. I said to Doris, "This way," and led her back to the servants' stairs. We saw no one.

The well-remembered house. I prowled now through the scenes of my pampered but miserable childhood. In this house, dominated by a robber-baron father and a giddy nitwit mother, I had grown up in the company of brothers and sisters of such stultifying banality that it can be no wonder that I clung to Doris, once I found her, as a drowning man clings to a passing life preserver.

But Doris hadn't preserved my life. She had created my life.

On the second floor, I led the way directly to my father's den. Father *is* a robber baron, with the robber-baron's necessary fear that someday All will become Known. For that reason he keeps a large amount of cash secreted under the false bottom of a desk drawer in his den. But of course nothing is hidden in a house containing a bored and curious child. I had known about that cache of getaway money — as I am convinced my mother *didn't* know, since Father would hardly think in terms of making an escape with *her* at his side — I had known about it since I was ten.

It was still there. Five thousand dollars in used hundreds. I stashed it inside my costume, put the false bottom back, closed the drawer so that its having been jimmied wouldn't be readily apparent, and on we went to my mother's bedroom.

In each instance I was the one who actually entered the room while Doris stood in the doorway to watch for intruders.

In Mama's room I moved aside the painting of autumn woods — it looked like a jigsaw puzzle — and there was the safe hidden away behind it. In it were most of Mama's jewels. She hadn't worn much by way of jewelry tonight, because of her costume. Although she should most appropriately have attended in the guise of a Mack truck, she had chosen instead to be Diana the Huntress, complete with the quiver of arrows on her quivering back.

From the doorway, Doris whispered, "How are you going to break into that? We don't dare blast it."

"I know where Mama keeps the combination," I whispered back. I went over to the telephone table, picked up the small address book there, and carried it over to the better light by the doorway. "Mama can't remember the combination," I told Doris. "So she writes it down in here, in the form of a phone number."

"That's incredible," said Doris. "What's it under? C for combination?"

"No. L for Locke. John Locke. Mother is literate."

"You mean literal," said Doris faintly.

I opened the address book, and there it was: John Locke, VAndyke 6-1233. The VA on the phone dial was 82, and the first number would be to the left. Therefore, the combination was L8, R26, L12, R33.

I went back to the safe and opened it. I put the jewels inside my costume, shut the safe, slid the painting back into place, and Doris whispered, "Somebody coming!"

I zipped under the bed. Doris stepped behind the door.

It was, unfortunately, Mama. She came into the room, switched on her small vanity lamp — Mama dislikes bright light in a bedroom — and went poking through her dresser drawers, the arrows rattling faintly in the quiver on her back.

Doris was in plain sight! Peeking from under the bed, I saw that the door was only half open, and that Doris was where Mama merely had to turn her head to see her.

But Mama didn't see her. Doris had put her black-garbed hands up in front of her face, covering the mirror and her eyes, so that she was now totally black. She blended into the shadow behind the door, as invisible as glass. The only reason I knew she was there was because, uh . . . well, because I knew she was there.

Finally Mama left, and a very few minutes later so did we. We returned to the main banquet room and both made ourselves conspicuous for a little while, dancing with this one and that one, joining the largest chattering groups, all as preface to a nice obvious smooth withdrawal. Thirty or forty people would see us leave, departing casually, openly, with not an apparent care in the world. Who would suspect such leave-takers of burglary?

But just as I was about to begin my farewells, a heavy hand closed on my arm and a familiar voice said, "Hold on, there. Somebody wants to see you."

I turned my head and it was my older brother Jocko, the football player, as huge and dense as ever, dressed in a Tarzan suit. I braced myself to pull out of his grip and try for the door, but then I saw he was smiling. He had not penetrated my disguise after all, but had approached me for some other reason.

I said, "What's up?"

"Just come along," he said, taking a childish delight in being mysterious. "You'll see."

I went with him, warily, ready to run. We walked down the side of the room to the bandstand, where I saw, milling about in some confusion, seven more Satans, plus Doris, plus — standing in front of the microphone — my Mama.

As Jocko placed me amid the other devils, Mama began to shout for attention, announcing, "It's time for prizes, everybody!"

Prizes?

When she had the attention she wanted, Mama went on to explain: "Instead of the usual prize for *best* costume," she yelled, "we thought it would be fun to give *two* prizes this year, one for the *most* original costume and one for the *least* original costume!"

Oh.

I very carefully avoided looking at Doris, but I didn't need to actually see her to know about the little triumphant smirk she would be wearing behind her mirror at the moment. Obviously she had been brought up here to be awarded the prize for the most original costume, which was all she'd needed to make her unbearable for weeks to come.

All she'd needed, but not all she was getting. What were we eight Lucifers here for, if not to be jointly — and quite properly, I must admit — awarded prizes for the least original costume? It would take me months to live this down, months.

My forebodings were correct. Mama announced the prize winner for most original costume to be "the young lady who came as *everybody else!*" Doris stepped up onto the platform, bowed prettily to the burst of applause, and accepted her prize, which turned out to be a little brooch watch.

They were giving Doris time. A chill sense of apprehension crept up my back, but I shrugged it away. They were

172

giving Doris a nice addendum to our haul, that's what they were doing, that and nothing more.

And then it was our turn, we eight scarlet fiends with scarlet faces, and sheepishly we trooped up onto the bandstand to get our prizes: blank identification bracelets.

I felt foolish, of course, standing there above the crowd, being hailed and applauded for my lack of originality while Doris smugly looked on, but a minute later I felt even more foolish as I began to hear the word the crowd was now shouting at us, over and over again:

"Unmask! Unmask!"

Well, I didn't get all the way to the door, but at least in the confusion Doris managed to get away, and if I know Doris she's already plotting some way to break me out of here. I don't know yet what it is, but I do know one thing about it.

It'll be original.

THE SWEETEST MAN
IN THE WORLD

I adjusted my hair in the hall mirror before opening the door. My hair was gray, and piled neatly on top of my head. I smoothed my skirt, took a deep breath, and opened the door.

The man in the hallway was thirtyish, well dressed, quietly handsome, and carrying a briefcase. He was also somewhat taken aback to see me. He glanced again at the apartment number on the door, looked back at me, and said, "Excuse me, I'm looking for Miss Diane Wilson."

"Yes, of course," I said. "Do come in."

He gazed past me uncertainly, hesitating on the doorstep, saying, "Is she in?"

"I'm Diane Wilson," I said.

He blinked. "*You're* Diane Wilson?"

"Yes, I am."

"The Diane Wilson who worked for Mr. Edward Cunningham?"

"Yes, indeed." I made a sad face. "Such a tragic thing," I said. "He was the sweetest man in the world, Mr. Cunningham was."

He cleared his throat, and I could see him struggling to regain his composure. "I see," he said. "Well, uh — well, Miss Wilson, my name is Fraser, Kenneth Fraser. I represent Transcontinental Insurance Association."

"Oh, no," I said. "I have all the insurance I need, thank you."

"No, no," he said. "I beg your pardon, I'm not here to *sell* insurance. I'm an investigator for the company."

"Oh, they all say that," I said, "and then when they get

inside they *do* want to sell something. I remember one young man from an encyclopedia company — he swore up and down he was just taking a survey, and he no sooner —"

"Miss Wilson," Fraser said determinedly, "I am *definitely* not a salesman. I am not here to discuss your insurance with you, I am here to discuss Mr. Cunningham's insurance."

"Oh, I wouldn't know anything about that," I said. "I simply handled the paperwork in Mr. Cunningham's real estate office. His private business affairs he took care of himself."

"Miss Wilson, I —" He stopped, and looked up and down the hallway. "Do we have to speak out here?" he asked.

"Well, I don't know that there's anything for us to talk about," I said. I admit I was enjoying this.

"Miss Wilson, there *is* something for us to talk about." He put down the briefcase and took out his wallet. "Here," he said. "Here's my identification."

I looked at the laminated card. It was very official and very complex and included Fraser's photograph, looking open-mouthed and stupid.

Fraser said, "I will *not* try to sell you insurance, nor will I ask you any details about Mr. Cunningham's handling of his private business affairs. That's a promise. Now, *may* I come in?"

It seemed time to stop playing games with him; after all, I didn't want him getting mad at me. He might go poking around too far, just out of spite. So I stepped back and said, "Very well then, young man, you may come in. But I'll hold you to that promise."

We went into the living room, and I motioned at the sofa, saying, "Do sit down."

"Thank you." But he didn't seem to like the sofa when he sat on it, possibly because of the clear plastic cover it had over it.

"My nieces come by from time to time," I said. "That's why I have those plastic covers on all the furniture. You know how children can be."

"Of course," he said. He looked around, and I think the entire living room depressed him, not just the plastic cover on the sofa.

Well, it was understandable. The living room was a natural consequence of Miss Diane Wilson's personality, with its plastic slipcovers, the doilies on all the tiny tables, the little plants in ceramic frogs, the windows with venetian blinds *and* curtains *and* drapes, the general air of overcrowded neatness. Something like the house Mrs. Muskrat has in all those children's stories.

I pretended not to notice his discomfort. I sat down on the chair that matched the sofa, adjusted my apron and skirt over my knees, and said, "Very well, Mr. Fraser. I'm ready to listen."

He opened his briefcase on his lap, looked at me over it, and said, "This may come as something of a shock to you, Miss Wilson. I don't know if you were aware of the extent of Mr. Cunningham's policy holdings with us."

"I already told you, Mr. Fraser, that I —"

"Yes, of course," he said hastily. "I wasn't asking. I was getting ready to tell you myself. Mr. Cunningham had three policies with us of various types, all of which automatically became due when he died."

"Bless his memory," I said.

"Yes. Naturally. At any rate, the total on these three policies comes to one hundred twenty-five thousand dollars."

"Gracious!"

"With double indemnity for accidental death, of course," he went on, "the total payable is two hundred fifty thousand dollars. That is, one quarter of a million dollars."

"Dear me!" I said. "I would never have guessed."

Fraser looked carefully at me. "And you are the sole beneficiary," he said.

I smiled at him, as though waiting for him to go on, then permitted my expression to show that the import of his words was gradually coming home to me. Slowly I sank back into the chair. My hand went to my throat, to the bit of lace around the collar of my dress.

"Me?" I whispered. "Oh, Mr. Fraser, you must be joking!"

"Not a bit," he said. "Mr. Cunningham changed his beneficiary just one month ago, switching from his wife to you."

"I can't believe it," I whispered.

"Nevertheless, it is true. And since Mr. Cunningham did die an accidental death, burning up in his real estate office, and since such a large amount of money was involved, the routine is to send an investigator around, just to be sure everything's all right."

"Oh," I said. I was allowing myself to recover. I said, "That's why you were so surprised when you saw me."

He smiled sheepishly. "Frankly," he said, "yes."

"You had expected to find some sexy young thing, didn't you? Someone Mr. Cunningham had been having an — a relationship with."

"The thought had crossed my mind," he said, and made a boyish smile. "I do apologize," he said.

"Accepted," I said, and smiled back at him.

It was beautiful. He had come here with a strong preconception, and a belief based on that preconception that something was wrong. Knock the preconception away and he would be left with an embarrassed feeling of having made a fool of himself. From now on he would want nothing more than to be rid of this case, since it would serve only to remind him of his wrong guess and the foolish way he'd acted when

I'd first opened the door.

As I had supposed he would, he began at once to speed things up, taking a pad and pen from his briefcase and saying, "Mr. Cunningham never told you he'd made you his beneficiary?"

"Oh, dear me, no. I only worked for the man three months."

"Yes, I know," he said. "It did seem odd to us."

"Oh, his poor wife," I said. "She may have neglected him but —"

"Neglected?"

"Well." I allowed myself this time to show a pretty confusion. "I shouldn't say anything against the woman," I went on. "I've never so much as laid eyes on her. But I do know that not once in the three months I worked there did she ever come in to see Mr. Cunningham, or even call him on the phone. Also, from some things he said —"

"What things, Miss Wilson?"

"I'd rather not say, Mr. Fraser. I don't know the woman, and Mr. Cunningham is dead. I don't believe we should sit here and talk about them behind their backs."

"Still, Miss Wilson, he did leave his insurance money to you."

"He was always the sweetest man," I said. "Just the sweetest man in the world. But why he would —" I spread my hands to show bewilderment.

Fraser said, "Do you suppose he had a fight with his wife? Such a bad one that he decided to change his beneficiary, looked around for somebody else, saw you, and that was that."

"He was always very good to me," I said. "In the short time I knew him I always found Mr. Cunningham a perfect gentleman and the most considerate of men."

"I'm sure you did," he said. He looked at the notes he'd been taking, and muttered to himself. "Well, that might explain it. It's nutty, but —" He shrugged.

Yes, of course he shrugged. Kick away the preconception, leave him drifting and bewildered for just a second, and then quickly suggest another hypothesis to him. He clutched at it like a drowning man. Mr. Cunningham had had a big fight with Mrs. Cunningham. Mr. Cunningham had changed his beneficiary out of hate or revenge, and had chosen Miss Diane Wilson, the dear middle-aged lady he'd recently hired as his secretary. As Mr. Fraser had so succinctly phrased it, it was nutty, but —

I said, "Well, I really don't know what to say. To tell the truth, Mr. Fraser, I'm overcome."

"That's understandable," he said. "A quarter of a million dollars doesn't come along every day."

"It isn't the amount," I said. "It's how it came to me. I have never been rich, Mr. Fraser, and because I never married I have always had to support myself. But I am a good secretary, a willing worker, and I have always handled my finances, if I say so myself, with wisdom and economy. A quarter of a million dollars is, as you say, a great deal of money, but I do not *need* a great deal of money. I would much rather have that sweet man Mr. Cunningham alive again than have all the money in the world."

"Of course," he nodded, and I could see he believed every word I had said.

I went further. "And particularly," I said, "to be given money that should certainly have gone to his wife. I just wouldn't have believed Mr. Cunningham capable of such a hateful or vindictive action."

"He probably would have changed it back later on," Fraser said. "After he had cooled down. He only made the change three weeks before before — he passed on."

"Bless his soul," I said.

"There's one final matter, Miss Wilson," he said, "and then I'll leave you alone."

"Anything at all, Mr. Fraser," I said.

"About Mr. Roche," he said. "Mr. Cunningham's former partner. He seems to have moved from his old address, and we can't find him. Would you have his current address?"

"Oh, no," I said. "Mr. Roche left the concern before I was hired. In fact, Mr. Cunningham hired me because, after Mr. Roche left, it was necessary to have a secretary in order to be sure there was always someone in the office."

"I see," he said. "Well —" He put the pad and pen back into the briefcase and started to his feet, just as the doorbell rang.

"Excuse me," I said. I went out to the hallway and opened the door.

She came boiling in like a hurricane, pushing past me and shouting, "Where is she? Where is the hussy?"

I followed her into the living room, where Fraser was standing and gaping at her in some astonishment as she continued to shout and to demand to know where *she* was.

I said, "Madame, please. This happens to be my home."

"Oh, does it?" She stood in front of me, hands on hips. "Well, then, you can tell me where I'll find the Wilson woman."

"Who?"

"Diane Wilson, the little tramp. I want to —"

I said, "I am Diane Wilson."

She stood there, open-mouthed, gaping at me.

Fraser came over then, smiling a bit, saying, "Excuse me, Miss Wilson, I think I know what's happened." He turned to the new visitor and said, "You're Mrs. Cunningham, aren't you?"

Still open-mouthed, she managed to nod her head.

Fraser identified himself and said, "I made the same mistake you did — I came here expecting to find some vamp. But as you can see —" And he gestured at me.

"Oh, I *am* sorry," Mrs. Cunningham said to me. She was a striking woman in her late thirties. "I called the insurance company, and when they told me Ed had changed all his policies over to you, I naturally thought — well — you know."

"Oh, dear," I said. "I certainly hope you don't think —"

"Oh, not at all," Mrs. Cunningham said, and smiled a bit, and patted my hand. "I wouldn't think that of *you,*" she said.

Fraser said, "Mrs. Cunningham, didn't your husband tell you he was changing the beneficiary?"

"He certainly didn't," she said with sudden anger. "And neither did that company of yours. They should have told me the minute Ed made that change."

Fraser developed an icy chill "Madame," he said, "a client has the right to make anyone he chooses his beneficiary, and the company is under no obligation to inform anyone that —"

"Oh, that's all right," I said. "I don't need the money. I'm perfectly willing to share it with Mrs. Cunningham."

Fraser snapped around to me, saying, "Miss Wilson, you aren't under any obligation at all to this woman. The money is legally and rightfully yours." As planned, he was now one hundred per cent on my side.

Now it was time to make him think more kindly of Mrs. Cunningham. I said, "But this poor woman has been treated shabbily, Mr. Fraser. Absolutely shabbily. She was married to Mr. Cunningham for — how many years?"

"Twelve," she said, "twelve years," and abruptly sat down on the sofa and began to sob.

"There, there," I said, patting her shoulder.

"What am I going to *do?*" she wailed. "I have no money,

nothing. He left me nothing but debts! I can't even afford a decent burial for him!"

"We'll work it out," I assured her. "Don't you worry, we'll work it out." I looked at Fraser and said, "How long will it take to get the money?"

He said, "Well, we didn't discuss whether you want it in installments or in a lump sum. Monthly payments are usually —"

"Oh, a lump sum," I said. "There's so much to do right away, and then my older brother is a banker in California. *He'll* know what to do."

"If you're sure —" He was looking at Mrs. Cunningham, and didn't yet entirely trust her.

I said, "Oh, I'm sure this poor woman won't try to cheat me, Mr. Fraser."

Mrs. Cunningham cried, "Oh, God!" and wailed into her handkerchief.

"Besides," I said, "I'll phone my brother and have him fly east at once. He can handle everything for me."

"I suppose," he said, "if we expedite things, we could have your money for you in a few days."

"I'll have my brother call you," I said.

"Fine," he said. He hesitated, holding his briefcase. "Mrs. Cunningham, are you coming along? Is there anywhere I can drop you?"

"Let the woman rest here awhile," I said. "I'll make her some tea."

"Very well."

He left reluctantly. I walked him to the front door, where he said to me, quietly, "Miss Wilson, do me a favor."

"Of course, Mr. Fraser."

"Promise me you won't sign anything until your brother gets here to advise you."

"I promise," I said, sighing.

"Well," he said, "one more item and I'm done."

"Mr. Roche, you mean?"

"Right. I'll talk to him, if I can find him. Not that it's necessary." He smiled and said goodbye and walked away down the hall.

I closed the door, feeling glad he didn't think it necessary to talk to Roche. He would have found it somewhat difficult to talk to Roche, since Roche was in the process of being buried under the name of Edward Cunningham, his charred remains in the burned-out real estate office having been identified under that name by Mrs. Edward Cunningham.

Would Roche have actually pushed that charge of embezzlement he'd been shouting about? Well, the question was academic now, though three months ago it had seemed real enough to cause me to strangle the life out of him, real enough to cause me to set up this hasty and desperate — but, I think, rather ingenious — plan for getting myself out of the whole mess entirely. The only question had been whether or not our deep-freeze would preserve the body sufficiently over the three months of preparation, but the fire had settled that problem, too.

I went back into the living room. She got up from the sofa and said, "What's all this jazz about a brother in California?"

"Change of plans," I said. "I was too much the innocent, and you were too much the wronged woman. Without a brother, Fraser might have insisted on hanging around, helping with the finances himself. And the *other* Miss Wilson is due back from Greece in two weeks."

"That's all well and good," she said. "But where is this brother going to come from? She doesn't have one, you know — the real Miss Wilson, I mean."

"I know." That had been one of the major reasons I'd

hired Miss Wilson in the first place aside from our general similarity of build — the fact that she *had* no relatives, making it absolutely safe to take over her apartment during my impersonation.

My wife said, "Well? What are you going to do for a brother?"

I took off the gray wig and scratched my head, feeling great relief. "I'll be the brother," I said. "A startling family resemblance between us."

She shook her head, grinning at me. "You are a one, Ed," she said. "You sure are a one."

"That's me," I said. "The sweetest man in the world."

A GOOD STORY

The big snake moved in its cage, getting hungry. Flat eyes watched Leon walk through and out of the barn; Leon pretended not to notice. There'd been nothing in the mail today, so he was free. He walked past the cages and cotes, past the sawdust-smelling shed where the crates were hammered together, past the long, low main house, with its mutter of air conditioning, and on down the dry dirt road into town, where he bought a beer in the cantina next to the church and stepped outside to enjoy the day.

The sun in the plaza was bright, the air clean and hot, and when he tilted the bottle and put his head back, the lukewarm beer foamed in his mouth. Stripped to the waist, T-shirt dangling from the back pocket of his cutoff jeans, moccasins padding on the baked brown earth, Leon strolled around the plaza, smiling up at the distant crown of the Andes.

Slowly he sipped his beer, enjoying the sensations. This town was so high above sea level, the air so thin, that perspiration dried on him as soon as it appeared. Eight months ago, when he'd first come to Ixialta, Leon had found that creepy and disconcerting, but now he liked the dry crackle and tingle on his flesh, the accretion of salt that he could later brush off like talcum powder.

Eight months; no time at all. The work he did was easy and the money terrific, and the temptation to just drift along with it was very strong — that's what Jaime-Ortiz counted on, he knew that much — but he'd promised himself to give it no more than a year. Tops; one year. Go home rich and clean and 24, with the world before him. Leon grinned, a tall,

185

sloping boy with wiry arms and the hard-muscled legs of a jogger, and was still grinning when the car appeared.

Except for Jaime-Ortiz' six vehicles, cars were a rarity in Ixialta. The dirt road winding up the jungled mountainside was a mere spur from the trans-Andean highway, dead-ending in this public square, surrounded by low stucco buildings.

In the past eight months, how many strangers had been here? A government tax man had come to talk with Jaime-Ortiz, had stopped for lunch and a bribe and had departed. A couple of closemouthed Americans had brought up the new satellite dish, hooked it up and showed Jaime-Ortiz how it worked.

And who else? A pair of British girls working for the UN on some hunger survey; two sets of dopers searching for peyote, going away disappointed; a couple of American big-game hunters who'd stayed three days, shot one alpaca and contracted dysentery; and one or two more. Maybe seven interventions from the outside world in all this time.

And now here was number eight, a dusty maroon rental Honda with a pair of Americans aboard. The 30ish woman who got out on the passenger side was an absolute drop-dead ice blonde. In khaki slacks, thonged sandals, pale-blue blouse and leather shoulder bag, she was some expensive designer's idea of a girl foreign correspondent. The big dark sunglasses, though, were an error; only Jackie O., in Leon's opinion, could wear Jackie O. sunglasses without loss of status. Still, this was a dream walking.

The man was something else. Wide-rumped in stiff new jeans, he wore office-style brown oxfords and a *long-sleeved* buttondown shirt. He was an office worker, a professor of ancient languages, a bank teller, and he didn't belong on this mountain. Nor with that woman.

Leon approached, smiling, planning his opening remark, but the woman spoke first, frowning as though he were the doorman: "What place is this?"

"Ixialta," he told her.

"The high Ixi," she said, unexpectedly. There was a faint roughness in her voice, not at all unpleasant. "What's an Ixi?"

"Maybe a god." Leon had never asked that question.

The man had draped himself with cameras. Blinking through clip-on sunglasses over his spectacles, he said, "Look at those cornices! Look at that door!"

"Yes, Frank," she said, uninterested, and pointed at Leon's beer. "That looks good."

"I'll get you one."

"And shade," she said, looking around.

"Table beside the cantina." He pointed. "In the shade, in the air, you can watch the world go by."

"Good." Setting off across the plaza, Leon beside her, the woman said, "Much of the world go by here?"

"You're it, so far."

Two small round white-metal tables leaned on the cobblestones beside the cantina, furnished with teetery ice-cream-parlor chairs and shaded by the bulk of San Sebastian next door. The woman chose the table without a sleeping dog under it, while Leon went inside. The few customers in the dark and ill-smelling place stopped muttering when he walked in, as they always did, and sat looking at their thick hands or bare feet. Leon finished his beer and bought two more. Putting his T-shirt on, he paid and carried the bottles outside.

Across the way, Frank was taking photos of cornices and doors. The woman had pushed her big sunglasses up on top of her head and was studying her face in a round compact mirror. She had good, level gray eyes, with something cool in them. Sitting across from her, he placed both bottles on the table and said, "I'm Leon."

"Ruth." She put the compact away and looked out at the empty plaza. "Lively spot."

"Come back on Sunday," Leon invited.

"What happens Sunday?"

"Paseo." Leon waved his arm in a great circle. "The boys walk around that way, the girls come the other way, give each other the eye. They come from all around the mountain here."

"The mating ritual," she said, picking up the bottle.

Leon shrugged. "It's the way they do it. All the Indian boys and girls." Across the way, Frank sat in the sunny dust, taking a picture of a stone step.

Ruth drank, head tipped back, throat sweet and vulnerable; Leon wanted to nibble on it. The thought must have showed on his face, because, when she lowered the bottle, the smile she gave him was knowing but distanced. "You're no Indian," she said.

"I'm an Indian's secretary," he said and laughed at the joke.

"How does that work?"

"There's a rich man up here. Owns a lot of land, has everything he wants."

"And he lives here?" The skepticism was light, faintly mocking.

"This is where his money comes from."

"He's a farmer, then."

"He sells animals."

"Cattle?" Confusion was making her irritable, on the verge of boredom.

"No, no," Leon said, *"wild* animals. Jaime-Ortiz sells them to zoos, circuses, animal trainers all around the world.

That's why he needs a secretary, somebody to write the letters in English, handle the business details."

She looked faintly repelled. "What kind of animals?"

"All sorts. This whole range around here — Peru, Bolivia, Paraguay — it's one of the last great wildlife areas. We've got puma, jaguar, all kinds of monkeys, llamas, snakes —"

"Ugh," she said. "What kind of snakes?"

"Rattlers. Anaconda. Boa constrictor. We got a huge boa up in the barn now, all ready to go."

She drank beer and shivered. "Some way to make a living."

"Jaime-Ortiz does OK," Leon assured her and grinned at what he was leaving unsaid.

She seemed to sense there was more to the story. Watching herself move the bottle around on the scarred metal top, she said, "And you do OK, too, I guess."

"Do I look like I'm complaining?"

She glanced at him sidelong. "No," she said, slow and thoughtful. "You look quite pleased with yourself."

Was she making fun? A bit defensive through the lightness, he said, "It's an interesting job here. More than you know."

"How'd you get it? Answer a want ad?"

Leon grinned, on surer ground. "Jaime-Ortiz doesn't put any want ads. He doesn't want some stranger poking around in his business."

"You already knew him, then."

"Family connection. Somebody in the business at the other end."

"An uncle," she said and smiled, showing all her teeth, as though he were a kid she didn't have to compose her face for.

"OK, an uncle," he said, getting really annoyed now. "That doesn't make me just a nephew."

Looking contrite but still smiling, she reached out to touch the tips of two red fingernails to the back of his hand, the nails slightly indenting the flesh. "Don't be mad, Leon," she said. "Take a joke."

Frank and his cameras were still across the plaza. Leon turned his hand, closed it with gentle pressure on her fingers. "I like to joke," he said.

"The wild-animal trainer." She withdrew her hand. "I'd get bored, playing zoo."

"There's better stuff." Suddenly nervous, he gulped beer, and when he lowered the bottle, she was looking at him.

Some instinct of caution made him hesitate. But the English girls had been *very* impressed. And what difference did it make if he talked? The strangers came and went, forgetting the very name of Ixialta. Looking away toward the mountains, he said, "This is also where the coca bush grows. All around here."

"Cocaine," she said, getting it, but then frowned: "What about the law?"

"Around here? You're kidding."

"No, the States, when you smuggle it in."

"That's the beauty," he told her, grinning. "You take your white powder, you see? You put it in your glassine envelopes. You feed your envelopes to your monkey."

"Monkey? But he'll digest it; he'll —"

"No," Leon said. "Because then you feed your monkey to your boa constrictor."

"Oh," she said.

"There isn't a Customs man in the world gonna look to see what's inside a monkey inside a boa constrictor."

"*I* wouldn't."

"The monkey has to go into the snake alive," Leon said, glad to see her eyes widen. "It takes the snake seven days to digest the monkey but only two days to be flown to Wilkinson, the wild-animal dealer in Florida." It was such a good story that he laughed all over again every time he told it. "As the fella says, it's all in the packaging."

"Yes," she said, her expression suddenly enigmatic. She stood, turning away, calling, "Frank! Frank!"

Leon said, "Look, uh. . . ."

"Just a minute." She was brisk and businesslike, utterly different.

Baffled, Leon got to his feet as Frank came trotting across the plaza, holding his cameras down with both hands. "Yeah?"

Nodding at Leon, Ruth said, "He's the one."

Frank looked surprised. "You sure?"

"He just told it to me."

"Well, that was quick," Frank said. His manner was suddenly also changed, less fussy, more self-assured. He walked toward Leon, making a fist. Leon was so bewildered he didn't even duck.

Someone pulled his hair. Leon jerked trying to stand, but was held down, rough ropes holding him to a chair. He opened his eyes, and Jaime-Ortiz stood in front of him, along with Paco and a couple of the other workers. They were all in the big barn, where the air was always cool, rich with animal stink, the hard-packed-earth floor crosshatched with broom lines.

Against the far wall, under the dim bulbs, stood the cages, only a few occupied. A red-furred howler monkey, big-shouldered and half the size of a man, sat with its back to everybody, the hairless tip of its long tail curled negligently around a lower bar, while next door a golden guanaco pranced nervously, its delicate ears back and eyes rolling.

Farther from the light, the big, skinny boa, pale brown with darker crossbars, its scaly head rearing up nearly three feet in the air, showed yellow underbelly as it stared through the bars and wire at everything that moved.

"Jaime?" Leon tugged at the hairy ropes, tasting old blood in his mouth, feeling the sharp stings around his puffy lips. "Jaime? What —"

"I got to be disappointed in you, Leon," Jaime-Ortiz said. He was a big, heavy man with a broad, round face and liquid-brown eyes that could look as soulful as that guanaco's — or as cold as stones. "You," he said, pointing a thick, stubby finger at Leon. "You got to be one real disappointment to me." He shook his head, a fatalistic man.

"But what did I — What's —"

"Little stories going around," Jaime-Ortiz said. He waggled the fingers of both hands up above his head, like a man trying to describe birds in flight. "Somebody talking about our business, Leon. Yours and mine. Making trouble for you and me."

"Jaime, please —"

"All of a sudden," Jaime-Ortiz said, "these drug agents, they come to our friend Wilkinson, they got a paper from a judge."

"Oh, my God." Leon closed his eyes, licking his sore lips. The rope was tied very hard and tight; he could barely feel his hands and feet.

"Who would make trouble for you and me and Wilkinson? Leon? Who?"

Eyes shut, Leon shook his head back and forth. "I'm sorry, Jaime. I'm sorry."

"Friends in New York ask me this," Jaime-Ortiz said. "I say it's not me, it's not Leon, it's not Paco. We all got too much to lose. They say they send somebody down, walk around, see who likes to tell stories."

"Jaime, I'll never, never —"

"Oh, I know that," Jaime-Ortiz said. "You can't be around here no more, Leon. I got to send you back to the States."

Hope stirred in Leon. He stared up at Jaime-Ortiz. "Jaime, I promise, I won't say a word, I'll never —"

"That's right," Jaime-Ortiz said. "You will never say a word. Not the way *you're* going back to the States."

Leon didn't get it until he saw Paco come toward him with the glassine envelope in his hand. "Open wide," Paco said.

BREATHE DEEP

Black stitching over the left pocket of his white-silk shirt read CHUCK in cursive script. His pale, wiry arms were crossed below the name; his large Adam's apple moved arrhythmically above. Before him on the small lima-bean-shaped green table the 200 playing cards were fanned out, awaiting fresh players.

It was 3:30 in the morning and fewer than half the tables in the main casino were staffed. A noisy crowd at one crap table gave an illusion of liveliness, but only four of the seven blackjack dealers on duty had any action. Chuck had stood here at the ten-dollar-limit table for nearly an hour; it was looking as though he wouldn't deal a single round before his break.

"Hey, Chuck."

At the left extreme of the table stood a small old man in a COORS cap, smiling, hands in raincoat pockets. The raincoat hung open, showing a white shirt, as sloppily knotted dark, thin tie and a bit of dark jacket. The old man had shaved recently but not well, and his gray eyes were red-rimmed and merry. The dealer saw not much hope here, but he said, "A game, sir?"

"Maybe in a while, Chuck," the old man said and grinned as though he were thinking of some joke. "Did you know I came out of the hospital just this morning?"

The dealer, his foot near the button that calls security, looked at the old man. He said, "Is that right, sir?"

"Sun City Hospital, right here in Las Vegas, Nevada. Fixed me up just fine. No more broken bones." That I-know-a-joke grin appeared again.

"Sir, if you're not interested in playing —"

194

"Oh, I *could* be, Chuck," the old man said. "I *might* be."

The night was slow, and the dealer's break was due in just a few minutes. So he didn't touch his foot to the button that calls security. "Take your time, sir," he said.

"That's all I've got," the old man said, but then he grinned again. "I love the big Strip hotels at night."

"You do, sir?"

"Oh, yeah. Oh, yeah. I hate Vegas, you know, but I love the hotels at night. I come in, I breathe deep, I'm a young man again. All the old words come back, run around inside my mind like squirrels. You know what I mean, Chuck?"

"Excitement," suggested the dealer, flat-voiced.

"Oh, sure. Oh, yes. By day, you know, I hang around downtown. You know those places. Big sign out front: PENNY SLOTS. FREE BREAKFAST. Penny slots." The old man made a laugh sound in his throat — heh heh — that turned into something like a cough.

"Sir," said the dealer, "I want to give you some friendly advice." He'd seen past the imperfectly shaved cheeks now, the frayed raincoat, the charity-service necktie. This was an old bum, a derelict, one of the many ancient, alcoholic, homeless, friendless, familyless husks the dry wind blows across the desert into the stone-and-neon baffle of Las Vegas. "You don't belong here, sir," he explained. "I'm doing you a favor. Security can get kind of rough, to discourage you from coming back."

"Oh, I know about that, Chuck!" the old man said, and this time he laughed outright. "I *belong* downtown, with those penny slots. Start all over again, Chuck! Build a stake on those slot machines down there, penny by penny, *penny by penny,* come back!"

"Sir, I'm telling you for your own good."

"Chuck, listen." Hands in raincoat pockets, the old man

leaned closer over the table. "I want to tell you a quick story," he said, "and then I'll go. Then *we*'ll go. OK?"

The dealer's eyes moved left and right. His shift boss was down by the active tables. His relief dealer was almost due. "Keep it short," he said.

"Oh, I will!" His hands almost came out of the raincoat pockets, then didn't. "Chuck," he said, "I *know* where I belong, but I just keep coming out to the Strip, late at night. It's a fatal attraction. You know what that is, Chuck?"

"I think so," the dealer said. He thought about showgirls.

"But what makes it, Chuck? Look around. No windows, no clocks, no day or night in here. But it's only at night I *like* these places. That's when they make me feel . . . good. Now, why's that?"

"I wouldn't know, sir."

The old man said, "Well, I was in here one time, and a couple of security fellows took me out back by the loading dock to *discourage* me a little. There were all these tall green-metal cans there, like if you have bottled gas delivered to your house out in the country, and I bumped into them and fell off the loading dock and all these big green-metal cans rolled off and landed on me. And that's why I was in the hospital."

The dealer looked at him. "But here you are back again."

"It's the old fatal attraction, Chuck."

"You'd better get over it."

"Oh, I'm going to." Once again, the old man's hands almost came out of his raincoat pockets but didn't. "But I thought I'd tell somebody first about those green cans. Because, Chuck, here's the funny part. They had them in the hospital, too."

"Is that right?"

"That's right. 'What's that?' I asked the nurse. 'Oxygen,' she said. 'Any time you see a tall can like that, if it's green, you know it's oxygen. That's a safety measure on account of oxygen's so dangerous. You get that stuff near any kind of fire and the whole thing'll burn like fury.' Did you know that, Chuck? About green meaning oxygen?"

"No, I didn't."

"Well, what I kept thinking was: Why does a big Strip hotel need about fifty cans of oxygen? And then I remembered the big hotel fire on the Strip a couple years ago. Remember that one?"

"I do," the dealer said.

"It said in the papers there was a fireball crossed six hundred feet of main casino in seventeen seconds. That's *fast*, Chuck."

"I suppose it is."

"In there, in the hospital," the old man said, "I had this thought: What if, late at night, here in the casino, with no windows and no clocks, air conditioning out of vents all over, what if . . . Chuck, what if they add oxygen to the *air?* The very air we breathe, Chuck, this air all around us." The old man looked around. "Here in this spider's parlor."

"I wouldn't know anything about that," the dealer said, which was the absolute truth.

"Well, I wouldn't *know*, either, Chuck. But what if it's true? Spice up the air at night with extra oxygen, make the gamblers feel a little happier, a little more awake?"

"I'm going to have to call security now," the dealer said.

"Oh, I'm almost done, Chuck. You see, those penny slots downtown, they won't lead me back anywhere. I threw myself away, and I'm not coming back at all. I would have checked out of this rotten life two or three years ago, Chuck, if it hadn't been for this *fatal attraction*. Come out to the Strip late at night. Breathe deep. Get a little high on that extra oxygen, begin to *hope* again, get roughed up by security."

"They don't do that with the oxygen."

"They don't? Well, Chuck, you may be right." The old man took his hands from his raincoat pockets. In his right hand, he held a can of lighter fluid; in his left, a kitchen match. "Let's see," he said and squirted a trail of lighter fluid onto the green felt of the table.

The dealer, wide-eyed, stomped down hard on the button. "Stop that!" he said.

The old man kept squirting lighter fluid, making dark puddles in the felt. "Security coming, Chuck?" he asked.

"Yes!"

"Good. I'd like them to travel with us," the old man said and scraped the match along the edge of the table.

LOVE IN THE LEAN YEARS

Charles Dickens knew his stuff, you know. Listen to this: "Annual income twenty pounds, annual expenditure nineteen nineteen six, result happiness. Annual income twenty pounds, annual expenditure twenty pounds ought and six, result misery."

Right on. You adjust the numbers for inflation and what you've got right there is the history of Wall Street. At least, so much of the history of Wall Street as includes me: seven years. We had the good times and we lived high on that extra jolly sixpence, and now we live day by day the long decline of shortfall. Result misery.

Where did they all go, the sixpences of yesteryear? Oh, pshaw, we know where they went. You in Gstaad, him in Aruba, her in Paris and me in the men's room with a sanitary straw in my nose. We know where it went, all right.

My name's Kimball, by the way, here's my card. Bruce Kimball, with Rendall/LeBeau. Account exec. May I say I'm still making money for my clients? There's a lot of good stuff undervalued out there, my friend. You can still make money on the Street. Of course you can. I admit it's harder now, it's much harder when I have only thruppence and it's sixpence I need to keep my nose filled, build up that confidence, face the world with that winner's smile. Man, I'm only hitting on one nostril, you know? I'm *hurtin'.*

Nearly three years a widow; time to remarry. I need a true heart to share my penthouse apartment (unfurnished terrace, unfortunately) with its grand view of the city, my cottage (14 rooms) in Amagansett, the income of my portfolio of stocks.

An income — ah, me — which is less than it once was. One or two iffy margin calls, a few dividends undistributed, bad news can mount up, somehow. Or dismount and move right in. Income could become a worry.

But first, romance. Where is there a husband for my middle years? I am Stephanie Morwell, 42, the end product of good breeding, good nutrition, a fine workout program and amazingly skilled cosmetic surgeons. Since my parents died as my graduation present from Bryn Mawr, I've more or less taken care of myself, though of course, at times, one does need a man around the house. To insert light bulbs and such-like. The point is, except for a slight flabbiness in my stock portfolio, I am a fine catch for just the right fellow.

I don't blame my broker, please let me make that clear. Bruce Kimball is his name and he's unfailingly optimistic and cheerful. A bit of a blade, I suspect. (One can't say *gay* blade anymore, not without the risk of being misunderstood.) In any event, Bruce did very well for me when everybody's stock was going up, and now that there's a — oh, what are the pornographic euphemisms of finance? A shakeout, a mid-term correction, a market adjustment, all of that — now that times are tougher, Bruce has lost me less than most and has even found a victory or two amid the wreckage. No, I can't fault Bruce for a general worsening of the climate of money.

In fact, Bruce . . . hmmm. He flirts with me at times, but only in a professional way, as his employers would expect him to flirt with a moneyed woman. He's handsome enough, if a bit thin. (Thinner this year than last, in fact.) Still, those wiry fellows. . . .

Three or four years younger than I? Would Bruce Kimball be the answer to my prayers? I do already know him and I'd rather not spend *too* much time on the project.

Stephanie Kimball. Like a schoolgirl, I write the name on the note pad beside the telephone on the Louis XIV writing table next to my view of the East River. The rest of that page is filled with hastily jotted numbers: income, outgo, estimated expenses, overdue bills. *Stephanie Kimball.* I gaze upon my view and whisper the name. It's a blustery, changeable, threatening day. *Stephanie Kimball.* I like the sound.

"There is a tide in the affairs of men, which, taken at the flood, leads on to fortune." Agatha Christie said that. Oh, but she was quoting, wasn't she? Shakespeare! Got it.

There was certainly a flood tide in my affair with Stephanie Morwell. Five years ago, she was merely one more rich wife among my clients, if one who took more of an interest than most in the day-to-day handling of the portfolio. In fact, I never did meet her husband before his death. Three years ago, that was; some ash blondes really come into their own in black, have you noticed?

I respected Mrs. Morwell's widowhood for a month or two, then began a little harmless flirtation. I mean, why not? She was a widow, after all. With a few of my other female clients, an occasional expression of male interest had eventually led to extremely pleasant afternoon financial seminars in midtown hotels. And now, Mrs. Morwell; to peel the layers of black from that lithe and supple body. . . .

Well. For three years, all that was merely a pale fantasy. Not even a consummation devoutly to be wished — now, who said that? No matter — it was more of a daydream while the computer's down.

From black to autumnal colors to a more normal range. A good-looking woman, friendly, rich, but never at the forefront of my mind unless she was actually in my presence, across the desk. And now it has all changed.

Mrs. Morwell was in my office once more, hearing mostly bad news, I'm afraid, and in an effort to distract her from the grimness of the occasion, I made some light remark, "There are better things we could do than sit here with all these depressing numbers." Something like that; and she said, in a kind of swollen voice I'd never heard before, "There certainly are."

I looked at her, surprised, and she was arching her back, stretching like a cat. I said, "Mrs. Morwell, you're giving me ideas."

She smiled. "Which ideas are those?" she asked, and 40 minutes later we were in her bed in her apartment on Sutton Place.

Aaah. Extended widowhood had certainly sharpened *her* palate. What an afternoon. Between times, she put together a cold snack of salmon and champagne while I roved naked through the sunny golden rooms, delicately furnished with antiques. What a view she had, out over the East River. To live such a life. . . .

Well. Not until this little glitch in the economy corrects itself.

"Champagne?"

I turned and her body was as beautiful as the bubbly. Smiling, she handed me a glass and said, "I've never had such a wonderful afternoon in my entire life."

We drank to that.

We were married, my golden stockbroker and I, seven weeks after I first took him to bed. Not quite a whirlwind romance, but close. Of course, I had to meet his parents, just the once, a chore we all handled reasonably well.

We honeymooned in Caneel Bay and had such a lovely time we stayed an extra week. Bruce was so attentive, so charming, so — how shall I put it? — ever ready. And he got along amazingly well with the natives; they were eating out of his hand. In no time at all, he was joking on a first-name basis with half a dozen fellows I would have thought of as nothing more than dangerous layabouts, but Bruce could find a way to put almost anyone at ease. (Once or twice, one of these fellows even came to chat with Bruce at the cottage. I know he lent one of them money — it was changing hands as I glanced out the louvered window — and I'm sure he never even anticipated repayment.)

I found myself, in those first weeks, growing actually fond of Bruce. What an unexpected bonus! And my warm feeling toward this new husband only increased when, on our return to New York, he insisted on continuing with his job at Rendall/LeBeau. "I won't sponge on you," he said, so firm and manly that I dropped to my knees that instant. *Such* a contrast with my previous marital experience!

Still, romance isn't everything. One must live as well; or, that is, some must live. And so, in the second week after our return, I taxied downtown for a discussion with Oliver Swerdluff, my new insurance agent. (New since Robert's demise, I mean.) "Congratulations on your new marriage, Mrs. Kimball," he said, this red-faced, portly man who was so transparently delighted with himself for having remembered my new name.

"Thank you, Mr. Swerdluff." I took my seat across the desk from him. "The new situation, of course," I pointed out, "will require some changes in my insurance package."

"Certainly, certainly."

"Bruce is now co-owner of the apartment in the city and the house on Long Island."

He looked impressed. "Very generous of you, Mrs., uh Kimball."

"Yes, isn't it? Bruce is so important to me now, I can't imagine how I got along all those years without him. Oh, but this brings up a depressing subject. I suppose I must really insure Bruce's life, mustn't I?"

"The more important your husband is to you," he said, with his salesman's instant comprehension, "the more you must consider every eventuality."

"But he's priceless to me," I said. "How could I choose any amount of insurance? How could I put a dollar value on *Bruce?*"

"Let me help you with that decision," Mr. Swerdluff said, leaning that moist red face toward me over the desk.

We settled on an even million. Double indemnity.

"Strike while the widow is hot." Unattributed, I guess.

It did all seem to go very smoothly. At first, I was merely enjoying Stephanie for her own sake, expecting no more than our frequent encounters, and them somehow the idea arose that we might get married. I couldn't see a thing wrong with the proposition. Stephanie was terrific in bed, she was rich, she was beautiful and she obviously loved me. Surely, I could find some fondness in myself for a package like that.

And what she could also do, though I had to be very careful she never found out about it, was take up that shortfall, those pennies between me and the white medicine that makes me such a winning fellow. A generous woman, certainly generous enough for that modest need. And I understood from the beginning that if I were to keep her love and respect and my access to her piggy bank, I must never be too greedy. Independent, self-sufficient, self-respecting, only dipping into her funds for those odd sixpences which would bring me, in Mr. Dickens' phrase, "result happiness."

The appearance of independence was one reason why I kept on at Rendall/LeBeau, but I had other reasons as well. In the first place, I didn't want one of those second-rate account churners to take over the Morwell — now Kimball — account and bleed it to death with percentages of unnecessary sales. In the second place, I needed time away from Stephanie, private time that was reasonably accounted for and during which I could go on medicating myself. I would never be able to maintain my proper dosages at home without my bride sooner or later stumbling across the truth. And beyond all that, I've always enjoyed the work, playing with other people's money as if it were merely counters in a game, because that's all it is when it's other people's money.

Four lovely months we had of that life, with Stephanie never suspecting a thing. With neither of us, in fact, ever suspecting a thing. And if I weren't such a workaholic, particularly when topped with my little white friend, I wonder what eventually might have happened. No, I don't wonder; I know what would have happened.

But here's what happened instead. I couldn't keep my hands off Stephanie's financial records. It wasn't prying, it wasn't suspicion, it wasn't for my own advantage, it was merely a continuation of the work ethic on another front. And I wanted to do something nice for Stephanie because my fondness had grown — no, truly, it had. Did I love her? I believe I did. Surely, she was lovable. Surely, I had reason. Every day, I was made happy by her existence; if that isn't love, what is?

And Stephanie's tax records and household accounts were a mess. I first became aware of this when I came home one evening to find Stephanie, furrow-browed, huddled at the dining-room table with Serge Ostogoth, her — our — accountant. It was tax time and the table was a snowdrift of papers in no discernible order. Serge, a harmless drudge with leather elbow patches and a pathetic small mustache, was patiently taking Stephanie through the year just past, trying to match the paperwork to the history, a task that was clearly going to take several days. Serge had been Stephanie's accountant for three years, I later learned, and every year they had to go through this.

So I rolled up my sleeves to pitch in. Serge was grateful for my help. Stephanie, with shining eyes, kept telling me I was her savior, and eventually we managed to make sense of it all.

It was then I decided to put Stephanie's house in order. There was no point mentioning my plan; Stephanie was truly ashamed of her record-keeping inabilities, so why rub her nose in it? Evenings and weekends, if we weren't doing anything else, not flying out to the cottage or off to visit friends or out to theater and dinner, I'd spend half an hour or so working through her fiscal accounts.

Yes, and her previous husband, Robert, had been no help. When I got back that far, there was no improvement at all. In fact, Robert had been at least as bad as Stephanie about keeping records, and much worse when it came to throwing money around. A real wastrel. Outgo exceeded income all through that marriage. His life insurance, at the end, had been a real help.

And so had Frank's.

It was a week or two after I'd finished rationalizing the Robert years — two of them, though in three tax years — that my work brought me to my first encounter with Frank. Another husband, last name Bullock. Frank Bullock died three and a half years before Stephanie's marriage to Robert Morwell. Oh, yes, and he, too, had been well-insured. And with him, too, insurance paid double indemnity for accidental death.

Robert had been drowned at sea while on a cruise with Stephanie. Frank had fallen from the terrace of this very apartment while leaning out too far with his binoculars to observe the passage of an unusual breed of sea gull; Frank had been an amateur ornithologist.

And Leslie Hanford had fallen off a mountain in the Laurentians while on a Canadian ski holiday. Hanford was the husband before Bullock. Apparently, the first husband. Leslie's insurance, in fact, had been the basis for the fortune Stephanie now enjoyed, supplemented when necessary or convenient by the insurance of her later husbands. After each accidental death, Stephanie changed insurance agents and accountants. And each husband had died just over a year after the policy had been taken out.

Just over a year. So that's how long my bride expected to share my company, was it? Well, she was right about that, though not in the way she expected. I, too, could be decisive when called upon.

Whenever the weather was good, Stephanie took the sun on our terrace. Although it would be plagiarizing a bit from my bride, I could one day, having established an alibi at the office. . . .

The current insurance agent was named Oliver Swerdluff. I went to see him. "I just wanted to be sure," I said, "that the new policy on my life went through without a hitch. In case anything happened to me, I'd want to be certain Stephanie was cared for."

"An admirable sentiment," Swerdluff said. He was a puffy, sweaty man with tiny eyes, a man who would never let suspicion get between himself and a commission. Stephanie had chosen well.

I said, "Let me see, that was — half a million?"

"Oh, we felt a million would be better," Swerdluff said with a well-fed smile. "Double indemnity."

"Of course!" I exclaimed. "Excuse me, I get confused

about these numbers. A million, of course. Double indemnity. And that's exactly the amount we want for the new policy, to insure Stephanie's life. If that's what I'm worth to her, she's certainly that valuable to me."

Call me a fool, but I fell in love. Bruce was so different from the others, so confident, so self-reliant. And it was so clear he loved me, loved *me,* not my money, not the advantages I brought him. I tried to be practical, but my heart ruled my head. This was a husband I was going to have to keep.

Many's the afternoon I spent sunbathing and brooding on the terrace while Bruce was downtown at the firm. On one hand, I would have financial security for at least a little while. On the other hand, I would have Bruce.

Ah, what this terrace could be! Duckboarded, with wrought-iron furniture, a few potted hemlocks, a gaily striped awning. . . .

Well, what of it? What was a row of hemlocks in the face of true love? Bruce and I could discuss our future together, our finances. A plan, shared with another person.

We would have to economize, of course, and the first place to do so was with that million-dollar policy. I wouldn't be needing it now, so that was the first expense that could go. I went back to see Mr. Swerdluff. "I want to cancel that policy," I said.

"If you wish," he said. "Will you be canceling both of them?"

LAST-MINUTE SHOPPING

When O'Brien answered the doorbell, it was Officer Keenan standing there. "Oh, no!" O'Brien cried. "Not on Christmas Eve! Besides, I didn't do anything!"

"Take it easy, O'Brien," Keenan said. "I'm not here to arrest you."

"You're not?"

"I'd like to come in," Keenan said.

"You're in," O'Brien agreed, and shut the door behind him.

Keenan looked around the neat but sparse living room. "Huh," he said. "Crime really doesn't pay."

"Is that why you came here, to tell me that?"

"No, O'Brien," Keenan said. "We've known each other over the years."

"You've arrested me over the years, you mean. And a lot of times it didn't stick."

"I do my job, you do yours." Keenan shrugged, and said, "Now I need your help."

"I don't fink," O'Brien said.

"Oh, you would, if the circumstance was right," Keenan said, "but that's not what I want. You may not know this, but I've had a steady lady friend for a few years now."

"She hasn't done much for your personality."

"I guess not," Keenan said, "because two weeks ago we had a major fight, we broke up, that was the end of it, and it was all my fault."

"I'm sorry to hear that," O'Brien said.

"Fellow feeling. I've always liked that about you." Keenan

nodded and said, "An hour ago, 10 P.M. on Christmas Eve, she calls me. She's sorry we broke up, she's been thinking about me, why don't we try to get back together. Sure, that'd be great, I been miserable for two weeks, I didn't know I'd ever get another chance. She's a waitress at a place in midtown, she took the Christmas Eve shift because there wasn't anybody for her to go home to, she'll get off at 11:30, she wants me to come to her place at midnight."

"An hour from now."

"That's the problem," Keenan said. "Laurie says — that's her name, Laurie. Laurie say she's been thinking about nothing but me for the last two weeks, but like a dope I've been trying to think about anything except her, making myself miserable. So what this means is, I know she's gonna have a really thoughtful terrific Christmas present for me when I get to her place, but I got nothing for her, and everything's closed, and I don't want to look like a bum when we're supposed to be making up and getting back together again."

"Tough," O'Brien said.

Keenan cleared his throat. "There's a jewelry store," he said, "called Henderson's."

"Hey, wait a minute!" O'Brien said, backing up. "We been getting along so well up to now."

"Take it easy, take it easy. I believe you know this jewelry store."

"Believe what you want," O'Brien said.

"I believe you've made a number of unofficial visits to Henderson's over the years," Keenan said.

"Prove it."

"I don't want to prove it," Keenan said. "Not now, not tonight. What I want is to get into Henderson's in the next half-hour."

O'Brien looked at him.

"Not to steal anything," Keenan said. "You can't give a person stolen goods for a Christmas present."

"Oh, yeah?"

"Yeah," Keenan said. "What I want to do, I want to go into Henderson's pick out something really nice, and leave the money for it."

"And you want me to get you in."

"Without busting anything. The kind of neat work you always do."

"Keenan," O'Brien said, "this is looking an awful lot like entrapment."

"I wouldn't set you up," Keenan said. "Come on, O'Brien, you know me. I've always been straight with you, and you've always been crooked with me. I'm not gonna change now. And after this, I'll owe you one. The time'll come, down the road, I'll take care of you."

"Call the owner of the store, ask him to open up."

"He's away for the holidays. You're my only hope."

O'Brien pondered. "You want me to break into Henderson's with you watching."

"I'll turn my back until the door's open."

"A cop standing right there, and I'm breaking into a jewelry store."

"It's my future happiness, O'Brien."

"And I've got no choice, do I?"

"Sure you do."

O'Brien brooded. Keenan said, "Don't you have a lady friend?"

"Yeah?"

"While we're in there, pick her up a little something."

O'Brien perked up. "I can?"

Keenan gave him a look. "And pay for it."

"Oh, right," O'Brien said. "You can't give stolen goods

for a Christmas present."

"That's right."

"It's very hard," Keenan whispered, "to pick out a nice piece of jewelry in the dark."

"Usually in this situation," O'Brien told him, "the perpetrator just takes a couple handfuls and goes."

"This isn't the usual situation," Keenan said. "Can't we have a little more light from that flash?"

"You wanna spend Christmas at the precinct, explaining your love life?"

"Well, aim it better, anyway."

Keenan leaned over the counters of brooches and rings, and O'Brien leaned over Keenan, shining the flashlight at the trays. Two strips of electrician's tape on the lens left only a narrow slit for light to come through. Gold and silver and semiprecious stones gleamed murkily in that amber light.

"Maybe over on this side," Keenan said, and they bumped each other as they turned to cross the store.

More trays of underlit goodies. O'Brien whispered, "How you gonna pay for this stuff? You can't use a credit card when the store's closed."

"I got cash. I grabbed what I had, and borrowed from guys at the station."

"Plan ahead, huh?"

"Yeah. Ouch! That's my foot under your foot, O'Brien."

"Sorry."

Finally, after a longer time than O'Brien usually spent in Henderson's, Keenan chose a nice bracelet, gold filigree with garnets, a nice Christmasy glow. "Six hundred bucks," he said, reading the tag. "Good, I thought it'd be more. I'll just leave the money where the bracelet was." He did, and said,

"What about you, O'Brien? Find anything for your lady friend?"

"I think over on the other side there was something. Hold the flashlight for me, okay?"

"Right. Ow!"

"Sorry."

"Rubbing his shin, Keenan said, "I thought you'd be better than that, in the dark."

"You mean, get like permanent night vision? It doesn't work that way. Shine it here, will you, Keenan?"

It wasn't long before O'Brien found what he wanted, a pretty brooch. "That goes with Grace's eyes," he said. "How much is it?"

Keenan squinted at the tag. "Four fifty."

"I think I can do that." O'Brien pulled out a wad, thumbed through it. "Yep. And thirty bucks left over."

He left the money, then eased them out of the store and hooked up the alarm again. "I appreciate this, O'Brien," Keenan said.

"It was easy," O'Brien said.

When Grace opened the door, her smiling face was framed by the lustrous Christmas tree across the room. It made her look like an angel. O'Brien said, "Grace, you're beautiful."

"What a sweet thing to say," Grace said, and shut the door, and kissed him.

O'Brien took the little box out of his pocket. "Merry Christmas," he said.

Grace looked at the little box and her smile faded. "What did you do, Harry?" she asked him.

"I got you a Christmas present. It's Christmas."

"You didn't — Harry, you promised me. You didn't. . . ."

"Steal it?" O'Brien laughed. "I wouldn't do that," he said.

"You can't give stolen goods for a Christmas present."

"That's right." Grace opened the box and gazed in pleasure at the silver brooch with the green stones. "It's beautiful."

"Like you."

Doubtful again, she said, "Harry? You don't have any money, I know you don't. How'd you pay for this?"

"I did some consultancy work for a cop tonight," O'Brien said, "and he paid me. He doesn't know he paid me, but he paid me." In his mind's eye came the memory of Keenan stumbling around in the dark, his pockets full of he couldn't be sure how much money. "The thing is," O'Brien said, as he pinned the brooch on his lady friend, "I got great night vision."

THE BURGLAR
AND THE WHATSIT

"Hey, Sanity Clause," shouted the drunk from up the hall. "Wait up. C'mere."

The man in the red Santa Claus suit, with the big white beard on his face and the big heavy red sack on his shoulder, did not wait up, and did not come here, but instead continued to plod on down the hall in this high floor of a Manhattan apartment building in the middle of a cold evening in the middle of December.

"Hey, Sanity! Wait *up*, will ya?"

The man in the Santa Claus suit did not at all want to wait up, but on the other hand he also did not at all want a lot of shouting in this hall here, because in fact he was not your normal Santa Claus but was something else entirely, which was a burglar, named Jack. This Jack was a burglar who had learned some time ago that if he were to enter apartment buildings costumed like the sort of person who in the normal course of events would carry on himself some sort of large bag or box or reticule or sack, he could probably fill that sack or whatever with any number of valuable items without much risk of his being challenged, questioned or — in the worst case — arrested.

Often, therefore, this Jack would roam the corridors of the cliff dwellers garbed as, for instance, a mailman or other parcel delivery person, or as a supermarket clerk pushing a cart full of grocery bags (paper, because you can see through plastic, and plastic bags don't stand up). Just once he'd been a doctor, with a stethoscope and a doctor's black bag, but that time he'd been snagged at once, for everybody knows doctors don't make house calls. A master of disguise, Jack even occasionally appeared as a Chinese restaurant delivery guy. The bicycle clip around his right ankle, to protect his pants leg from the putative bicycle's supposed chain, was the masterstroke of that particular impersonation.

But the best was Santa Claus. First of all, the disguise was so complete, with the false stomach and the beard and the hat and the gloves. Also, the Santa sack was more capacious than almost anything else he could carry. And finally, people *liked* Santa Claus, and it made the situation more humane, somehow, gentler and nicer, to be smiled upon by the people he'd just robbed.

The downside of Santa was that his season was so short. There was only about a three-week period in December when the appearance of a Santa Claus in an apartment building's public areas would not raise more questions than it would answer. But those three weeks were the peak of the year for Jack, when he could move in warmth and safety and utter anonymity, his sack full of gifts — not for the nearby residents but from them. And all in peace and quiet, because people leave Santa Claus alone, when they see him they know he's on his way somewhere, to a party or a chimney or something.

So they leave Santa *alone*. Except for this drunk here, shouting in the hallway. Jack the burglar didn't need a lot of shouting in the hallway, and he didn't want a lot of shouting in the hallway, so with some reluctance he turned around at last and waited up, gazing at the approaching drunk from eyes that were the one false in the costume: They definitely did not twinkle.

The drunk reeled closer and stared at the burglar out of his own awful eyes, like blue eggs sunny-side up. "You're just the guy I need," he announced, inaccurately, for clearly what he most urgently needed was both a 12-step program and a whole lot of large, humorless people to enforce it.

The burglar waited, and the drunk leaned against the wall to keep the building from falling over. "If anybody can get the goddamn thing to work," he said, "it's Sanity Clause. But don't talk to me about batteries. Batteries not included is *not* the problem here."

"Good," the burglar said, and then expanded on that: "Goodbye."

"Wait!" the drunk shouted as the burglar turned away.

The burglar turned back. "Don't shout," he said.

"Well, don't keep going away," the drunk told him. "I got a real problem here."

The burglar sighed through his thick white beard. One of the reasons he'd taken up this line of work in the first place was that you could do it alone. "All right," he said, hoping this would be short, at least. "What's the problem?"

"Come on, I'll show you." Risking all, the drunk pushed off from the wall and tottered away down the hall. The burglar followed him, and the drunk touched his palm to an apartment door, which clicked and swung open — *that* was cute — and they went inside. The door swung shut, and the burglar stopped dead and stared.

Jack the burglar had seen a lot of living rooms in his business, but this one was definitely the strangest. Nothing in it looked right. All the furniture, if that's what it was, consisted of hard and soft shapes from geometry class, in a variety of pastel colors. Tall narrow things that looked like metal plants might have been lamps. Short wide things that crouched could have been chairs. Some of the stuff didn't seem to be anything in particular at all.

The drunk tottered through this abstract landscape to an inner doorway, then said, "Be right back," and disappeared.

The burglar made a circuit of the room, and to his surprise

found items of interest. A small pale pyramid turned out to be a clock; into his sack it went. Also, this avocado with ears seemed to be a CD player; pop, in it went.

In a far corner, in amazing contrast to everything else, stood a Christmas tree, fat and richly green and hung with a million ornaments, the only normal object in sight. Or, wait a minute. The burglar stared and frowned, and the Christmas tree shimmered over there as though it were about to be beamed up to the starship *Enterprise*. What was wrong with that tree?

The drunk returned, aglow with happy pride. Waving at the wavering Christmas tree, he said, "Whaddya think?"

"What *is* it, that's what I think."

"A hologram," the drunk said. "You can walk all around it, see all the sides, and you never have to water it, and it never drops a needle and you can use it next year. Pretty good, huh?"

"It isn't traditional," the burglar said. He had his own sense of the fitness of things.

"Tra-*dish*-unal!" The drunk almost knocked himself over, he rocketed that word out so hard. "I don't need tradition, I'm an *inventor!*" Pointing at a whatsit that was just now following him into the room, he said, "See?"

The burglar saw. This whatsit was a metal box, pebbly gray, about four feet tall and a foot square, scattered all over with dials and switches and antennas, plus a smooth dome on the top and little wheels on the bottom that hummed as the thing came straight across the bare gray floor to stop in front of the burglar and go, "Chick-chick, chillick, chillick."

The burglar didn't like this artifact at all. He said. "Well what's this supposed to be?"

"That's just it," the drunk said and collapsed backward onto a trapezoid that just possibly could have been a sofa. "I don't know *what* the heck it is."

"I don't like it," the burglar said. The thing buzzed and chicked as though it were a supermarket scanner and Jack the burglar were equipped with a bar code. "It's making me nervous."

"It makes *me* nervous," the drunk said. "I invented the darn thing, and I don't know what it's for. Whyn't you sit down?"

The burglar looked around. "On what?"

"Oh, anything. You want an eggnog?"

Revolted, the burglar said, "Eggnog? No!" And he sat on a nearby rhomboid, which fortunately was more comfortable than it looked.

"I just thought, you know, the uniform," the drunk said, and sat up straighter on his trapezoid and began to applaud.

What's he got to applaud about? But here came another whatsit, this one with skinny metal arms and a head shaped like a tray. The drunk told it, "I'll have the usual." To the burglar he said, "And what for you?"

"Nothing," said the burglar. "Not, uh, on duty."

"OK. Give him a seltzer with a slice of lime," he told the tray-headed whatsit, and the thing wheeled about and left as the drunk explained, "I don't like to see anybody without a glass."

"So you got a lot of these, uh, things, huh? Invented them all?"

"Used to have a lot more," the drunk said, getting mad, "but a bunch got stolen. Goddamn it, goddamn it!"

"Oh, yeah?"

"If I could get my hands on those burglars!" The drunk tried to demonstrate a pretend choke in midair, but his fingers got all tangled together, and in trying to untangle them he fell over on his side. Lying there on the trapezoid, one eye visible, he glared at the domed whatsit hovering near the burglar and snarled, "I wish they'd steal *that* thing."

The burglar said, "How can you invent it and not know what it is?"

"Easy." The drunk, with a lot of arm and leg movements, pushed himself back to a seated position as the bartender whatsit came rolling back into the room with two drinks on its head/tray. It zipped past the drunk, who grabbed his glass from it on the fly then paused in front of the burglar on the rhomboid, who accepted the glass of seltzer and suppressed the urge to say "Thanks."

Tray-head wheeled around the enigmatic whatsit and left. The drunk frowned at the whatsit and said, "Half the things I invent I don't remember. I just do them. I do the drawing and fax it to my construction people, and then I go think about other things. And after a while, dingdong, United Parcel, and there it is, according to specifikah— speci— plan."

"Then how do you find out what anything's for?

"I leave myself a note in the computer when I invent it. When the package shows up, I check back and the screen says, 'We now have a perfect vacuum cleaner.' Or, 'We now have a perfect pocket calculator.' "

"How come you didn't do that this time?"

"I did!" A growl escaped the drunk's throat and his face reddened with remembered rage. "Somebody stole the computer!"

"Ah," said the burglar.

"So, here I am," the drunk went on, pointing with his free hand at himself and the whatsit and his drink and the Christmas tree and various other things, "here I am, I got this thing — for all I know it's some sorta boon to mankind, a perfect Christmas present to humanity — and I don't know what it is!"

"But what do you want from me?" the burglar asked, shifting on his rhomboid. "I don't know about inventions."

"You know about *things,*" the drunk told him. "You know about *stuff.* Nobody in the world knows *stuff* like Sanity Clause. Electric pencil sharpeners. Jigsaw puzzles. *Stuff.*"

"Yeah? And? So?"

"So tell me stuff," the drunk said. "Any kinda stuff that you can think of, and I'll tell you if I did one yet, and when it's something I never did we'll try out some commands on Junior here and see what happens."

"I don't know," the burglar said, as the whatsit at last wheeled away from him and out into the middle of the room. It stopped, as though poised there. "You mean, just say *products* to you?"

"S'only thing I can think off," the drunk explained, "that might help." Then he sat up even more and gaped at the whatsit. "Looka that!"

The whatsit was extruding more aerials. Little lights ran around its square body. A buzzing sound came from within. The burglar said, "It isn't gonna explode, is it?"

"I don't think so," the drunk said. "It looks like it's broadcasting. Suppose I invented something to look for intelligence on other planets?"

"Would you want something like that?"

The drunk considered, then shook his head. "No. You're right, it isn't that." Perking up, he said, "But you got the idea, right? Try me, come on, tell me stuff. We gotta get moving here. I gotta figure out what this thing's supposed to do before it starts doing it all on its own. Come on, come on."

The burglar thought. He wasn't actually Santa Claus, of course, but he was certainly familiar with stuff. "A fax machine," he said, there being three of them at the moment in his sack on the floor beside the rhomboid.

"Did one," the drunk said. "Recycles newspapers, prints on it."

"Coffee maker."

"Part of my breakfast maker."

"Rock polisher."

"Don't want one."

"Air purifier."

"I manufacture my own air in here."

They went on like that, the burglar pausing to think of more things, trying them out, bouncing them off the drunk, but none of them right, while the whatsit entertained itself with its chirruping and buzzing in the middle of the room, until at last the burglar's mind had become drained of artifacts, of ideas, of things, of *stuff.* "I'm sorry, pal," the burglar said, after their final silence. Shaking his head, he got up from the rhomboid, picked up his sack and said, "I'd like to help. But I gotta get on with my life, you know?"

"I appreciate all you done," the drunk said, trying but failing to stand. Then, getting mad all over again, he clenched his fists and shouted, "If only they didn't steal my computer!" He pointed an angry fist toward a keypad beside the front door. "You see that pad? That's the building's so-called burglar alarm! Ha! Burglars laugh at it!"

They did. Jack himself had laughed at several of them just tonight. "Hard to find a really good burglar al—" he said, and stopped.

They both stared at the whatsit, still buzzing away at itself like a drum machine with the mute on. "By golly," breathed the drunk, "you got it."

The burglar frowned. "It's a burglar alarm? That thing?"

"It's the perfect burglar alarm," the drunk said, and bounced around with new confidence on his trapezoid. "You know what's wrong with regular burglar alarms?" he demanded.

"They aren't very good," the burglar said.

"They trap the innocent," the drunk told him, "and they're too stupid to catch the guilty."

"That's pretty much true," the burglar agreed.

"A *perfect* burglar alarm would sense burglars, know them by a thousand tiny indications, too subtle for you and me, and call the cops before they could pull the job!"

Behind his big white Santa Claus beard, Jack the burglar's chin felt itchy all of a sudden. The big round fake stomach beneath his red costume was heavier than before. Giving the whatsit a sickly smile, he said, "A machine that can *sense* burglars? Impossible."

"No, sir," said the drunk. "Heavier-than-air flight is impossible. Sensing guilt is a snap, for the right machine." Contemplating his invention, frowning in thought, the drunk said, "But it was broadcasting. Practicing, do you suppose? Telling me it's ready to go to work?"

"Me, too," the burglar said, moving toward the door.

"Go to work. Nice to —"

The doorbell rang. "Huh," the drunk said. "Who do you suppose that is at this hour?"

SKEEKS

The jangle of the telephone eventually dragged the miserable Boy Cartwright up to the surface of the planet earth from his drug-induced sleep — the only kind of sleep he ever got — to find himself in his own rumpled bed in his own unspeakable room, with Florida sunlight like radiation poisoning at the edges of the thick, dark window shades. To one side of him sprawled in wanton stupor a reporter named Trixie, or so she claimed, while on the other side stood a half-empty — nothing in Boy's life was half-full — bottle of flat champagne and the squawking telephone. The phone could wait. First, Boy finished the champagne.

This must be a Saturday or a Sunday. Otherwise, he would have awakened at work with the sudden twitch-jump that told his co-workers at the world's most successful (and therefore most reprehensible) supermarket tabloid that the decayed Boy Cartwright brain had yet again chosen to rejoin the decaying Boy Cartwright body. So if this was a weekend, and if the telephone would not stop that noise, the *Weekly Galaxy* itself must be calling with news of the world. A task. Another opportunity for Boy Cartwright, maggot-infested Englishman, to prove himself the star on the *Galaxy* staff.

Champagne ingested, Boy at last picked up the phone: "Are you there?"

"Are you awake?"

"Ah, Mr. Scarpnafe," Boy said. "Delightful to hear your voice."

"Skeeks is dead," Scarpnafe announced. He had, in fact, a voice like a ferret with a hernia.

"Ah," said Boy, knowing that sooner or later someone would tell him what that sentence meant.

"In Los Angeles."

That was no help. "Ah," Boy said.

"We'll want the whole thing. Get there before the cremation."

"Yes, of course."

"And we'll definitely want the body in the box."

"Consider the matter done," Boy said and reached out to tug at Trixie's nether hair. "I'm assembling my team already."

"Good Boy," Scarpnafe said, and hung up the phone.

Trixie grumbled. She said, "Are you ever going to do anything pleasant with that hand?"

"Of course. Who is Skeeks?"

"A dog. A German shepherd. With a great big tongue, like yours."

The *Galaxy* stringer who met Boy and his team of four reporters at LAX was a personal trainer named Jim Jemmy, who would have been much more successful at his chosen career were it not for his insuppressible body odor, a personal tragedy that forced him to supplement his income with other less savory tasks, such as working for the *Galaxy*. "I got us a house in Venice," he announced as Boy and the team approached him and then stepped back. "Less than two miles from Skeeks' place in Santa Monica."

"Wonderful," said Boy. "Lead on."

On the plane coming out, Boy had been brought up to speed on the late Skeeks, who had been, it seemed, a lovable German shepherd, as if there could be such a thing. For three years Skeeks had portrayed the adorable pooch on an extremely successful sitcom, and when the human male lead of that show decided to throw it all in for the glories of failure as a motion picture star, the mail bemoaning the disappearance of Skeeks from the nation's screens (they're that stupid, and yet they can read and write, marveled Boy) was so overwhelming (the word avalanche was used in all press releases on the subject) that the network brought Skeeks back the next season with his very own sitcom, called *Skeeks*, in which he portrayed the dog in a man-and-dog vaudeville act. The idea at the heart of this series — that there is, at this moment, in the secondary cities of America, a thriving circuit of vaudeville theaters — was not the most outlandish suggestion ever made on television, and it was accepted without a murmur, as was Skeeks' partner on *Skeeks*, a comedian named Bill Terry, who when sober could juggle, sing, ride a unicycle and remember jokes.

Skeeks was now in its fifth year, its popularity through the roof and still climbing. Just this year a third regular had been added, little Tommy Little, a winsome child, already another audience darling. Skeeks himself was a robust nine-year-old with his own production company to handle the details of endorsements and other residual income. Away from the set, he lived quietly on an estate in Santa Monica just a few blocks from the sea. He was said to be the cast favorite among the writers.

And now Skeeks was dead, unexpectedly, calamitously. A stunned nation mourned the dog it had taken to its heart. The president had been quoted on the morning news shows as saying, "Thank God my mom passed away before this happened. It would have killed her."

Celebrity deaths, along with celebrity weddings, celebrity hanky-panky, improbable diets, visits from outer space and dubious arthritis cures, were the bread and butter of the *Galaxy*. When a celeb went down, the entire career could be rehashed just one more time. Earlier sins and scandals could be evoked in order to express forgiveness at this time of grief, and a final photo of the departed, lying in a casket, would be featured on the front page of the next issue: seven days of waxy dead flesh, in color, next to the cough drops at the cash register.

Frequently, the selfish and narrow-minded friends and relatives of the deceased didn't want that particular picture taken and might even take steps to prevent it. The pic of the body in the box was thus often a difficult and expensive proposition, with bribes to pay, bones to set, reporters to be bailed out of the slammer. Of all the *Galaxy*'s talented and unscrupulous staff, Boy Cartwright was the most consistently successful in getting the body in the box. This time would be no exception.

A dog would be different. There would be no list of marriages to go through, no extramarital affairs or history of support for wimpy environmental causes, no statements on record to demonstrate the decedent's nobility or earthiness or Americanism. No stock photos of this celeb playing golf with Glen Campbell.

Nevertheless, Boy now understood that Skeeks was (a) beloved and (b) a star. The funeral, in Forest Lawn's Wee Kirk o' the Heather, would be the largest send-off there since that tramp what's-her-name. There would be a full day of viewing the body — what a challenge for the hairdresser that would be! — and then the flames. This was a major celebrity death, no matter the species of the celebrity, and Boy intended to give it the full treatment.

Beginning with the house. Whenever there was a top-of-the-line story like this, the *Galaxy*'s first move was to send a local stringer out to rent a house, a modest, plain, ordinary house in a modest, plain, ordinary neighborhood. Eight to 12 phone lines would be put in, most of the furniture taken out, the local authorities reassured that this was not a bookie's office, and then the regular *Galaxy* staffers would fly in from Florida, ready to do battle: The morons of the world deserve the facts!

Why a house? Why not rooms in some hotel or motel? The *Galaxy* needs privacy, and the *Galaxy* well knows how easy hotel staffers are to bribe. *Galaxy* phone calls should not go through a hotel switchboard, the people the *Galaxy* interviews should not be seen in a hotel lobby. Believing in privacy for no one else, the *Galaxy* absolutely requires it for itself.

The house for the Skeeks offensive was a flea-bitten one-story stucco cottage near one of the nonexistent canals that give Venice, California its name. Occupied by an ever-shifting bevy of flight attendants, the house was always available for profitable short-term rental, since these young women never lacked entirely for alternate accommodations. Normally, the house looked exactly like a den of iniquity, but with its beds replaced by phones, fax machines and long tables bearing rows of telephones and notebook computers, with its largest bathroom converted to a darkroom, the place looked like no fun at all.

Here Boy assembled his team: Trixie and three other staffers, Jim Jemmy, three local photographers who often did piecework for the *Galaxy*, plus two more longtime stringers, one a bartender and the other a famous limousine driver. "At ease, ladies and gentlemen," Boy said unnecessarily. Gazing around with the slow insolent smile of command he said, "You are in good hands now. Boy will lead you. Trixie, did Skeeks ever father a child?"

"No idea." She appeared to be a bit hungover.

"Learn, dear," Boy said and went on to give the other peons their initial assignments: cause of death, disposition of the estate, friends and enemies, rivals (if any), ownership of the animal (even millionaire dogs, like senators, belong to somebody), future of the program, future of Bill Terry.

When the reporters had scattered, leaving Boy with Jim Jemmy and the photographers, Boy rubbed his hands together in expectant satisfaction and said, "And now, the body in the box."

Jim came closer, lowering his voice. "There's a fellow at the vet, he's —"

"Tell you what, dear. Let's chat on the porch."

"Oh. OK."

Out on the tiny sagging porch, with its unimpeded view of the canal, Boy sat on the untrustworthy railing, some distance from Jim, and said, "Tell me about it, dear."

"I have a contact at the vet, but he's being a little funny. He wants money."

"They all do, dear, and that's why we're here. To provide money."

"I think he's got something else. He wants more, he wouldn't talk to me. He seems to want, you know, more money."

The body in the box was always a delicate task. Boy had sent photographers into funeral homes disguised as priests, as nuns, as firemen, as long-lost offspring of the deceased and, on one memorable occasion, as a process server determined to press divorce papers on the corpse. Each case was different, and to each case Boy responded with his usual grimy savoir faire.

The simplest way, in the present instance, would be to insert a photographer into the veterinary hospital after the late Skeeks had been arranged in his coffin, but before the dog and coffin had been transported to Forest Lawn. That would require no more than the suborning of one employee.

Jim Jemmy had clearly done the first part of the job in finding a bribable employee, but now there was going to be some sort of problem.

Sighing, Boy saw he would have to deal with this veterinary lowlife himself. "How do I make contact?"

"I can call his home and leave him a message."

"Do, dear boy. And don't look so worried. Boy is here, and joy shall prevail."

They have met at a small outdoor restaurant on the Malibu coast. Driftwood had been imported from as far away as Tierra del Fuego to construct this restaurant in which you were guaranteed to get splinters. Boy, with clip-on sunglasses clipped on his sunglasses and a dark blue Moon Mission cap pulled low over his pasty brow, remembered again just what it was he hated about Los Angeles: everything.

The outdoorness of the restaurant was necessary, given the redolence of both his companions. Jim Jemmy continued to smell like Jim Jemmy, and Carlo, the squat Incan from the vet, smelled like the vet. He was a janitor, a man who knew every scrubbed inch of the place as well as he knew his own toilet, and his news was not good. "Sports department," he announced, hunched over the hamburger with sprouts the *Galaxy* was buying him.

"Ah," said Boy, squinting behind all his dark glass.

"Dey got dese jackets, you know what I mean? Color like a raspberry. On da pocket, by da heart, dey got dis network sign —"

"Logo," Boy edited.

Carlo crumpled his face like a fender. "Huh? No, man, a logo's a wolf. Dis on da jacket, dis what you see on da TV."

"Understood," Boy assured him.

"Dey all useta be football players, now dey work da sports

department at da network. Dey on guard, man."

"Guarding Skeeks?"

"For da pikchas, man. Dey know about you guys and your papers, dat you do da pikchas. Dey say, 'No way.' "

"*You* could skip past —"

But Carlo was shaking his woolly head, sending clouds of formaldehyde to compete across the table with essence of Jemmy. "Dey search me, man. Dey find da camera, dey drop-kick my ass back to Peru."

Boy sighed. While he loved a challenge, of course, he preferred his challenges to be easier than they looked. He said, "Carlo, one understood you had something to sell, something more than the picture, not something less."

"Dis *is* more. But you gotta pay, man."

"We'll pay what it's worth," Boy assured him.

Carlo thought about that, then decided to risk it. Whispering so low that Boy could barely hear him, he said, "Somebody offed da dog."

More gibberish. But then Jim Jemmy, utterly shocked, cried, "Skeeks was *murdered?*" and all became clear.

To the entire restaurant. Bouncing in his chair, Carlo cried, "Cool it, man! *Jesucristo!*"

"Oh, I beg your pardon!" Jim covered his mouth with both hands.

Boy said, "Class. Students. Let us have order here. Carlo, what do you mean? Do you have proof?"

"I done da cleanup, man, I know what I'm cleanin'. Dat dog got poisoned. I heard da doctors, dey don't wanna tell nobody."

"Why not?"

"Couple scandals last year, man. Dat place, movie stars keep deir dogs and cats and gerbils and all deir pets dere while dey go away, make a movie, come back, it's dead, man, wrong

231

food, wrong medicine. Dey afraid dey gonna get blamed."

"So no one knows this interesting news," Boy concluded, "except the veterinarians, and you, and us."

Carlo looked sullen. "And all dose people at d'udder tables."

"I *am* sorry," Jim said.

"I think we can ignore that," Boy decided. "This is a restaurant in Los Angeles, after all." Reaching into a side pocket, he brought out a wad of bills folded in half and held with a red rubber band. Removing the rubber band, he peeled off five $100 bills and handed them to Carlo. "This is for our exclusive use of your information."

"That's OK," Carlo agreed. The money disappeared.

Boy took a tiny camera that looked like a cigarette lighter from his other pocket. "If by chance you do happen to get Skeeks' final photo, there'll be another $1000 in it for you."

But Carlo wouldn't touch the camera. "Dem sports guys from da network, man," he said, "in dem raspberry coats, man, dey big. Big and mean."

Sneering, Boy said, "You're afraid of men in raspberry coats?"

"You look at 'em, man," Carlo said. "You'll never eat a raspberry again."

Back at the *Galaxy* nest in Venice, Boy debriefed his team, standing to demonstrate the quality of command and also because he had a long splinter in his bum. Trixie's news was that Skeeks had been rendered unfit for fatherhood as a youth, before his fame could protect him from such indignities; ergo, no progeny. The others had also been busy gleaning data, and this is what Boy learned:

Skeeks did have an owner, a holding company in Houston

called Shunbec International. Several of the Shunbec princi-
pals were deeply involved in the S&L mess, and Skeeks had
been just about their last viable asset. On the other hand, the
beast had been insured like the Hope diamond.

Closer to home, the comedian Bill Terry was known to be
unhappy, in his sober moments, at playing second fiddle to a
dog. Without the dog, of course, Bill Terry wasn't even dog
meat, but actors have been known to have egos. Other news
about Terry was said to be on its way from headquarters in
Florida.

Keeping Terry comparatively calm and happy was his
live-in girlfriend, Sherry Cohen, a co-producer of *Skeeks* who
was credited with being most of the brains behind the show.
She'd been a television professional for 15 years and had persuaded the network to hire Bill Terry despite his drinking
problem. "I'll take care of that," she had reportedly told
them, and so she had. If there was one reason the show had
lasted five years, other than the pitiable state of the American
mind, it was Sherry's control of Terry.

Another human close to Skeeks was his housekeeper,
Mayjune Kent, a former Miss America runner-up who had a
successful career as an auto show model, standing in long
gowns on all those turntables, until a crazed fan threw acid in
her face, reasoning that since he couldn't have her, no one
else should. The fan received a very light sentence since
Mayjune publicly and often forgave him, saying, "He only
did it for love."

However, when the fan was released from prison 17
months later, Mayjune ran over him in a rented automobile,
explaining she'd been blinded by tears of joy at seeing him a
free man. She was put on trial, nevertheless, for manslaughter
and given probation and assistance in finding employment.
Several human employers had agreed they could overlook her

history, but when they met her they realized they'd never be able to overlook that face. Skeeks was the only employer in southern California able and willing to give the unfortunate young woman housing and a decent job, and Mayjune was said to be devoted to the animal.

"Well, children," Boy said, "you have done reasonably well. Material for several stories here, particularly if Bill Terry has been cheating on Sherry Cohen or vice versa. However, none of this matters if we don't get the body in the box, and I am assured that any number of homicidal ex-footballers stand between us and that goal. When the going gets tough, as you've heard, the tough proceed, and I do believe one has found the answer." Then he dropped his bombshell: "One has learned, through an unimpeachable source, that Skeeks was murdered."

"No!" everybody cried. "Who? Why? Are you sure?"

"Yes," Boy replied. "Don't know yet. Don't know yet. Yes. The veterinary hospital is keeping the fact quiet for its own reasons. We know and no one else."

Jim Jemmy blushed.

"How," Boy asked rhetorically, "may we use this information? One is glad you asked. We shall find the murderer, in the next 24 hours. Anyone close enough to poison the beast can get close enough to take his picture. We shall confront the murderer and demand the photo as our price for silence."

Trixie's jaw dropped. "You mean, we won't print the story about the murder?"

"Of course we will. But the photo first. I didn't say we wouldn't publish, I said we'd *say* we wouldn't publish."

"Oh, that's all right, then," Trixie said.

"This is a manhunt," Boy told his team, "or possibly a womanhunt. Go, seek, find. And, Trixie?"

"Yes?"

"I'll want you in my office. You do have tweezers, one hopes?"

The voice of Don Grove, a Florida-based member of the team, murmured in Boy's ear, and Boy took notes as he rode along in the backseat of the limo steered randomly around Santa Monica by their driver-stringer, Portnikuff. "I m going over the wall now," murmured Don, and some blocks away he was doing it, slipping into Dungowrie, half a square block of expensive Santa Monica real estate, residence of the late Skeeks.

As Boy rode and listened, Don penetrated deeper into the place, describing what he saw. Within the tall tan stucco walls stood a modest two-story Mission-design house, a U-shaped swimming pool, a number of short specimen palm trees and a space Don described as looking like a miniature golf course, actually Skeeks' exercise area, with bouncing balls on strings, sticks that threw and returned themselves and a small sand box of carrion for the star to roll in, replenished weekly.

The main point here was description, so communication was one-way and Don didn't have too much to carry — just the microphone clipped to his turned-up collar and the power pack in his pocket. Forward he went, murmuring, to a pair of French doors, and on into the house.

"Freeze!"

Boy had written *Fr* before he got his wits about him. That was a different voice, female and harsh. Mayjune, the house-keeper?

"Don't move!" Don't turn around! You don't want to see me!"

The housekeeper, check. And Don was caught.

When Don spoke in a normal voice, as he did now — "I'll go quietly" — it about took Boy's head off. He scrabbled at his ear to remove the tiny speaker but stopped when he heard the woman say, "You won't go anywhere. Not till the police get here. You hit an electric eye on top of that wall, and I'm holding a gun on you. So it isn't that easy, is it?"

"I'm just a reporter!" Don bellowed into Boy's quaking ear.

"Don't lie to me! Don't you think I know what you're up to? You can tell her, you can tell all of them —"

Yes? Yes? Boy waited, pencil poised. A siren sounded, separately, in both his ears.

The woman spoke again: "Hear that siren?"

"Yes," Boy said. "Home, James," he told the driver.

"The name's Hubert."

Don's voice roared through Boy's head: "I'm turning around. I want to explain —"

"Don't! You'll be sorry!"

"I just want you to know I'm — Aaakkk!"

A police car hurtled by, siren roaring, but the bug-eyed Boy couldn't hear it. By the time his ears recovered from that last shtick, the limo was halfway to Venice, and from the speaker embedded in Boy's ear came only a gurgle, a grumble, a rush, a slosh.

Mayjune. Don Grove, with one look at her, had swallowed the microphone.

ARMED RESPONSE, said the hexagonal sign mounted on the brick wall just above the front doorbell. But why offer a doorbell if you then threaten to shoot anyone who uses it? "America," Boy decided. He pressed his pale, fat thumb to the button and, of course, nothing happened. All bluster, these people.

"What?"

Bending to speak into the grid from which that aggressive

word had rocketed, Boy, at his most British, plummily answered, "Alasdair Smythe here, of Lloyd's."

"Don't want any."

"Afraid it's not your choice, old bean. The insured has passed over."

A brief silence and then, "What?"

"Are we going back to square one, old crumpet? The animal Skeeks, insured by Lloyd's of London, is no more. I am the claims examiner."

A longer pause this time and then, "Wait."

Boy waited. The sleepy hills of Bel Air reposed around him, the curving roads dotted with grubby gardeners' trucks, the residents presumably all within, on their Stair Masters. Behind this high brick wall, with its wide electric gate, a gleaming blacktop drive angled up a grassy slope toward a lesser Tara. And down the drive, in an electric cart, came a burly sullen fellow in tan uniform and dark sunglasses, pistol in holster on hip. The armed response, at last.

Dismounting from his trusty cart, this hollow threat approached the gate, gazed through it at Boy and said, "You got ID?"

"Of course."

Of course. Boy could prove himself to be anybody you wanted. After brooding over the impressive Smythe ID, the armed responder wordlessly opened the gate, then offered Boy a lift to the house several feet away.

In front, on the lawn, a man in shorts and Gold's Gym sweatshirt juggled Indian clubs, not very well; as Boy watched the man hit himself on the head. "Stop," bade Boy, and he stepped off the cart before it halted. Ignoring the indignant words from behind him he approached the juggler. "William Kampledown, I believe."

The man hit himself again with several clubs, which then

fell to the ground. He stared openmouthed at Boy. "What did you say?"

The background information on Bill Terry, long known but not previously found useful, had arrived from Florida. Boy said, "Wanted for manslaughter in Canada. The plastic surgeon who made you comical instead of recognizable is now a well-paid consultant for a television network."

"It was all a mistake," the man said, kicking the fallen clubs in his agitation. "I was drunk. Somebody else was driving. It wasn't me anyway. I never heard that name before."

"And now you're Bill Terry, drinking to forget, a TV star beloved by millions, though not as beloved as Skeeks."

"What the hell is going on out there?"

Boy turned in the direction of that squawk and saw, on the rose-trellised porch of the pocket Tara, an apparition: Atop a slender body, a perfectly ordinary cheerleader's face had been given to South American tribesmen to shrink. Then it had been shellacked and had zircons placed in its eye sockets. Scary but sexy. "Ah, madam," Boy began, approaching her, "I am —"

"Not selling insurance, I hope."

"Of course not, madam, I am —"

But she was glaring past him at the man on the lawn, snarling at him. "What are you standing around for? You have to be able to keep those goddamn things in the air by next Wednesday, when *The Bill and Tommy Show* starts to tape!"

"Maybe we can get some with helium in them," the man suggested.

"All the helium we need," she answered, "is in your head." Switching her glare to Boy, she demanded, "What does Lloyd's of London want from us?"

"We are the insurer of —"

"Well, we're not the owners. We're not putting in any claims."

On the lawn, Bill Terry once again flung Indian clubs about. Boy said, "I take it I am addressing Ms. Sherry Cohen. Ms. Cohen, Lloyd's would like to extend its condolences at —"

"Save them," she suggested.

Something short in bib overalls that was either a depraved cherub or the Nicaraguan bantamweight champion now came out onto the porch and whined, "Well, are we playing Scrabble or not?"

"Be right there, Tommy," Sherry Cohen said, her irritation at once deliquescing. She couldn't have gazed on the tiny tot with more ardor if he'd been a T-bone steak. "We're just saying goodbye to the insurance man." The zircon eyes swung around in the snake head. "Goodbye."

"Madam, if I could —"

"I'll ride you to the gate," offered the armed responder as woman and child swept into the house and Bill Terry continued to bean himself.

"I believe I can find it," Boy said.

Back at the *Galaxy* nest, Boy went over what had been learned. None of the businessmen of Shunbec International had been in Los Angeles at the key moment, all being under subpoena in Texas for something or other to do with business legality. Bill Terry, Sherry Cohen and Mayjune Kent were all without alibis, and no one else could have been close enough to the animal at the appropriate moment to do him in. (A trainer normally accompanied Skeeks between Dungowrie and the studio, but *Skeeks* had been on a two-month hiatus in filming, so the trainer had been gone for a week on safari in Tanzania.)

"These are our suspects," Boy announced to his motley crew. "We want to know where they were, minute by minute, over the past three days. We want to know what stores they went to, whom they visited, what doctors are their friends. We want their credit card receipts. We want to know which of these three dispatched the lovable pooch, and we want it by nine tomorrow morning because the cadaver will be limoing Kirk-ward by 11."

This was a unique position in which the Galaxians found themselves; they were turning their talents to good. The same rapacious tenacity with which they tracked star adultery, UFO sightings and arthritis cures would now be lasered into solving a fiendish, not to say heinous crime. Is it any wonder their sallow cheeks glowed with something similar to health, their dead eyes came to life, or something very like life?

Yoicks and away; Nemesis has nothing on the *Weekly Galaxy*.

Palindrome Productions occupied the upper floor of a two-story building in downtown Santa Monica. Here were the offices of all the company members except Skeeks, who never had much involved himself in decision making at his firm. And outside, at four that afternoon, the fellow up the telephone pole, with the telephone company hard hat and the telephone equipment dangling from his utility belt and the telephone company identification clipped to his work shirt, had, of course, nothing to do with the phone company at all but was Chauncey Chapperrell of the *Weekly Galaxy*. Other Galaxians, in California and Florida, were busily rooting into the suspects' lives, records and garbage cans, but Chauncey hit pay dirt with this conversation:

"Palindrome Productions."

"Sherry, please."

"Who shall I say is calling?"

"Mayjune."

"One moment, please."

Chauncey, whose usual assignment for the *Galaxy* was outer space, took the opportunity here to survey the world from a second-story level and found it good. No wonder that UFO aliens come here so often; it's a fun place when seen from above.

"I'm sorry, Ms. Kent, but Ms. Cohen is unavailable at the moment."

"She'd better be available. Or should I call the district attorney?"

"One moment, please."

Chauncey was taping this conversation but he wasn't listening to it. He was grooving on reality instead, as seen from 15 feet up. It had been a while since he had concentrated so totally on the mother planet.

"Mayjune? What the hell is all this about?"

"I want you to come right over here, Sherry."

"I'm busy here. Do you have any idea what a mess we have on our hands?"

"It's nothing next to the mess you *will* have. Be here in half an hour." And Mayjune Kent hung up.

So did Chauncey.

After Don Grove's experience at Dungowrie — the fellow was still in jail, have to do something about that eventually — Boy knew that over the wall was not the way to enter the estate. Not that he was much of a wall-scaler anyway. He was lucky if he could scale a curb.

Fortunately, money makes a fine substitute for muscle. Having hired a burglar known as Rack, Boy now sat comfortably in the rear of the limo piloted by Hubert Portnikuff and waited. Yonder, Rack, shielded from passing curious eyes by Chauncey and Trixie, who were engaged in long and sprightly conversation on the sidewalk in front of him, was dismantling the burglar alarm. Next he would unlock the ornamental iron front gate, override the call-the-police secondary alarm system by the inner door and finally snick open that last barrier.

There, done it. Having repacked his tools into his capaciously pocketed jacket, Rack sauntered away, a tune and a cigarette on his lips, while Trixie and Chauncey strode off in the opposite direction. Boy at last clambered stiffly out of the limo, strolled over to the estate entrance and eased on inside.

Everything in here was familiar from Don Grove's description. Boy moved past the pool, the palms, the exercise area — phew, carrion — and around to the French doors at the right side, one pair of which stood open to the evening air. Boy inserted himself into the house.

Voices. Female voices, some distance off. Were the servants at home or away? (None lived in, only Mayjune and Skeeks ever actually being in residence here.) Following that peremptory summons from Mayjune, Sherry Cohen had been in here for 20 minutes now. What could they be talking about? Boy needed to know. He filtered the house like a bad case of tar and nicotine, and the voices gradually grew louder.

There. A sort of Moorish living room, with arches and pillars everywhere, a few low couches and low tables, hanging lamps and a big round doggy bed in the middle of the floor. Peering from the semidarkness behind a pillar, Boy beheld the two women seated near each other, on sofas at right angles, with a low table between them. Boy blinked; they were drinking tea and eating cookies.

Really? The tape Boy had heard of Mayjune's phone call hadn't sounded like an invitation to tea. But here they were, just the two of them, murmuring together, munching cookies sipping tea. Sherry Cohen, on the left, looked softer than when Boy had last seen her, at the house she shared with Bill Terry — and Tommy Little? — in Bel Air. Or if not softer at least less sure of herself.

And then there was Mayjune. Oh my. The Phantom of the Opera's sister. If Boy Cartwright had a painting in his attic, that's what it would look like. How could she be sure where to insert that cookie?

Firmly watching Sherry and not Mayjune, Boy listened:

"More tea?"

"Thank you."

"Cookie?"

"I shouldn't." Pause. "Mayjune?"

"Yes?"

"Why?"

"I beg your pardon?"

"You were pretty tough on the phone, but now you just want to sit and have girl talk. I don't get it."

"I didn't want to rush into things. You and I never really got to know each other, Sherry."

"I always felt you didn't *want* to know people."

"I suppose so. Because of my face."

An uncomfortable silence; uncomfortable for Boy, anyway.

"Mayjune? Would you come to the point?"

"I suppose, really, that Skeeks was all I needed, not people at all. I took this picture of him at the vet, after they put him in the coffin."

Boy started, and stood up as straight as it was possible for him to stand. Mayjune handed a color 8 x 10 to Sherry.

"Oh, look at that. He looks, um, like he's asleep, doesn't he?"

"Dreaming," Mayjune said with her version of a poignant smile.. "Chasing rabbits."

"Chasing Nielsen households, you mean."

"When I saw he'd been poisoned —"

"*What?*"

"Oh, come on, Sherry, you can't hide anything from me. Skeeks was murdered, and you did it."

"That's — that's ridiculous!"

"Of course it is. You wouldn't get what you wanted, anyway."

"What I wanted?" Guardedly: "What was that?"

"For Tommy Little to take Skeeks' place. Then Bill would get star billing, and he might stop drinking himself to death. Of course, it would never work. You love Bill too much. You can't see he really isn't up to carrying the show."

"This is crazy!"

"Sherry, I watched you maneuver Tommy Little into place, and I knew you wanted Skeeks off the program. But I never thought you'd resort to murder."

"Mayjune, he was an animal! You can't say he — besides, why say it was me? I mean, if it even happened."

"I didn't do it, and Bill doesn't have the guts, and who else is there? You did it for love, Sherry. I know you did, for the love of Bill. But I loved Skeeks, and that's why you're going to die now."

Jumping to her feet, Sherry cried, "What are you talking about? I'm not going to die!"

"We both are, Sherry. Skeeks was the only one in my life. You took him away from me. I have no reason to live."

"Mayjune! For God's sake, what have you done?"

"The same poison you used," Mayjune said, as calm as voice mail. "It's in the cookies, and the tea. We both have less than half an hour to live."

"No!" Sherry turned away, stumbling, arms out as though to push open a lot of doors.

But Mayjune said, "I waited, Sherry, until it was too late before I told you."

"Stomach pumps! Antidotes!"

"Too late. Too late, Sherry. Sit down, dear, be calm. We'll wait together."

Sherry turned back, to stare with her zircon eyes at the placid Mayjune. "You did this? You did this for a dog?"

"My only friend, Sherry."

Sherry dropped into her seat, despair shriveling her features even more. The two women sat gazing at each other.

Boy looked at his watch. Half an hour eh? Fine. He tiptoed away found the kitchen and the cold chicken and white wine in the refrigerator. Mayjune had struck him as being a thrifty little gargoyle. She wouldn't poison everything in the house just the stuff she meant to feed Sherry.

He would phone the police, of course, once he had collected the photo and was well away from the house and after he'd called in his story to the *Galaxy*. In the meantime, snack on the kitchen table at his elbow, women expiring at the other end of the house, he pulled out notebook and pen and began the lead for this week's story:

"They did it for love."

TAKE IT AWAY

"Nice night for a stakeout."

Well *that* startled me, let me tell you. I looked around and saw I was no longer the last person on line. Behind me now was a goofy-looking guy more or less my age (thirty-four) and height (six feet) but maybe just a bit thinner than me (190 pounds). He wore eyeglasses with thick black frames and a dark-blue baseball cap turned around backward, with bunches of carroty-red hair sticking out under it on the sides and back.

He was bucktoothed and grinning, and he wore a gold-and-purple high school athletic jacket with the letter X hugely on it in Day-Glo white edged in purple and gold. It was open a bit at the top, to show a bright lime-green polo shirt underneath.

His trousers were plain black chinos which made for a change, and on his feet were a pair of those high-tech sneakers complete with inserts and gores and extra straps and triangles of black leather here and there that look as though they were constructed to specifications for NASA. In his left hand he held an *X-Men* comic book folded open to the middle of a story. He was not, in other words, anybody on the crew or even *like* anybody on the crew. So what was this about a stakeout? Who *was* this guy?

Time to employ my interrogation techniques, which meant I should come at him indirectly, not asking "Who are you?" but saying "What was that again?"

He blinked happily behind his glasses and pointed with his free hand. "A stakeout," he said, cheerful as could be.

I looked where he pointed, at the side wall of this Burger Whopper, where it was my turn tonight to get food for the crew, and I saw the poster there advertising this month's special in all twenty-seven hundred Burger Whoppers all across the United States and Canada, which was for their Special Thick Steak Whopper Sandwich, made with U.S. government-inspected steak guaranteed to be a full quarter-inch thick.

I blinked at this poster, with its glossy color photo of the special Thick Steak Whopper Sandwich, and beside me the goofy guy said, "A steak out, right? A great night to come out and get one of those steak sandwiches and take it home and not worry about cooking or anything like that because, who knows, the electricity could go off at any second."

Well, that was true. The weather had been miserable the last few days, hovering just around the freezing point, with rain at times and sleet at times, and at the moment — 9:20 P.M. (2120 hours) on a Wednesday — outside the picture windows of the Burger Whopper, there was a thick, misty fog, wet to the touch, kind of streaked and dirty, that looked mostly like an airport hotel's laundry on the rinse cycle.

Not a good night for a stakeout — not my kind of stakeout. All the guys on the crew had been complaining and griping on our walkie-talkies, sitting in our cars on this endless surveillance, getting nowhere, expecting nothing, except maybe we'd all have the flu when this was finally over.

"See what I mean?" the goofy guy said, and grinned his bucktoothed grin at me again and gestured at that poster like the magician's girl assistant gesturing at the elephant. See the elephant?

"Right," I said, and I felt a sudden quick surge of relief. If our operation had been compromised, after all this time and energy and effort, particularly given my own spotty record, I don't know what I would have done. But at least it wouldn't have been my fault.

Well, it hadn't happened, and I wouldn't have to worry about it. My smile was probably as broad and goofy as the other guy's when I said, "I see it, I see it. A steak out on a night like this — I get you."

"I'm living alone since my wife left me," he explained, probably feeling we were buddies since my smile was as moronic as his. "So mostly I just open a can of soup or something. But weather like this, living alone, the fog out there, everything cold, you just kinda feel like you owe yourself a treat, know what I mean?"

Mostly, I was just astonished that this guy had ever *had* a wife, though not surprised she'd left him. I've never been married myself, never been that fortunate, my life being pretty much tied up with the Bureau, but I could imagine what it must be like to have *been* married, and then she walks out, and now you're not married anymore. And what now? It would be like if I screwed up *real* bad, much worse than usual, and the Bureau dropped me, and I wouldn't have the Bureau to go to anymore — I'd probably come out on foggy nights for a steak sandwich myself and talk to strangers in the line at the Burger Whopper.

Not that I'm a total screwup — don't get me wrong. If I were a total screwup, the Bureau would have terminated me (not with prejudice, just the old pink slip) a long time ago; the Bureau doesn't suffer fools, gladly or otherwise. But it's true I have made a few errors along the way and had luck turn against me, and so on, which in fact was why I was on this stakeout detail in the first place.

All of us. The whole crew, the whole night shift, seven guys in seven cars blanketing three square blocks in the Meridian Hills section of Indianapolis. Or was it Ravenswood?

How do I know? — I don't know anything about Indianapolis. The Burger Whopper was a long drive away from the stakeout site — that's all I know.

And we seven guys, we'd gotten this assignment, with no possibility of glory or advancement, with nothing but boredom and dyspepsia (the Burger Whopper is not my first choice for food) and chills and aches and no doubt the flu before it's over, because all seven of us had a few little dings and dents in our curricula vitae. Second-raters together, that's what we had to think about, losing self-esteem by the minute as we each sat alone there in our cars in the darkness, waiting in vain for François Figuer to make his move.

Art smuggling: Has there ever been a greater potential for boredom? Madonna and Child, Madonna and Child, Madonna and Child. Who cares what wall they hang on, as long as it isn't mine, those cow-faced Madonnas and fat-kneed Childs? Still, as it turns out, there's a lively illegal trade in stolen art from Europe, particularly from defenseless churches over there, and that means a whole lot of Madonnas *und Kinder* entering America rolled up in umbrellas or disguised as Genoa salamis.

And at the center of this vast illegal conspiracy to bore Americans out of their pants was one François Figuer, a Parisian who was now a resident of the good old U.S. of A. And he was who we were out to get.

We knew a fresh shipment of stolen art was on its way, this time from the defenseless churches of Italy and consisting mostly of the second-favorite subject after M&C, being St. Sebastian — you know, the bird condo, the saint with all the arrows sticking out of him for the birds to perch on. Anyway, the Bureau had tracked the St. Sebastian shipment into the U.S. through the entry port at Norfolk, VA, but then had lost it. (Not us seven — some other bunch of screwups.) It was on its way to Figuer and whoever his customer might be, which is why we were there, blanketing his neighborhood, waiting for him to make his move. Meanwhile it was, as my goofy new friend had suggested, a good night for a steak out.

Seven men, in seven cars, trying to outwait and outwit one wily art smuggler. In each car we had a police radio (in case we needed local backup); we had our walkie-talkie; and we had a manila folder on the passenger seat beside us, containing a map of the immediate area around Figuer's house and a blown-up surveillance photo of Figuer himself, with a written description on the back.

We sat in our cars, and we waited, and for five days nothing had happened. We knew Figuer was in the house, alone. We knew he and the courier must eventually make contact. We watched the arrivals of deliverymen from the supermarket and the liquor store and the Chinese restaurant, and when we checked, they were all three the normal deliverymen from those establishments. Then we replaced them with our own deliverymen and learned only that Figuer was a lousy tipper.

Did he know he was being watched? No idea, but probably not. In any event, we were here, and there was no alternative. If the courier arrived with a package that looked like a Genoa salami, we would pounce. If, instead, Figuer were to leave his house and go for a stroll or a drive, we would follow.

In the meantime we wailed, with nothing to do. Couldn't read, even if we were permitted to turn on a light. We spoke together briefly on our walkie-talkies, that's all. And every night around nine, one of us would come here to the Burger Whopper to buy everyone's dinner. Tonight was my turn.

Apparently everybody in the world felt thick fog created a

good night to eat out, to counteract a foggy night's enforced slowness with some fast food. The line had been longer than usual at the Burger Whopper when I arrived, and now it stretched another dozen people or so behind my new friend and me. A family of four (small, sticky-looking children, dazed father, furious mother), a young couple giggling and rubbing each other's bodies, another family, a hunched fellow with his hands moving in his raincoat pockets, and now more in line beyond him.

Ahead, however, the end was in sight. Either the Whopper management hadn't expected such a crowd on such a night, or the fog had kept one or more employees from getting to work; whatever the cause, there was only one cash register in use, run by an irritable fat girl in the clownish garnet-and-gray Burger Whopper costume. Each customer, upon reaching this girl, would sing out his or her order, and she would punch it into the register as if stabbing an enemy in his thousand eyes.

My new friend said, "It can get really boring sitting around in the car, can't it?"

I'd been miles away, in my own thoughts, brooding about this miserable assignment and without thinking I answered, "Yeah, it sure can." But then I immediately caught myself and stared at the goof again and said, *"What?"*

"Boring sitting around in the car," he repeated. "And you get all stiff after a while."

This way true, but how did *he* know? Thinking, What is going *on* here? I said, "What do you mean, sitting around in the car? What do you mean?" And at the same time thinking, Should I take him into protective custody?

But the goof spread his hands, gesturing, at the Burger Whopper all around us. and said, "That's why we're here, right? Instead of four blocks down the street at Radio Special."

Well, yes. Yes, that was true. Radio Special, another fast-food chain with a franchise joint not far from here, was set up like the drive-in deposit window at the bank. You drove up to the window, called your order into a microphone and a staticky voice told you how much it would cost. You put the money into a bin that slid out and back in, and a little later the bin would slide out a second time with your food and your change.

A lot of people prefer that sort of thing because they feel more secure being inside their own automobile, but us guys on stakeout find it too much of the same old same old. What we want, when there's any kind of excuse for it, is to be *out* of the car.

So I had to agree with my carrot-topped friend. "That's why I'm here, all right," I told him. "I don't like sitting around in a car any more than I have to."

"I'd hate a *job* like that, I can tell you," he said.

There was no way to respond to that without blowing my cover, so I just smiled at him and faced front.

The person ahead of me on line was being no trouble at all, for which I was thankful. Slender and attractive, with long, straight, ash-blond hair, she was apparently a college student and had brought along a skinny green loose-leaf binder full of her notes from some sort of math class. Trying to read over her shoulder, I saw nothing I recognized at all. But then she became aware of me and gave a disgusted little growl, and hunched farther over her binder, as though to hide her notes from the eavesdropper. Except that I realized she must have thought I was trying to look down the front of her sweater — it would have been worth the effort, but in fact I hadn't been — and I suddenly got so embarrassed that I automatically took a quick step backward and tromped down squarely on the goof's right foot.

"Ouch," he said, and gave me a little push, and I got my feet back where they belonged.

"Sorry," I said. "I just — I don't know what happened."

"You violated my civil rights there," he told me. "That's what happened." But he said it with his usual toothy grin.

What *was* this? For once, I decided to confront the weirdness head-on. "Guess it's a good thing I'm not a cop, then," I told him, "so I *can't* violate your civil rights."

"To tell you the truth," he said, "I've been wondering what you do for a living. I know it's nosy of me, but I can't ever help trying to figure people out. I'm Jim Henderson, by the way. I'm a high school math teacher."

He didn't offer to shake hands and neither did I, because I was mostly trying to find an alternate occupation for myself. I decided to borrow my sister's husband's. "Fred Barnes," I lied. "I'm a bus driver. I just got off my tour."

"Ah," he said. "I've been scoring math tests. Wanted to get away from it for a while."

Mathematicians in front of me and behind me — another coincidence. It's all coincidence, I told myself, nothing to worry about.

"I teach," Jim Henderson went on, "up at St. Sebastian's."

I stared at him. "St. Sebastian's?"

"Sure. You know it, don't you? Up on Rome Road."

"Oh, sure," I said.

The furious mother behind us said, "Move the line up, will ya?"

"Oh, sorry," I said, and looked around, and my girl math student had moved forward and was now second on line behind the person giving an order. So I was third, and the goof was fourth, and I didn't have much time to think about St. Sebastian's.

★ ★ ★ ★ ★

Was something up, or not? If I made a move and Jim Henderson was merely Jim Henderson, just like he'd said, I could be in big trouble, and the whole stakeout operation would definitely be compromised. But if I *didn't* make a move, and Jim Henderson actually turned out to be the courier or somebody else connected to François Figuer, and I let him slip through my fingers, I could be in big trouble all over again.

I realized now that it had never occurred to any of us that anybody else might listen in on our walkie-talkie conversations, even though we all knew they weren't secure. From time to time, on the walkie-talkies, we'd heard construction crews, a street-paving crew, even a movie crew on location, as they passed through our territory, talking to one another. But the idea that François Figuer, inside his house, might have his own walkie-talkie, or even a scanner, and might listen to us had never crossed our minds. Not that we talked much, on duty, back and forth, except to complain about the assignment or arrange for our evening meal. . . .

Our evening meal.

Who was Jim Henderson? What was he? I wished now I'd studied the picture of François Figuer more closely, but it had always been nighttime in that damn car. I'd never even read the material on the back of the picture. Who was François Figuer? Was he the kind of guy who would do . . . whatever this was?

Was all this — please, God — after all, just coincidence?

The customer at the counter got his sack of stuff and left. The math girl stood before the irritable Whopper girl and murmured her order, her voice too soft for me to hear — on purpose, I think. She didn't want to share *anything*, that girl.

★ ★ ★ ★ ★

I didn't have much more time to think, to plan, to decide. Soon it would be my turn at the counter. What did I have to base a suspicion on? Coincidence, that's all. Odd phrases, nothing more. If coincidences didn't happen, we wouldn't need a word for them.

All right. I'm ahead of Jim Henderson, I'll place my order, I'll get my food, I'll go outside, I'll wait in the car. When he comes out, I'll follow him. We'll see for sure who he is and where he goes.

Relieved, I was smiling when the math girl turned with her sack. She saw me, saw my smile and gave me a contemptuous glare. But her good opinion was not as important as my knowing I now had a plan, I could now become easier in my mind.

I stepped up to the counter, fishing the list out of my pants pocket. Seven guys and we all wanted something different. I announced it all, while the irritable girl spiked the register as though wishing it were *my* eyes, and throughout the process I kept thinking.

Where did Jim Henderson live?

Could I find out by subtle interrogation techniques? Well, I would say to him, we're almost done here. You got far to go?

I turned. "Well," I said, and watched the mother whack one of the children across the top of the head, possibly in an effort to make him as stupid as she was. I saw this action very clearly because there was no one else in the way.

Henderson! Whoever! Where was he? All this time on line and just when he's about to reach the counter, he *leaves?*

"That man!" I spluttered at the furious mother, and pointed this way and that way, more or less at random. "He — Where — He —"

The whole family gave me a look of utter, unalterable,

255

treelike incomprehension. They were going to be no help at all.

Oh, hell, oh, damn, oh, gol*darn* it! Henderson, my eye! He's, he's, he's either Figuer himself or somebody connected to him, and I let the damn man escape!

"Wenny-sen foyr-three."

I started around the family, toward the distant door. The line of waiting people extended almost all the way down to the exit. Henderson was nowhere in sight.

"Hey!"

"Hey!"

The first "hey" was from the irritable Whopper girl, who'd also been the one who'd said "Wenny-sen foyr-three," and the second "hey" was from the furious mother. Neither of them wanted me to complicate the routine.

"You gah *pay* futhis."

Oh, God, oh, God. Time is fleeting. Where's he gotten to? I grabbed at my hip pocket for my wallet, and it wasn't there.

He'd picked my pocket. Probably when I stepped on his foot. Son of a *gun*. Money. ID. . . .

"Cancel the order!" I cried, and ran for the door.

Many people behind me shouted that I couldn't do what I was already doing. I ignored them, pelted out of the Burger Whopper, ran through the swirling fog toward my car, my face and hands already clammy when I got there, and unlocked my way in.

Local police backup, that's what I needed. I slid behind the wheel, reached for the police-radio microphone and it wasn't there. I scraped my knuckles on the housing, expecting the microphone to be there, and it wasn't.

I switched on the interior light. The curly black cord from the mike to the radio was cut and dangling. He'd been in the car. *Damn* him. I slapped open the manila folder on the passenger seat and wasn't at all surprised that the photo of François Figuer was gone.

Would my walkie-talkie reach from here to the neighborhood of the stakeout? I had no idea, but it was my last means of communication, so I grabbed it up from its leather holster dangling from the dashboard — at least he hadn't taken *that* — thumbed the side down and said, "Tome here. Do you read me? Calling anybody. Tome here."

And then I noticed, when I thumbed the side down to broadcast, the little red light didn't come on.

Oh, that bastard. Oh, that French —

I slid open the panel on the back of the walkie-talkie, and of course the battery pack that was supposed to be in there was gone. But the space wasn't empty, oh, no. A piece of paper was crumpled up inside there, where the battery pack usually goes.

I took the paper out of the walkie-talkie and smoothed it on the passenger seat beside me. It was the Figuer photo. I gazed at it. Without the thick black eyeglasses, without the buckteeth, without the carroty hair sticking out all around from under the turned-around baseball cap, this was him. It was *him*.

I turned the paper over, and now I read the back, and the words popped out at me like neon: "reckless," "daring," "fluent, unaccented American English," "strange sense of humor."

And across the bottom, in block letters in blue ink, had very recently been written:

"THEY FORGOT TO MENTION 'MASTER OF DISGUISE.' ENJOY YOUR STEAK OUT. — FF"

COPYRIGHTS AND ACKNOWLEDGMENTS